Enchanted hour

Armand waited in the moonlight, an urgency in his heart that could not be denied. Would she come again, the exquisite Rève, as she had the night before?

Suddenly, he heard a movement behind him, and she was there. When he went towards her, he could only put out his arms and hold her close to him.

She could not resist. Her head went back against his shoulder; he saw her eyes looking up into his, her lips waiting. He kissed her then, first tenderly and gently as one might caress a child, and then growing fiercer, more passionate, more demanding.

Now sh

LOVE IS
AN EAGLE

Barbara Cartland

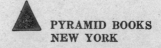

PYRAMID BOOKS
NEW YORK

LOVE IS AN EAGLE

A PYRAMID BOOK

Copyright 1951 by Barbara Cartland

Pyramid edition published June 1973
  Fourth printing, October 1975

ISBN 0-515-03047-3

Printed in the United States of America

Pyramid Books are published by Pyramid Communications, Inc. Its trademarks, consisting of the word "Pyramid" and the portrayal of a pyramid, are registered in the United States Patent Office.

Pyramid Communications, Inc.,
919 Third Avenue, New York, N.Y. 10022

1

The Earl of Morden paced restlessly up and down the cabinet room of No. 10 Downing Street.

The chairs pushed sideways, papers left disarranged on the table, the ink-stained pens and an overturned sand-box were evidence that the room had recently been the scene of a conference.

The afternoon was drawing to a close and in another part of the house Lady Morden was waiting for her husband, a silver kettle at the boil ready for his favourite cup of tea.

But Lord Morden had obviously no intention of leaving the cabinet room for the moment. Slowly he walked the room, pausing occasionally to stare with unseeing eyes through the long windows which opened into the garden.

Once he drew his watch from his vest pocket, compared the time with the hands of the Buhl clock on the marble mantelshelf, then resumed his pacing.

He must have waited twenty minutes before the door was flung open and a flunkey in gold-embroidered livery announced:

"The Viscount Sheringham, m'lord."

There was a perceptible pause after the echo of his voice had died away before Lord Sheringham appeared.

Immaculately dressed, his dark hair skilfully arranged in the very latest windswept fashion as set by the Prince, he wore a coat of dark blue superfine cloth cut by the great Swartz himself and Hessian boots polished with a judicious mixture of blacking and champagne until their shining surface reflected the golden rays of the afternoon sunshine.

His cravat was a masterpiece, the fit of his breeches

5

almost a miracle—in fact, his lordship was a Dandy. He came slowly into the room and Lord Morden's eyes rested heavily and without relief upon the countenance of his only son.

Lord Sheringham's expression was one of fashionable boredom, his eyelids half closed, the corners of his mouth slightly down-turned as if in disdain; but the face which bore this expression was arrestingly handsome.

The features were clear-cut and unmistakably aristocratic, yet giving an unusual and unexpected impression of intelligence.

Beneath the drooping lids there was a glint of either mischief or fire which somehow betrayed his languid airs and deliberately affected movements.

His voice, however, was tuned to perfection to the drawling notes of those bucks and dandies who divided their time between Carlton House and the more fashionable clubs of St. James's.

"You sent for me, Father?" Lord Sheringham asked. "Your message came at a curst ill-chosen moment, for I held the best hand at cards I have had for a week! But imagining that something untoward had occurred —such as your approaching demise or a petition of bankruptcy—I hurried here as swiftly as your carriage could carry me."

He paused, then continued.

"Incidentally, while I think of it, you had best allow me to buy you some more carriage horses at Tattersall's for those chestnuts of yours are damned slow."

"Thank you, Armand, but I am perfectly capable of choosing my own horses," Lord Morden replied. "I must apologise if I chose an inopportune moment to demand your presence here, but as it happens it is of the utmost consequence that I should speak with you immediately."

He walked across the room as he spoke, turned at the window and walked back again. Lord Sheringham raised his quizzing glass, regarded his father through it for a moment, then stood waiting motionless. Lord Morden came to a standstill.

"You know, of course, the matter about which I must speak?"

"I have a vague idea, Sir."

"I thought you would have," Lord Morden said grimly. "The Prussian Ambassador's formal complaint to the Foreign Secretary was brought to the Cabinet meeting and we discussed it at some length."

For the first time since he had entered the room Lord Sheringham looked respectful.

"That must have been deuced uncomfortable for you, Sir!"

"It was a good deal more than a question of my discomfort," Lord Morden replied testily. "Armand, how could you have been such a fool, such a damned fool?"

Lord Sheringham's chin went up at his father's tone, but he made his reply slowly and without apparently being on the defensive.

"The fellow has no sense of humour, my dear Father, or he would have taken it in good part."

"No Prussian has a sense of humour," Lord Morden said, "but that is no excuse for your behaviour."

"It was not intended as an insult," Lord Sheringham replied. "Freddie Ainsby and I were discussing food two nights ago at Whites' and I bet him a thousand guineas that I would produce a dinner which was a perfect culinary effort and yet, because of the way it was served at table, would prove completely unpalatable. Knowing my Chef, Freddie accepted the wager and the dinner party was arranged."

There was a moment's pause before Lord Sheringham added with a faint smile:

"I won my bet. Freddie's note of hand for a thousand guineas is in my pocket at this momnet. We started with oysters, the very best and fattest Colchesters. They were served to my guests in spittoons and were sent away untouched. They were followed by soup of a most delectable and rare flavour, but it was brought to the table in an ordinary domestic ch——"

Lord Morden held up his hand.

"That is enough, Armand! I have no desire to hear

7

further details. They have already been discussed freely at this very table."

Lord Sheringham's eyes rested for a moment on the empty chairs.

He could visualise the members of the Cabinet all too clearly—chief among them Canning, the Foreign Secretary, pushing, theatrical, superficially brilliant and devastatingly impulsive.

Lord Castlereagh of the War Department, the shrewd Ulsterman with an instinctive understanding of Foreign Affairs; Lord Hawkesbury, the lugubrious Home Secretary with the longest neck in England who looked as if he had been on the rack three times and saw the wheel being prepared for the fourth.

And Spencer Perceval, Chancellor of the Exchequer and Leader of the House of Commons, a cheerful, modest little man of narrow education and principles, an evangelical of extreme Protestant views.

Lord Sheringham could imagine the various ministers' reactions to his latest whimsicality—resentment, astonishment, shocked indignation, and perhaps in the case of one or two of them a touch of envy.

There was no mistaking the twinkle in Lord Sheringham's eyes as he looked at his father.

"I admit, Sir, that it was a mistake to include the Prussian Ambassador among my guests, but it was a last-minute impulse. He had been making himself peculiarly objectionable and I merely invited him to a dinner worthy of his reputation."

"Without explaining the circumstances in which it was given?" Lord Morden asked.

The twinkle in Lord Sheringham's eyes deepened.

"I am afraid that small detail must have been overlooked, Sir."

The eyes of father and son met, and for a moment it seemed as if Lord Morden would smile too. Then as if impatient at his own weakness he turned away and resumed his pacing up and down the floor.

"It is no use, Armand," he said, "This time you have gone too far. I warned you before that you were overstepping the bounds of all decency and propriety. God

8

knows I've tried to be patient with you, but this time you have really excelled yourself. Canning is annoyed, seriously annoyed, and who can blame him?"

Lord Sheringham shrugged his shoulders, then he said quietly:

"If Canning were a strong man, he would tell the Prussian Ambassador to go to hell."

"Canning isn't strong and never has been," Lord Morden replied, almost as if he spoke to himself rather than to his son. "If only Pitt were alive!"

He stood still with his back to the room and repeated the words softly:

"Yes, if only Pitt were alive!"

"But he isn't!" Lord Sheringham said. "And Canning isn't the only weak person in the Cabinet, Father!"

"I know that," Lord Morden replied. "I know if only too well, yet who else is there? Who else, I ask you?"

His voice rose for a moment almost on a note of despair, then he turned back towards his son, an expression of resolution on his face.

"Don't try to side-track me, Armand; I know your methods only too well. I brought you here not only to reproach you for what you did last night, but to tell you of the decision I have made regarding your future."

Lord Sheringham raised his eyebrows.

"That will be interesting hearing, Father. May I sit down? I find it vastly fatiguing to stand for a long time."

Lord Morden brought his fist down suddenly on the Cabinet table with a violence which rattled the pens and papers.

"Blister it, Armand," he said. "Why will you always behave in this spineless, affected fashion? I loathe your dandified airs and graces, the way you yawn your way through life and behave as if nothing is worth doing or saying. I speak to you of your future, and you tell me you are too tired to listen to it standing up. Have you no feelings, no emotions?"

Lord Sheringham sank languidly down in a chair and thrust out his long legs in front of him.

9

"The last time you sent for me, Father, it was to accuse me of having too many feelings and emotions."

"On that occasion we were talking about women," Lord Morden replied. "Where they are concerned your reputation has sank to the lowest depths of degradation. Lady Coldsworth has threatened to complain to the Queen of the way you have treated her daughter, and your parties at Morden House are the talk of the town."

"People have to talk about something," Lord Sheringham remarked mildly.

"Well, they won't talk about you much longer, my boy," Lord Morden said grimly. "Now listen to me!"

"I would remind you, Father, that I have been doing that for some considerable time," Lord Sheringham said affably.

Lord Morden's expression hardened and he seated himself in the arm-chair at the head of the Cabinet table. From there he stared across the room at his son.

They were not much alike, in fact there was little similarity other than a certain squareness of their jaws and in the breadth of their shoulders.

Beneath Lord Sheringham's exquisitely fitting clothes it was possible to guess at the strength of his arms and the wiry fitness of his figure which made him appear to be lighter than he was.

Lord Morden, heavier and bigger boned than his son, had nevertheless been a great athlete in his youth. He was proud of his strength, proud of referring to the days when he rode in steeplechases, fought with Gentleman Jackson and was acknowledged one of the best swordsmen in the country.

He had never cared for London and it was an increasing irritation to him that his son should spend so much time in the raffish world of fashion which circulated round the Prince.

"At our meeting this afternoon," Lord Morden began, his voice raised a little as if he were addressing a number of people rather than one elegant young man sprawled in the only comfortable chair in the room, "we discussed two things at some length. One was a

10

letter from the Prussian Ambassador concerning your party last night, and the other our information from France."

"Both obviously depressing subjects," Lord Sheringham ejaculated.

"I agree with you," Lord Morden replied. "They were depressing subjects, but both unfortunately have to be considered."

"As regards the one which concerns myself," Lord Sheringham said, "would a personal apology be of any avail?"

"It will be required, of course," Lord Morden replied, "both to the Ambassador and to Canning who has to deal with the matter. But as it happens, the other subject concerns you also."

"Me?" Lord Sheringham's voice was surprised.

"Yes, you," Lord Morden said. "I need not reiterate to you, Armand, the position that we find ourselves in at the moment. Since Fox's death last year our information from France is growing less month by month and becoming also increasingly unreliable. Fox, as we all knew, had his own methods of learning of matters which were of great import to this country."

He paused as if expecting a reply but his son said nothing.

"With his death those communications ceased or became comparatively useless and Napoleon started a blockade of Britain last November. We laughed in 1806 when he declared that the British Isles were to be placed in a state of blockade. We didn't believe it possible, but in 1807 we no longer laugh. The blockade is proving itself more effective than we anticipated.

"Every country in Europe is gradually being made submissive to France's commands, and today we have heard that Napoleon is seeking to provide for the closing of the ports of Spain and Portugal.

"If this is true, the position will be even more serious than it is at the moment. What we have got to find out is if this is true, and also what steps can be taken in the matter. Napoleon's armies are widely dispersed.

"Will he be strong enough to force the position on

11

the Portuguese and the Spanish? And what about the other countries with whom we are still in communication?

"These questions have got to be answered and we have no one in France at the moment on whom we can rely for the information."

Lord Morden ceased speaking and there was a long pause. Lord Sheringham did not move or stir from the position of languid relaxation in which he had thrown himself. His eyes were nearly closed and he might have been asleep except for a sudden tightening of his lips.

"Well?"

Lord Morden made the single word a question.

Lord Sheringham opened his eyes. His father waited but he did not speak. After a few seconds the tension was too great for the older man.

"Speak, boy," he said testily. "What have you got to say for yourself?"

Lord Sheringham looked surprised.

"I thought your decision was final, Sir, and that any protestations on my part would be useless."

For a moment it seemed as if Lord Morden was going to burst out into angry abuse, then the expression on his face changed and his eyes softened.

"Armand, my boy," he said in a quieter tone than he had used hitherto, "it has not been an easy thing for me to do, to suggest that you, my only son, should undertake such a mission. It was not entirely as a punishment—or should I say as a penalty?—that I suggested it, but for other reasons which you know only too well.

"Your mother was French. You are very like her and you speak French as fluently as you speak English. In France no one would question your being anything else but a Frenchman. You had also, before you took up with this tomfool set you are in now—a brain.

"Only last night I was looking over some of your reports from Eton and Oxford. There was not one but spoke of you as having an exceptionally brilliant future. As I read them, I wondered if I had failed in some way

12

to develop those talents which in the last five years you have managed to conceal most effectively."

Lord Sheringham sat up in his chair with a sudden jerk.

"No, Father," he said sharply, and for a moment he forgot to drawl. "You are not to reproach yourself. If I have behaved badly in the past five years, it is not in the slightest degree your fault. I think the explanation lies in the fact that I have been so damned lonely and excessively bored."

At his words Lord Morden rose from his chair and walked towards the window. He stood for some seconds with his back to his son, then in voice strangely unlike his own he said:

"You sounded very like your mother then. I have heard her use those very same words. 'I am bored, Bruno,' she would say to me—remember how she called me 'Bruno' because I was so big and she was so small? 'I am bored, Bruno! Life is too tedious to be endured!' Then she would go away and do something utterly outrageous."

Lord Morden's voice died away. He still stood staring out into the garden and was suddenly startled to feel his son's hand on his shoulder. He had not heard him move from the chair.

"I, too, have been outrageous, Sir," Lord Sheringham said quietly, "and now to make amends I will go to France and get the information you require."

"It will not be easy," Lord Morden said.

"I know that."

"It may indeed be very dangerous."

"Would you have me admit to being afraid of a few Frogs?"

Lord Morden turned his head and the two men looked at each other, then they both laughed.

"God bless you, my boy! I was not mistaken in you," Lord Morden said a little unsteadily.

Lord Sheringham linked his arm through that of his father.

"Let us discuss my plans," he said. "Have we any contacts that I can make in France?"

13

"There are one or two in Paris," Lord Morden replied, "but we are sure of none of them. Canning thinks, and I agree with him, that it would be best for you to strike out entirely on your own. Find out what you can, discover all that it is possible for you to discover and then return to us.

"When we are not certain whom to trust, to send you armed with letters or introductions may merely be to put your head into a noose. We can, of course, give you a certain amount of information, but it would be wisest for you to distrust everybody until they have proved themselves and even then to be cautious."

"I understand, Father," Lord Sheringham said. "What arrangements have you made to get me there?"

"You will cross the Channel in a Man-Of-War," Lord Morden replied. "You will be rowed ashore and put down on the coast of Normandy. You will be provided, of course, with plenty of money.

"You can buy yourself a horse or carriage and proceed leisurely towards Paris. Canning is making inquiries among his agents about the families of Normandy who have lived in comparative obscurity since the Revolution.

"There is certain to be one among them who has a son about your age who is either dead or incapacitated in some way. You will assume his name and, appearing as him, you should cause little or no comment in Paris."

"A good plan," Lord Sheringham approved, "provided it is well done. It would be uncomfortable to encounter at a dinner party the gentleman whose name and pedigree I had filched without apology."

"We will see that that does not happen," Lord Morden said. "Well, Armand, what do you think of the proposal? And have you any views as to the method of its execution?"

Lord Sheringham smiled.

"It is decent of you to ask my opinion, Father. I am willing to go. As you told me a little while back, I have spent five years in London, dissolute and raffish years if you like to put it that way. I am twenty-six and

14

so far I have achieved nothing and learned little save that women are desirable until they surrender, and that gambling is an expensive and artificially stimulated excitement."

Lord Morden threw back his head and laughed.

"A cynic!" he ejaculated. "And at twenty-six! My poor Armand!"

"It's the truth, nevertheless," Lord Sheringham protested. "Perhaps it's my French blood, Sir, which makes me so restless. I have to find new excitements, new ways to keep myself amused even at the risk of offending Ambassadors!"

"You will not forget that matter," Lord Morden said.

"Indeed I have not forgotten it," Lord Sheringham replied. "Can't you see, Sir, that in a way it is providential? Obviously you are extremely annoyed with me, and the whole fashionable world will agree that you are entirely justified in the course you have taken in sending me to the country and closing Morden House for a few months."

"Yes, I see," Lord Morden said softly. "We shall have to have an explanation of your absence from England."

"From London, Sir," Lord Sheringham corrected. "You have estates in Norfolk. As far as the gossips are concerned, I have been sent there to rusticate. No women, no cards—the shooting of the partridges when they come into season to be my only entertainment."

"Excellent," Lord Morden approved.

"If I may make a suggestion, Sir," Lord Sheringham continued, "I think it would be wiser if no one save yourself, Mr. Canning and the Members of the Cabinet who were here this afternoon, know where I have gone. I would rather that you do not even tell my stepmother. I am devoted, as you know, to Lady Morden, but women gossip for they have so little else to do."

"Her ladyship shall be told that you are in Norfolk," Lord Morden said. "But what of your own friends, my boy, especially the female ones?"

15

"They will be told the same. Tonight the whole of London will know of your harshness and severity. I shall abuse you over the port and even weep a tear or two, I dare say, against some white shoulder. Then tomorrow I can be on my way."

Lord Morden put out his hand.

"Thank you, Armand."

"On the contrary, my dear Father, it is for me to thank you. For the first time for months I have something to do which really interests me."

"Are you trying to tell me," Lord Morden asked in mock severity, "that you have not been interested in all those lovely ladies with whom your name has been coupled with such repugnant and regrettable publicity?"

"They interest me to a point," Lord Sheringham answered, "but that point, Sir, has always been very fine-edged about the hour of dawn."

Lord Morden laughed, but his eyes as they rested on his son's handsome face were sad.

It was nearly dawn three days later when Monsieur Armand de Ségury landed on the shores of France. The sailors who rowed him ashore according to instructions did not speak as he waved his hand in farewell.

They watched him spring lightly from the bow of the boat on to the sand, and waited until his tall figure disappeared into the shadow of the cliffs.

Then they rowed quickly away back to their ship.

Armand made his way slowly and without hurry to a small hamlet situated about one mile from the coast. He strolled into the Inn about breakfast time, ordered himself a good meal and told the landlord a long and complicated story.

His coach had broken down some ten miles away, he had managed to get a lift in a farm cart as far as the village, but that a horse must be procured for him immediately as he had urgent business in Rouen.

His story was accepted without suspicion and the country-side was combed for a suitable mount.

Fortunately it was easy to purchase an animal with

a quite passable pedigree. The local Châtelain, impoverished by the Revolution, had turned horse-breeder and was finding it difficult to dispose of the animals he bred at any reasonable price.

He could, of course, sell them to the Army, but there he was beaten down to the very last sou. In fact he often lost on the sale of a horse rather than gained by it.

When he realised that Armand was rich enough to pay a decent price he was almost pathetically eager to accommodate him.

After some negotations which ended pleasantly in a bottle of wine Armand continued his journey, riding a spirited black stallion which had a touch of Arab in its blood.

He was not surprised to see the country-side well cultivated, the people in the villages looking happy, the children rosy-cheeked and well fed. The villainous *sans culottes* and bloodstained scenes of Gilray's cartoons which had made all England shudder had been replaced by clean streets and orderly citizens.

In the villages the women in their red camlet jackets and high aprons with long flying lappets to their white caps had a friendly word for anyone who visited the markets to purchase their brightly painted eggs.

Their wooden sabots with scarlet tufts clattered gaily over the cobbles and in the inns they served fragrant coffee, frothy yellow omelettes and long crisp rolls with all their accustomed skill.

But in the provincial towns there was a very different story to be told. Napoleon was already feeling the severity of the economic war he had begun. It spelt ruin to thousands of French subjects.

There was no outlet for surplus production, taxation rising on a declining consumption was crushing, the hordes of starving beggers increased day by day.

As an appropriate background for this were the castles and *châteaux* ruined during the Revolution, the churches sacked and desolate, the tombs desecrated, the pews and altars used for firewood.

17

Only in the fields, from where all the young men had been taken by conscription, was there full employment. Here if nowhere else the years of neglect and destruction were being speedily rectified.

Armand was in no hurry to get to Paris. He was well aware of the dangers and difficulties which lay ahead of him and that the part he would play would be fraught with danger.

He remembered the story one of the Dons at the University used to tell of how he had tried to get to Mecca by pretending to be an Arab pilgrim.

"The first art of disguise," he told the attentive undergraduates, "is to think in the language you are speaking."

Armand had never forgotten his words, and now as he rode through France he was training himself to think only in French. It was not as difficult for him as it would have been for anyone else.

His mother had talked to him in French when he was a tiny boy; in fact his very first words had been a mixture of French and English. Always when they were together they had talked only in French, and often she had said to him affectionately:

"You must be my son as well as your father's. He can give you so much—your position, your title, the great wealth which will come to you one day—but I too can give you something valuable. I can give you the secret of living fully, I can teach you the art of being able to laugh at yourself and I can tell you of the joy and pain of being in love."

He remembered then how she would throw back her head, her whole body arched a little as if with yearning, as she exclaimed:

"*Teins!* but these English! They do not know how to love! When you are older, Armand, I will tell you so much about it."

But when he was old enough to understand such things, she was not there. She had died, his fascinating, adorable, little French mother, when he was just seventeen.

18

He could recall all too vividly the shock of learning that she was dead. He remembered staring at a bowl of spring flowers in the drawing-room—a room which had been particularly her own—and thinking that they too would die and their loveliness depart even as she had gone.

He had not blamed his father for marrying again. He had understood how the emptiness of the rooms where his mother had laughed and played had seemed hollow and lonely beyond endurance.

He could understand how his father had felt that any companionship, however commonplace, would be better than sitting alone listening for a voice which never came, for the sound of a footfall which could not be heard, for the rustle of a gown which its owner would never wear again.

He, too, had known what it was to feel the aching want of something which had gone from his life never to return.

He, too, had stretched out his arms to the skies and wondered if life could ever be the same without the person who had made it seem so full, so glorious, so exciting an adventure.

She had been lovely, his mother, and yet he could see his own likeness to her was there, that he resembled her more than he did his father, and that she had had every reason to laugh and call him "My own little French baby".

For a year or so after she had died he could not bear even to think of her.

He would not speak French or listen to it being spoken; but when the first agony of her loss was made easier by the passing of time, he began to treasure every memory of her, every word he could recall her having spoken.

Now they all came back to him, every sentence, the little exclamations, the fascinating and amusing little idioms she had used which invariably made him chuckle.

As he jogged over the broad acres of the land which had been hers, he felt her presence beside him, guiding him in this, the greatest adventure he had ever undertaken.

It was ten days before he drew near to Paris. The weather was perfect, warm, and yet not too sultry, a faint breeze sweeping over the land so that even at midday it was not too hot to travel.

Now Armand was impatient to arrive at his destination. He had no plans, no idea what would happen when he reached Paris, yet he felt a sudden urgency creeping over him to get there.

He wanted to begin the work he had undertaken, he wanted to get, as it were, his teeth into it. His days of travelling had given him, he felt, a chance to be armoured against surprise, to be ready for anything, however strange, however unexpected.

It was Wednesday evening when he rode down the long straight road which led to the village of St. Benis. The stars were coming out, the moon was rising. Armand drew his watch from his pocket and saw that the hands pointed to a quarter to ten.

Both he and his horse were tired. He should really have dined and slept some ten miles back, but he was impatient and he knew that St. Benis was but twenty-five miles from Paris, and therefore decided to stay the night there.

It was a lovely country-side, the grass verdant and lush, great trees shading the roads and the undulating hillside.

Armand reached his destination and found, as he had expected, that the Inn was small and sparsely furnished. It was, however, clean and the patron hurried to procure him supper and a bottle of wine.

Neither tempted him to linger over the consumption of them, and when his hunger was satisfied he walked to the stables to see if his horse had been properly rubbed down and bedded.

Finding it had, he passed leisurely down the village street. After riding all day it was pleasant to stretch his legs, and presently Armand turned off the cobbles down a narrow lane which he saw was bordered by a high wall.

It was a wall of formidable proportions, nearly twelve feet high, and surmounted by iron spikes which were an obvious deterrent to trespassers. But it was not such an impregnable obstacle as it looked, for farther on it had partly collapsed, leaving a gap through which one could easily have passed a horse and cart.

Curious, Armand looked through the trees and bushes which lay beyond the wall, and saw in the far distance the glimmer of silver.

For no reason save that he had nothing better to do he climbed over the fallen stones, and walking on the soft carpet of pine needles and moss which lay beneath the trees, he entered a garden.

After the fallen wall, he had expected to see a ruined *Château* such as he had passed, only too often, on his journey from the coast; but though he walked for some time there was no sign of a building and the trees thinned to reveal only a small lake fed by an artificial waterfall and overshadowed by towering trees.

This was the glimmer of silver he had seen in the distance, and for a moment he stood still, astounded at the beauty of it.

Where Armand emerged from the wood he was facing the waterfall, and he guessed that above it would be another lake, with perhaps another and yet another.

To the left of the waterfall there was a small Grecian Temple built of marble which once must have been of ivory white, but which now had mellowed to a weather-beaten opalescent beauty and up whose pillars grew a profusion of honeysuckle and roses.

The moonlight was full on the little Temple as it stood flanked by dark trees. From it there were stone steps leading down to the lake. Everything was very quiet and the only sounds were the soft music of the waterfall and the magical, gentle movements which can always be heard in a wood at night.

Armand stood very still. It was not only the beauty of the place which seemed to hold him motionless.

It was almost as if an enchantment was laid upon

some instinctive sixth sense told him that this
was of vast importance and that something
out to happen.

As he watched and as a strange unaccountable presentiment of having known this would happen swept over him, down the steps from the Temple there came a woman.

She moved very slowly and she held draped about her a white and diaphanous wrap. As Armand watched, she reached the last step which led from the Temple to the water.

She stood still, looking about her as if she would drink in the loveliness of the scene, then slowly, so slowly that it was almost like the mists vanishing before the morning sun, the garment that she wore dropped to her waist, then on to the ground at her feet.

She threw back her head, raised her face towards the moon as it shone over the trees. She was completely naked and her beauty was indescribable.

White and perfect, and yet glowing like the warmth of a pearl against the grey stone on which she stood, she was reminiscent of a piece of ancient Greek statuary.

But there was nothing ancient in the pulsating roundness of her high breasts, in the slender length of her thighs and in the proud strong line of her back.

Her waist could be spanned by a man's two hands and her neck, long and graceful, seemed to give her lovely head a distinction which was visible even from a distance.

For a full second she stood poised, then she dived into the water beneath her. She swam across the lake, turned, swam back and climbed the steps again to stand shimmering in the moonlight iridescent on the drops of water which fell from her body.

Her hair was dark against her shoulders, and reaching up her arms, she twisted it with a timeless gesture into a long coil to wring it dry.

Then, as unexpectedly as she had come, she moved up the steps and disappeared into the shadow of the Temple.

22

Armand drew a deep breath. He had not breathed as he stood there watching her, spellbound by a beauty such as he had never imagined possible—the moonlight, the silver water, the dark trees, that lovely exquisite, perfect figure.

For a moment he thought he must have dreamt it, and then from where he stood he could see a pool of water dark and wet on the stone steps—water which had touched her body.

Slowly, almost as if he were drawn against his will, he started to walk towards the Temple.

2

The Temple was larger than Armand had realised from the distance. Partially ruined, it had in the moonlight a strange and dramatic appearance as if it were the setting of a dream.

The pathway led him to the centre of the steps, some of which ascended into the opening between the marble pillars whole the others descended into the cool, silver and now undisturbed water. He stood waiting.

Far away in the darkness of the trees a nightingale was singing. He was conscious of the fragrance of roses and of the other flowers whose more exotic perfumes he did not recognise. Everything was very still and it seemed as if even the trees and flowers waited.

Suddenly she appeared, and although he had been expecting her, it was almost startling to see her.

She stood there flanked on either side by the pillars, her feet making no sound as she moved forward from the darkness of the doorway into the moonlight.

She was humming a little tune to herself, and now that the silence was broken it was almost as if a full orchestra crashed into a paean of triumph.

She was lovely! Armand, who had known many beautiful women in his life, caught his breath at the sheer untouched perfection of her loveliness.

She was not tall, but the grace with which she carried herself and the exquisite manner in which her head was poised on her long neck gave an impression both of height and dignity.

Her face was heart-shaped, her dark hair growing into a distinct point in the centre of her smooth white forehead. Her eyes were very large with dark-fringed eye-lashes, and between them was a tiny straight patrician nose which was somehow at variance with the warm and inviting curves of her red mouth.

Her lips were parted, her eyes wide and shining as she stared up for a moment at the moon, quite oblivious that anyone was watching her.

She was wearing a robe of some diaphanous material, caught beneath her breasts with silver ribbons, and round her bare arms and over one shoulder was thrown a wrap of white velvet trimmed with swansdown.

It seemed to Armand watching her that it was fitting that she should come from the Temple and never had a goddess who had stepped from Olympus been better fitted to play the part.

The little tune she was humming died away. She looked again at the moon and sighed as if she breathed a wish or a prayer and watched it wing its way towards the heavens. But some instinct must have told her that she was being watched.

She turned her head quickly and saw Armand. For a moment neither moved, and then the girl's hand went towards her breast as if to quieten the sudden beating of her heart.

"Who are you? What are you doing here?" she inquired, her voice low and sweet though slightly tinged with fear.

Armand stood bare-headed and bowed.

"I am a trespasser in fairyland, Mademoiselle."

"Trespasser, certainly," was the cold reply. "Please leave immediately the way you came."

"You could not be so cruel," Armand protested.

Without waiting for her to speak again he walked up the steps and stood by her side so that she could see him clearly by the light of the moon.

She looked him squarely in the face for a moment or two before she spoke. Then she asked:

"What do you want?"

"Nothing!" Armand replied. "I am a traveller who has lost his way, or should I say found it into an enchanted world of make-believe?"

It seemed for a moment as if his answer reassured

25

her. It was as if she had been expecting something more formidable. Her hand no longer trembled at her breast and she replied calmly and in unhurried tones:

"These grounds are private! You will please withdraw."

"May I first ask on whose authority you give such orders?" Armand asked.

The girl drew herself up and her voice was proud as she replied:

"On my own! I am the Comtesse Rêve de Valmont, and the grounds are mine."

"Rêve!" Armand repeated softly. "Then I am not mistaken! This is a dream and you are the dream within it."

"A dream, Sir, to which there will be a rude awakening if you do not leave immediately."

"And if I refuse?" Armand asked.

His eyes met hers for a moment and then quickly she looked away. She looked round the dark silence of the wood and he knew that she was aware of the futility of her own threats. He saw the sudden sense of her own helplessness sweep over her and instantly he took a step backwards.

"Forgive me!" he said. "I was but teasing you. If you wish me to go, I will go at once."

Now that he had capitulated so completely, it seemed that her curiosity was aroused. She looked him up and down, noting his handsome face, the well-cut, expensive clothes and the flash of diamonds on his little finger.

"You say you are a traveller, Sir. Perhaps you have lost your way?"

"Not my way," Armand replied, "but something infinitely more valuable."

"Indeed!"

Her eyebrows were arched in interrogation.

"It is something which has never happened to me before," Armand said; "yet as I stood among the distant trees, having, I admit, Mademoiselle, climbed into your property through a broken wall, I saw something so beautiful, so exquisite, that my heart flew from my body and is, I believe, lost to me for ever."

26

Her hands fluttered and her eyes could not look at his.

"You—you mean you—you have been here—for some—time?" she stammered.

"For a few seconds—for the whole of eternity. In fact for a moment that cannot be measured by the mundane confines of the passing hours."

He watched the colour rise in her cheeks, making her if possible more beautiful, and then at length with a gesture which somehow combined both pride and a sweet shyness, she said:

"I must ask you, Sir, to remember that you were trespassing and that what you saw was not intended for your eyes or for anyone else's."

"I can remember nothing save that you are the most beautiful person I have ever seen in my whole life."

His voice was very low and though she looked at him in sudden fright she did not move away. They were both of them conscious of some under-current which drew them together, some magnetism which passed between them both, making everything seem strange and yet pulsatingly alive.

It changed the very words they uttered and charging them with an excitement and a magic which utterly transformed the sense of everything that was said.

For a moment neither could move. They could only stand looking at each other, their eyes held by a power stronger than that of their own wills and of their own thoughts.

Armand was conscious that his own heart was beating quickly. He could see a pulse throbbing in the white throat of the girl who faced him and knew that her breath was coming quickly between the sweetness of her parted lips.

Now in a voice hardly above a whisper she asked:

"Who are you?"

It was a tremendous effort to bring himself back to reality.

"I am Armand de Ségury," he replied, "travelling to Paris from my hone in Normandy."

"Armand de Ségury," she repeated. "How strange!

27

My brother's name is also Armand, and I am awaiting his arrival."

"Tonight? At this moment?" Armand asked for no particular reason save to prolong the conversation.

What did it matter what they said aloud when their hearts were speaking a very different language?

"Tonight, tomorrow, or as you say at this very moment! Who knows?" the Comtesse replied. "He is coming from a long distance and should have been here some days ago. But this will not interest you, Sir! It is only the coincidence that your names are the same which made me mention it."

"On the contrary, I am extremely interested," Armand replied.

"Why?"

The question was quite artless. He smiled as he replied:

"Do you really need an answer to that question?"

She flushed again and then, as if she made a desperate effort to recall convention, she said:

"I must return to the house. It is growing late."

"I beg you not to leave me."

His words were impulsive, insistant.

"But I must! Good-bye, Monsieur."

She held out her hand, but he did not kiss it conventionally. Instead he took it in both his and held it closely in a warm, firm grasp.

"Listen," he said. "Sometimes in life things happen which are too extraordinary for one ever to have thought about or imagined them. There come moments which are unique, wonderful and perhaps heaven-sent.

"We should be stupid indeed if we were to ignore such moments, such occurrences, or to treat them as anything but miraculous. Tonight a miracle has happened to me. I stepped into the wood over there a very different person from what I am at this moment.

"Can you leave me now and expect me to go to Paris as if nothing had happened?"

He felt her fingers tremble beneath his, but he would not release her hand.

"Your journey is doubtless of importance, Sir."

"Nothing is important save that I should see you again," Armand insisted.

"But that is impossible!"

"Why?"

She hesitated before she replied.

"There are so many reasons why! You are a stranger, I do not know you! If I allowed you to call, how could I explain our acquaintance? My Great-Aunt, who chaperons me, would ask questions. Besides, my brother is expected."

"So many excuses," Armand muttered, "and yet I would swear humbly and without conceit that you wish to see me again even as I wish to see you."

She glanced up at him and the words with which she would have replied died away on her lips. She was all too conscious of that strange unaccountable magnetism between them, of a tingling sensation which seemed to run like fire through his fingers to invade her whole body.

She felt as if he were drawing her relentlessly nearer to him and with a sudden sense of panic she wrenched her hand from his and turned her face away.

"Please go!"

She spoke pleadingly. Armand knelt suddenly on one knee, took her hand in his again and pressed his lips against it.

"I shall come again tomorrow night and wait," he said quietly. "If you are not there, I shall know that this has been in all truth—a dream."

He rose, and without looking at her again walked away down the path by which he had approached the Temple.

Only when he reached the end of the lake and saw the way through which he had entered the wood did he look back. But she was gone!

The Temple in the moonlight looked empty and lonely.

Back at the Inn Armand found the Innkeeper stifling his yawns as he waited up for him.

"Who lives in the estate on the other side of the village?" Armand asked.

"It had been given back to the de Valmont family," the Innkeeper replied, adding: "What's left of them!"

"Did they forfeit it in the years of the Terror?" Armand inquired.

The Innkeeper nodded.

"The Count went to the guillotine. I'm not saying that there wasn't things against him, but he weren't a bad master for all that. However, he died, as did most of the cursed aristocrats in these parts. But the Emperor, just man that he is, has given the estate back to the Count's daughter, the Comtesse Rêve. She lives there with her aunt, the old Duchess."

"And what about the son of the family?" Armand inquired.

The Innkeeper looked surprised.

"Son? There ain't no son, not that I know of! One child was all the Count and Countess had, and she's there at the *Château* now, as you can see for yourself if you care to drop in tomorrow on your way to Paris."

"I'll consider it," Armand said languidly, "and by the way, I shall not be leaving for Paris tomorrow. My horse needs a rest and so do I. I shall stay here another night."

The Innkeeper, at the thought of further business, instantly became obsequious.

"But certainly, Monsieur. It will be an honour, Monsieur. If Monsieur will mention his favourite dishes in the morning, my wife will cook a meal fit for the Emperor himself."

Long before the Patron had finished speaking Armand was half-way up the stairs *en route* to his bedroom.

It was a sparsely furnished apartment, the candle throwing dark shadows on the big beamed ceiling and showing up the uneven boards and cracks on the uncarpeted floor.

But Armand's thoughts were far from his surroundings, and when finally he lay down on the bed made of

30

home-plucked goose feathers he fell asleep almost immediately and slept without stirring until the morning.

The sun coming through the uncurtained window woke him, and for a moment he lay still with his eyes closed, remembering the events of the night before.

In retrospect they seemed fantastic, not actually because of what had occurred—the act of trespassing in a wood, of seeing a young woman bathing in a silver pool—but because of the emotions which had been aroused within him, emotions which he had never expected to experience.

He tried to tell himself it was all an illusion, and yet he knew, even as he formulated the excuse, that it was not true.

As if impatient at the very hours he had spent in sleep, Armand got out of bed with a swiftness and determination which was very unlike his usual languid movements.

After breakfasting he walked out into the cobbled village streets where the peasants were busy marketing their wares.

Oblivious of the curious glances turned towards him, Armand walked through the village the way he had travelled the night before until he reached the narrow road bordered by the high wall.

This time instead of turning left he went right, following the wall until he came to some huge iron gates flanked by stone columns and surmounted by heraldic devices.

Through the gates was a drive, untidy and overgrown with weeds, but bordered by a magnificent avenue of poplars.

At the far end of them stood the *Château*. It was very impressive in the morning sunshine, its towers and turrets glittering against the blue sky, its windows flashing as iridescently as the lake which encompassed it about on three sides.

Armand stood staring at it for some time, then turning walked slowly back to the Inn. The Patron was nowhere to be seen, but finding his way from the front of the house to the back.

Armand discovered the Innkeeper's wife in a big, low-ceilinged kitchen, plucking a couple of ducklings.

"Bonjour, Monsieur," she said, her eyes lighting up at the sight of him, her expression one of admiration as he bowed his head to enter the low doorway.

"Bonjour, Madame," Armand replied. "Tell me, what is the name of the aunt who chaperons the Comtesse Rêve de Valmont?"

"Madame la Duchesse de Malessene," she replied. "Great-Aunt she is to the little one and of a great age, Monsieur, but she has all her faculties about her. My own niece, who works at the *Château,* tells me that nothing escapes her eagle eye. Yes indeed, she is of the old school and there are not many like them these days."

"Why, *Citoyenne,* would you praise the aristocrats?" Armand teased.

He noticed that she glanced over her shoulder as if in fear before she laughed back at him.

"I'm not saying I regret the old days, Monsieur," she said. "We would be ingrates indeed to do so when our beloved Emperor has made France the greatest nation on the earth and the most feared. But there are some who take advantage of the new conditions and the new freedom.

"It's all very well to do away with religion and all the old rules by which we were brought up, but are the young people any better for it? That's what I sometimes ask myself."

She finished plucking one duck, trussed it and set it down on the table; then she took up the other.

"I've no quarrel with those who live at the *Château,"* she said. "The Count was kind enough to my family and the little Comtesse has never been anything but an angel. God bless her! But you'll find some in this village, Monsieur, who are murmuring against the Emperor himself because he gave the *Château* back to the de Valmonts."

"I imagine they would not dare do anything else but murmur?" Armand asked.

"Indeed not," was the reply. "Who are they, one

would like to know, to question the Emperor's decisions? There's impudence for you, and ingratitude! But as I've said often enough to my own good man, you can give some people fine positions and fine clothes, but you won't make them any better than the pigs they were when they were born."

"True enough," Armand said gravely, "And there is no one else at the *Château* but the Comtesse and her Great-Aunt?"

"No one at the moment, I believe, Monsieur, except Antoinette."

"And who is Antoinette?" Armand inquired.

"Oh, she is only a servant, but a character—a real character. Nurse she was to the little Comtesse when she was born, and when the Terror came she smuggled her out of the *Château* at the very moment when the citizens were storming the gates.

"No one knew what had happened to the *pauvre petite* for many years, but Antoinette kept her safe, although it's said they roamed the country-side like gipsies. Then two years ago the blessed Emperor gives the *Château* back to the little Comtesse and the old house comes to life again."

"It's almost like a fairy story," Armand said, "and let us hope it has a happy ending."

Madame laughed.

"Ah-ha," she said roguishly. "Monsieur would have my story finish with a romance. Well, Monsieur will not be disappointed, for 'tis whispered that the little Comtesse is soon to be affianced to a very great gentleman and one of vast importance."

"Indeed."

Armand's tone was cold. The heat of the kitchen, the scent of the cooking were suddenly nauseating. He turned towards the door, yawning as he went, and Madame stared after him with a puzzled expression as he left without another word.

On leaving the kitchen Armand went purposefully and without hesitation to where his horse was stabled. He called an ostler, told him to saddle the stallion and waited impatiently while he did so.

"Monsieur is leaving?" the ostler inquired.

"Certainly not! I shall be back within a few hours," Armand replied as he swung himself into the saddle.

The black stallion, fresh after a night's rest, reared and wheeled round the yard. When finally Armand had mastered him, he set off at a sharp trot towards the *Château*.

The weeds neglected on the drive were echoed on closer acquaintance by the shabbiness of the house itself. Panes of glass were missing, the lintels were sadly in need of paint, and the flower gardens which sloped down to the lake were wild and untended.

Yet it was beautiful, its grey walls reflected in the water, its lovely proportions unaffected by superficial blemishes.

Armand dismounted at the front door and pulled the bell-chain, which was rusty. It was a long time before the door was opened.

He heard slow shuffling footsteps cross the floor, the rattle of chains and locks, and finally the oak door swung open to reveal an old servant in a stained and patched uniform, his wig awry, his eyes short-sighted and bleary.

"Oui, Monsieur?"

"I have come to call on Madame la Duchesse de Malessene," Armand said.

"Certainly, Monsieur. Will Monsieur be pleased to step inside?"

The old man opened the door a little wider, but Armand looked at his horse. The old man became flustered.

"Monsieur is riding! Now how can I get the groom? . . . 'Tis a long way—I shall keep Monsieur waiting."

They stood undecided, a worried expression on his face; and then, as Armand said nothing, he stepped forward and put his hand on the horse's bridle.

"I myself will take Monsieur's horse to the stables. Enter, Monsieur, and go straight along the passage. You will find Madame in the Purple Salon overlooking the lake. You must excuse us, Monsieur, but we were not expecting visitors and we are short-handed—very short-handed."

The old man led the horse away, muttering to himself as he went, and Armand with a faint smile on his face entered the *Château*.

He laid his hat down on the hall table. The furniture was good, he noticed. But the passage was uncarpeted and unbrushed and his feet echoed noisily as he passed through a high marble hall out of which an elaborate staircase ascended.

There was no one to be seen. He hesitated a moment for there were a number of doors opening out of the hall. It was difficult to guess which might be the Purple Salon, but at last, making his choice, he turned the handle of a door and found himself in a huge room with tapestry covered walls but otherwise completely unfurnished.

He was about to retreat when he heard voices and saw that a door was open in the far corner of the room.

He crossed the floor and saw through the half-open doorway that the room beyond was furnished with chairs and hangings of purple silk.

The voices came from the window, and he saw that seated in the sunshine from an open casement in a high-backed chair of purple velvet was an elderly woman. This Armand guessed was the Duchess.

She was very small but excessively formidable. Her skin was withered and creased into a thousand wrinkles from which her high-bridged aristocratic nose emerged like a bridge of discoloured ivory. Her eyes small, shrewd and penetrating, were perpetually moving as if she were afraid she might miss something.

She wore the clothes of a bygone generation, a vast hooped skirt, a low cut, ornately decorated bodice, and on her head a monstrous red wig bedecked with jewels.

She would have been a laughable figure save for an inbred dignity, which made anyone who spoke to her instantly forget her appearance, and a sense of humour, which to herself and for all who knew her was an endless joy and amusement.

35

On a stool beside the Duchess, a piece of embroidery on her lap, was Rêve, wearing a gown of white muslin trimmed with blue ribbon.

"Do you think he will come today?" Armand heard her ask.

The old lady made an expressive gesture with her thin hands, the sunlight glittering on her rings as they moved.

"Who can anticipate what a young man will do?" she said in a dry, cackling voice. "Besides, he has a wearisome way to come."

"That is true!" Rêve replied, "and there are so many dangers on the way which might have delayed him. I wonder——"

Her voice broke off and her eyes widened in astonishment, for she had suddenly caught sight of Armand standing in the doorway.

For a moment she stared at him as if she could hardly believe her eyes, then she rose slowly to her feet, her cheeks crimsoning as she did so.

She was even more beautiful in the sunlight, Armand decided. The moon had not been strong enough to reveal the exquisite purity of her white skin or the fact that her eyes, fringed with their dark lashes, were an unusual shade of green flecked with amber.

But as Armand advanced into the room, he looked not at Rêve but at the older woman who, at his approach, raised a gold-framed lorgnette to her eyes.

Armand walked with the utmost composure up to the Duchess's chair; then he bowed and said:

"Your Grace must pardon my arriving unannounced, but your servant, who has taken my horse to the stables, told me I should find you here."

"And your name, young man?" the Duchess inquired.

"I am Armand de Ségury," Armand replied, "my father, Maurice de Ségury, told me to call on you and pay my respects."

"Maurice de Ségury," the Duchess repeated as if she strove to remember the name.

"It is many years, Ma'am, since you met my father,"

Armand said, "but he has often spoken of your wit and beauty, and I can well understand, now that I have seen you, that it would be easier for him to remember you than you him."

The Duchess chuckled.

"Your father has at least taught you to be a skilful flatterer, young man. For the moment I cannot recall your father, but when one is my age one's memory plays strange tricks."

She chuckled again and glanced at Rêve.

"Let me present you to my great-niece, the Countess Rêve de Valmont."

Armand bowed. Rêve put out her hand as she curtsied and he touched it for a moment with his lips. Her fingers were very cold.

"And what are you doing in this part of the world?" the Duchess asked, *"En route* for Paris, I'll be bound."

"You are quite right, Ma'am. I journey towards Paris."

"In search of excitement, adventure and, of course —beautiful women," the Duchess said.

"Again, Madame, your supposition is entirely right, though it seems there is no need for me to go to Paris in search of the latter."

He glanced at Rêve as he spoke, but her eyes were veiled by her lashes and she would not look at him.

"Your father is well?" the Duchess asked. "Your estates in Normandy unimpaired?"

There was no need to ask what she meant by the last part of her question.

"We are very fortunate," Armand replied. "We live in a very isolated part of the country and the peasants there were not unduly infected by the fever which swept over much of France."

"And now?" the Duchess asked.

"Like the rest of France our men are serving the Emperor," Armand replied.

The Duchess nodded.

"Yes, it is the same everywhere. Napoleon is insatiable for men—men, and more men, more blood to be shed, more lives to be lost."

She spoke the last words vehemently, and Rêve gave her a startled glance before putting her hand on her arm.

"Be careful, Madame," she said in a low voice, then looking at Armand she said: "Her Grace is very frank in expressing her opinions, Monsieur."

"And why not?" Armand asked. "I am not an informer, Mademoiselle."

"Of course you are not," the Duchess said quickly before Rêve could speak. "You don't look like one! Besides, you are a gentleman, one can see that with half an eye. You are not like those common jumped-up *parvenus* who strut about the Tuileries being invested with ridiculous titles to cloak their inbred vulgarity."

"Madame! Madame!" Rêve admonished anxiously;

But Armand threw back his head and laughed. The Duchess joined in.

"A perfect description, Madame," he said, "but one which will hardly commend itself to the Emperor's sense of humour."

"Pshaw!" the Duchess snorted. "He hasn't got one. No soldier ever had, and certainly no Corsican."

"Yet France pays him homage and offers him absolute adoration," Armand said.

"Rightly so, for he has saved France from herself," replied the Duchess. "But will he be content with what he has already achieved?"

Armand did not reply and after a moment she continued:

"No—for such as he can never stand still, he must always press onward—onward—and to what?"

"He is ambitious, Madame!"

"Ambitious!" the Duchess snorted. "There are three things, boy, which turn a man from a human being into a god—or a devil; three things which make a man's spirit soar like the flight of an eagle—ambition, religion—and love."

"So love is an eagle," Armand said softly, his eyes on Rêve.

"Indeed it is," the Duchess retorted. "And who cares a fig for your cooing doves? But remember, an eagle

38

may be beautiful in the sky, but he can be terrible and fierce and treacherous at close quarters."

"And the crest of Napoleon Bonaparte is an eagle—soaring," Armand smiled.

"Exactly—but one day his wings will tire."

The Duchess laughed her high cackle as at a prophecy of ill omen.

Rêve walked to the window and looked out over the lake.

"You forget, Ma'am," she said, "the the Emperor has returned to me the home of my ancestors and has honoured me with his friendship. Laughing at him is hardly a becoming way of showing our gratitude."

The Duchess smiled at her and held out her hand with an impulsive gesture.

"All right, child," she said. "I am a garrulous old woman! I will strive to keep my tongue in check, but I have lived too long to try to pick and choose my words like a hen looking for a grain of wheat. For eighty-five years I have said what has come into my head and I shall continue to do so whatever the consequences."

There was something pathetic rather than defiant in the Duchess's words, and Rêve, turning towards her, took her outstretched hand and laid it against her cheek.

The gesture was exquisite, and the white blue-veined fingers glittering with rings were in startling contrast to the ivory smoothness of the magnolia cheek.

The moment of sentiment passed quickly. The Duchess withdrew her hand and said sharply:

"We are forgetting our manners. Wine for our visitor. You will join me in a glass of Madeira, Sir?"

"I should be honoured," Armand said.

Rêve crossed the room. She moved so swiftly that Armand had to hurry to open the door for her before she reached it. As he did so their eyes met and for a moment she was still, arrested in the very movement of departure. Then she drew in a deep breath and went from the room.

Armand was aware that the Duchess was watching him closely. He moved back to her side.

"Maurice de Ségury," she said reflectively. "I wish I could remember him. Are you like your father, boy?"

"No, I resemble my mother," Armand answered truthfully.

"She must have been a very pretty woman," the Duchess said, and again in all truthfulness Armand replied:

"She was!"

He was expecting further questions regarding his family when the Duchess said unexpectedly:

"You admire my grand-niece?"

"But of course, Your Grace. Who could fail to admire anyone so exquisite."

"She is a sweet child," the Duchess said, "and by no means as simple as she appears. She has suffered and experienced many strange things during the years when she was in hiding. You have perhaps heard about her adventuring?"

"A little," Armand admitted. "There were many such stories, I believe, of the children of aristocratic families wandering the country-side in fear of their lives, attended only by some loyal servant who eventually smuggled them away to safety."

"Yes, there were many tales like that," the Duchess said, "but, as always in life, one is concerned with a particular instance, the one which concerns oneself. I was in Italy when the Revolution broke out, and I suppose that prevented me from embracing *Madame Guillotine,* but I heard that my nephew had been taken to Paris and executed. It was ten years before I finally learned what had happened to my great-niece. Ten years, Monsieur! It is a long time!"

"But she was safe!" Armand said.

The Duchess nodded.

"Yes, safe, thanks to the devotion of a maidservant. But who knows what the future will be! She has missed the sheltered, disciplined life which every French girl of decent family should enjoy. Sometimes I worry about her; sometimes, when she is chiding me for being frank and impetuous, I think there is no reason for me to worry."

The Duchess's voice sank almost to a whisper, and then with a sudden cackling laugh, which was startling as it echoed round the room, she said:

"But why should I bore a handsome young man with this? Tell me about yourself, Sir. There is no subject more interesting to a man."

"But I would far rather talk about you, Madame," Armand said. "I find my own history often insufferably boring, but yours should be stimulating."

The Duchess was laughing when Rêve came back into the room, carrying a silver tray on which reposed two glasses and a decanter of wine.

Armand and the Duchess drank together and when his glass was finished Armand rose to say good-bye. The few sentences he exchanged with Rêve were conventional, and yet he read much from the expression in her eyes, from the touch of her fingers as he raised them to his lips.

The Duchess dismissed him jokingly, teasing him about the gay time he would have in Paris; and when at length he was riding down the drive away from the *Château,* he was not certain what he had gained or lost by the boldness of his visit.

The rest of the day passed slowly, and it was with an impatience which in itself was a novel sensation that Armand watched the hours tick by until darkness would fall.

He dined early and allowed himself far too long for the walk through the village and down the lane which led to the gap in the wall. Indeed, he found his feet carrying him more swiftly than he had walked for some time.

He tried to laugh at himself, saying that the French air and the French wine must have gone to his head, but he knew that in truth his urgency was deep-rooted in his heart and would not be denied.

The little lake among the trees, which he knew now was the last of a long chain of lakes reaching from the *Château* to the wood, was as still and silver as on the night before.

Only the moon on the Temple was brighter, seeming

41

almost dazzling in its brilliance and making the contrast of the dark trees even more mystical.

Armand found the Temple deserted as he had expected, and sitting down on the steps, he prepared to wait. He tried to think, to analyse the feelings and emotions of the last twenty-four hours, but he found it impossible to do so.

He could only wait, every muscle in his body tense until the moment when Rêve would appear. For some agonising moments he began to think she would not come and to wonder what he would do, when suddenly he heard a movement behind him.

He turned to see her standing above him, between the pillars of the Temple.

He had not expected her to come that way. For a moment he did not rise but just sat motionless looking at her. She was wearing an evening gown of satin embroidered with tiny pearls and her hair was dressed high on her head and bound with a ribbon.

She stood there waiting for him to speak, and when finally he rose to his feet and went towards her, there was nothing left to say. He could only put out his arms and hold her close to him.

She could not resist him. It was as if she could no longer fight something more powerful and more insistent than convention. Her head went back against his shoulder, he saw her eyes looking up into his, her lips waiting.

He kissed her then, his mouth seeking hers, first tenderly and gently as one might caress a child, and then growing fiercer, more passionate, more demanding, until at length he felt the flame within himself igniting a response within her.

They clung together, drawing closer and closer until it seemed as if they were united one with the other, indivisible and for all time.

3

Rêve woke, and opening her eyes, lay for some time watching the sunshine percolating in narrow golden streams from behind the heavy curtains screening the windows of her bedroom.

She had slept in this room when she was a child and it was not only sentiment which made her choose it again when she returned to the *Château*. It was a fervent desire to recapture the happiness, contentment and peace of those years before the Revolution.

She had felt that the white walls patterned with gold roses, the ceiling painted with plump, smiling cupids and the windows overlooking the lake had a magic that would waft her back through time into the enchanted past.

But a room could not give her what she sought, nor indeed could she find within the walls of her old home anything but a yearning for her lost childhood and an apprehension for the future.

More than that, she was haunted by her memories of the Terror—memories which lay like an unhealed, aching scar beneath all she did and thought.

There was never a day, as she passed through the hall and up the exquisitely tapered staircase, when she did not remember the hoarse shouts and the banging on the outer doors which had heralded the approach of the revolutionaries.

She could see again her father coming slowly down the stairs, exquisitely dressed as always, the diamonds at his throat glittering in the light of the chandeliers, his thin fingers holding his gold snuff-box as nonchalantly as if he were about to entertain a number of welcome friends.

43

When they met on the staircase, he stopped and as Rêve looked up at him, her face white with fear, he put two fingers under her chin and turned her face to his. For a moment his eyes looked into hers before he said quietly:

"There is only one thing of which to be afraid, *ma fille,* and that is of being afraid."

Rêve had hardly heard him. Little though she was, she knew something momentous and terrifying was threatening her very existence.

She put out her arms to cling to her father, unaware that she was trembling, conscious only that the shouts outside and the thumping on the outer doors were becoming noisier and more violent.

The Count bent and kissed her and for a moment his lips lingered against her forehead, then with a faint smile he turned towards her nurse who was standing behind.

"*Allons,* Antoinette!" he said briefly and proceeded downstairs.

After that everything had been a nightmare of incoherence and terror. Antoinette had smuggled Rêve down a secret staircase into an ancient passage, damp and stinking from long disuse, which had been tunnelled beneath the lake.

When they had emerged gasping into the open, twenty minutes later, the air had seemed unexpectedly sweet and fresh after the foul atmosphere of the passage. And after they had filled their lungs, they had stood within the shelter of the wood to look back at the *Château.*

Every window was ablaze with light. In some of them the light came from the tapers normally lit at this hour in the great crystal chandeliers and crested silver sconces, but in others the tar-dipped torches of the revolutionaries gleamed red as blood.

It was some years before Rêve learned how her father had met and greeted the drunken, murderous rabble with courtesy and dignity which for the moment checked their lust for blood.

His indomitable courage had indeed saved his life

for a short while; but after he had been taken to Paris and imprisoned there, the death sentence was pronounced and he ascended the guillotine with a jest on his lips.

The *Château* had been sacked of most of its contents.

But when Rêve returned and took up residence again in the home of her forefathers, she grew used to hearing that those in the household who rose first in the morning had discovered little piles of furniture, drapery and various other articles outside the front door, deposited there by some conscience-stricken citizens under the darkness of the night.

Once when she was shopping in the village she had seen through an open door in a shop a gilt-framed mirror which had hung in her father's bedroom. She had stared at it but said nothing, and the shopkeeper, noticing her glance, went crimson with embarrassment.

Next morning the mirror lay outside the door of the *Château*. It was little things like this which touched her and made her feel that she was amongst her own people again.

Yet the agonies she had suffered in those years when, homeless and a fugitive, she roamed the country-side with Antoinette, were not easily forgotten.

At first she had been child enough to live from day to day; but as she grew older she had begun to realise how much she was missing of the life she should have enjoyed, the companions she should have had, and the position she should have held.

It was only after Napoleon Bonaparte had risen to power and France was once again behaving in a decent and civilised fashion that Rêve's life underwent a second transformation.

Antoinette had by this time managed to get in touch with some of Rêve's relatives in Paris. They were dull, poverty-stricken cousins who were not important enough to incite the anger of the revolutionaries and had therefore lived through the years of Terror undisturbed and unnoticed.

They made Rêve as welcome as they could, but it was perfectly obvious both to her and to Antoinette

45

that they had no wish to provide a permanent home for a beautiful girl of sixteen and her old nurse.

They talked things over frankly and her cousin, François, a middle-aged man whose only real interest in life was in the collection of ancient coins, consulted an advocate with whom he was on friendly terms.

The latter informed him that the *émigrés* had been permitted to return home and that Napoleon was in the process of restoring to some of them the property and houses of which they had been deprived during the Revolution.

Following this information it had been decided what would be the best for Rêve to do—to make an application through the civil courts, to approach the great Napoleon in person, or to return and attempt to take up residence in the *Château* which was known to be empty and unoccupied. It was Rêve who made the final decision.

"I will speak to the Emperor myself," she said.

At the Tuileries, where Napoleon had taken up his official residence, she managed by the usual method of bribery and cajolery of the Court officials to gain entrance to the ante-chamber where those desirous of an audience with the Emperor waited their turn, sometimes fruitlessly for months on end.

After years of living among peasants, of having neither money nor belongings of any value, she was at first overcome by the magnificence and luxury of the Palace—the green and gold livery of the servants, the pages with their gold chains and medals, the gorgeously be-gilt peace officers, were all as dazzling as the illustration to a fairy story.

There were, too, the furnishings of the different salons—in one the hangings were of blue lilac lustring embroidered with a honeysuckle pattern with maroon.

In another yellow satin and brown had been selected with fringes of *sang de bœuf* and the looking-glasses were all draped instead of framed, while beneath them stood beautiful porphyry and other fine marble tables holding vases of exquisite Sèvres china and of granite mounted in ormolu.

46

Treasures beyond price graced the walls for with Napoleon's endless increasing conquests it was little wonder that all his Palaces began to look like Aladdin's Cave.

There were Rembrandts and Van Dycks taken from the Dutch, antique armour from the Vienna collection, the sword of Frederick the Great from the Prussians —only from England were there as yet no spoils.

It was all very bewildering to a girl who for so many years of her life had only known ragged clothes and a straw mattress, who had often been hungry for the crusts of coarse black bread, who had thought of a cup of milk as a luxury, of a new-laid egg as a feast.

The contrast was bitter, too, not only for herself but for those who befriended her, knowing as she did the struggle they had to scrape a living from the soil and to pay the many taxes which were imposed upon them.

For a moment she had a wild desire to denounce this Corsican adventurer, who had risen to power by the ladder of the Revolution and who now surrounded himself with those very extravagances which had originally caused the flame of revolt.

But something cynical, or perhaps it was something sensible, made her choke back the feelings within her. She had come to get something and only by being calm and intelligent could she hope to gain it.

She waited three weeks before finally her opportunity came.

The Emperor, his audience at an end, was passing through the ante-chamber, and while the others stood back respectfully, Rêve rushed forward and flung herself on her knees before him.

Before the officials could remove her from his path, she had looked up into his face and said softly:

"I crave a favour, Sire."

He looked down at her and his cold, steel-gray eyes noted both her youth and her beauty. Napoleon never could resist a beautiful woman.

"Who are you?"

His voice was sharp and there was almost a military command about it.

"I am the Comtesse Rêve de Valmont," she replied, "and I have come to beg that my estates at St. Benis may be returned to me."

An official moved forward. He was a pompous, middle-aged man with a hard supercilious expression.

"This claim, Your Majesty, can be dealt with in orderly fashion by the commissioners you have appointed to investigate such matters. There is no reason for this young woman to trouble you personally."

Napoleon ignored the interruption. His eyes were on Rêve's heart-shaped face and the appeal in the big eyes raised to his.

"De Valmont!" he said slowly. "Was your father— Count Maxime de Valmont?"

"Yes, Sire."

"He is alive?"

"No, Sire. He died by the guillotine."

"If he had lived, how old would he have been?"

Rêve considered for a moment.

"He was born in 1761."

Napoleon nodded his head.

"I thought so! He was at the military school at Brienne with me. I remember him! He was kind to me once. He invited me to sup with him when I was hungry. Your estates shall be restored to you. See to it!"

The order was to the official who had tried to intervene, and then almost before Rêve had recovered from her surprise or could know the relief of having obtained that which she sought, the great man had passed on and the ante-chamber was emptying behind him.

Her first elation at coming back to the *Château* was short-lived. There was a great deal to be done to the place before it was even habitable, and there was very little money with which to do it.

Through her cousins she got in touch with her Great-Aunt, the Duchess of Malessene; but while the old lady was prepared to act as a chaperon to Rêve and to bring a great deal of her own furniture to the *Château,* like all the rest of the aristocracy whose position and power had been swept away by the flood tide of the Revolution she had pathetically little money to spend.

However, they managed; and it would not have been as easy as it was had there not been many guilty consciences in the village of St. Benis. Carpenters and bricklayers came to the *Château* and put in an abnormal amount of work for just a few sous in payment.

Painters and stone-masons seemed willing to work while the hours of daylight lasted, yet their accounts were equally as small. Gradually the holes in the roof were mended, the windows glazed, the doors rehung.

In fact it was possible to live in the *Château* even if it was but a shabby ghost of its former glory. And when the Duchess's furniture arrived from the south it began to recapture a little of its lost elegance.

Even so there was no point in unpacking too much, for the indoor staff consisted only of old Jacques and his wife, who had served the Count, Antoinette and two or three village girls who were too half-witted to find any other more lucrative form of employment.

Jacques was getting very old. He had been about to retire when the Revolution swept away his chance of a comfortable pension. But how thankful they were to have him there!

He knew how things ought to be done, and though he grumbled incessantly, mourning the loss of the old days and deprecating the improvisations and make-shifts which had to be used for everything they found that under his experienced jurisdiction there was at least some semblance of formality in the attentions they received from the indoor staff.

Sometimes Rêve would feel the whole thing was a farce, that the life she was trying to re-create among the ruins of the past was empty and meaningless.

At such times it was only the Duchess's magnificent sense of humour which kept her from seeming near to despair.

Gradually, as an ordered existence came out of chaos, other complications arose which made her apprehensive and not a little afraid. Yes, afraid; and lying now in her bed, Rêve admitted to herself that she was terribly afraid of—the future.

Impulsively, as if galvanised by her own thoughts, she sprang from the bed and drew back her curtains. She looked out over the clear water of the lake which lay directly beneath her bedroom window.

It was then that the full realisation of what had occurred last night came flooding back to her mind, and she raised her hand to her cheeks as if she would hide the crimson tide of colour which swept into them.

How wonderful, how unexpectedly miraculous it had been! She had not known it was possible to feel so happy, to know such an ecstasy within herself.

So this was love! This was love, soaring, as the Duchess said, like an eagle until one's very humanity was lost in the dazzling blue of a translucent joy— a joy which made one tremble with shyness, yet leapt as a burning flame to consume that very timidity.

Rêve drew a deep breath. She was happier than she had ever been before in the whole of her life.

She was in love! And yet there was still a shadow, a cloud hovering darkly in the background. There had been no time to talk last night.

There had indeed been not a moment for words as their whole beings responded one to the other, and she had known that all she wished to hear was Armand's heart beating in unison with hers, all she wished to feel was the insistence of his lips on hers and the tender pressure of his hands.

How could she even remember there was anything else in the wonder of knowing her own response, in the breathless happiness of seeing the flame of passion in his eyes and of knowing that he desired her?

How could they speak except in the broken murmurings of love, as soft and musical as the evening breeze in the pine trees?

"Je t'adore!"

"So lovely—so perfect!"

"Again!"

"Oh God—again!"

There had been no need, no time for conversation;

50

but now in the clear morning light Rêve realised how much they had to tell each other.

It was now that she regretted that she knew so little about Armand or he about her. They knew all that was essential, that they loved each other, that they belonged one to the other as they must have belonged in a former life.

It was not a question of love at first sight, but rather a reunion between two people who must indeed have been together in some previous existence and had now found each other again in this.

From the first moment she had set eyes on him, Rêve thought Armand seemed familiar. She did not know whether it was his handsome face, his dark eyes, the firm squareness of his jaw, or the way his mouth curved at the corners when he was amused.

All she knew was that it seemed impossible now that there had been a time when she had not known him, when she had not loved him; and she knew without being told it that he felt the same about her.

They had found each other, and their bodies had recognised what their memories and brains had forgotten.

"Your hair!"

Armand had touched it gently as if it were some delicate substance that might be injured by the strength of his fingers. She had known what he asked of her, and with hands which trembled with the ecstasy within her breast she had taken the pins from the dark, shining coils.

Her face burned again as her hair fell softly over her naked shoulders as it had done the night before. She had known of what he was thinking as he stepped back to look at her.

Then reverently, in what seemed to her almost an act of adoration, he had dropped on one knee and taking only one slender curl in his hand, he had pressed his lips to it.

For a moment she was half afraid, as if he had withdrawn from her into some sacred place where she could not follow him; then he was on his feet again and she was once more in his arms.

She felt the fiercely possessive strength of him compel her subservience; she knew the fury of the fire she had awakened within him and was aware that only an iron self-control kept him from carrying her by force into the dark shadows of the Temple.

"My little—love!"

His voice broke on the words; then his lips sought hers hungrily, the need for her making his caress almost cruel in its very existence.

Rêve felt the sun warm on her lips and felt again that kiss of exquisite pain and ecstasy.

At the very thought she felt her whole body tingle and as the flickering flame of desire rose within her she was aware of the sweet heaviness of her eyelids and the burning warmth of her mouth. Soon, soon, she told herself, she would see him!

At the thought her heart leapt, as she had so often seen the stags leap, wild and untrammelled, as they strove to attack the hinds.

She would see him again; and then, as if a cloud swept over the brilliance of the sun; she remembered that today might bring her half-brother to the *Château*.

She had waited for him so long. She had anticipated his arrival hour by hour, and yet now for the first time she dreaded his coming and wished she had prevented her aunt from writing to him.

Armand, Marquis d'Augeron, was the son of Rêve's mother by her first husband. She had been desperately unhappy in a marriage which had been contracted before she left school with a man old enough to be her father, and on her husband's death she had returned to her own home.

But her husband's relations had prevented her from taking her child with her and the boy, who had succeeded to the title, had been brought up on the Polish estates of his grandparents. After his mother had married the Count de Valmont, all communications between them ceased.

Rêve had never met her half-brother. She knew that

52

he was fifteen years older than she was, and that the mention of him had made her mother very sad.

She learned this from Antoinette, for her mother had died when Rêve was only two years old of some obscure agonising disease for which the doctors could find neither cure nor relief.

It was the Duchess who had insisted that Rêve's half-brother should be informed that she had returned to the *Château* and be asked to visit her.

She had mooted this suggestion several times before Rêve agreed to do as she wished, and only when the question of her marriage arose did she allow the Duchess to write the letter which invited Armand d'Augeron to Valmont.

"It is not fitting," the Duchess said, "that I should negotiate your marriage when you have a nearer relative. If your brother did not exist, then perforce I should do my best for you, child, but when it comes to marriage, more than anything else it is of the utmost importance that one should be conventional as well as shrewd. I am getting old;

"I find finance and figures makes me feel giddy and I cannot grasp them. This offer for your hand is made by a very rich man and the settlement which he must make on you should be a large one, but I am afraid to undertake such delicate negotiations. Let us ask your half-brother to come here for a visit.

"He holds a position of importance and his lands and properties will not have been affected by the Revolution. He will obviously make the arrangements far better than I can. Be guided by me in this if in nothing else."

Rêve had agreed and one of the reasons for her agreement was that while they were waiting for Armand's arrival the arrangements for her wedding must be held up too. She knew nothing about the Comte de Durieux who had offered for her hand.

To the best of her belief she had never set eyes on him, although the information was conveyed to the Duchess by a friend that he had seen her when she was in Paris and had fallen in love with her.

The Duchess was so old, so out of touch with the

modern world, that she knew as little about the Count and his family as did Rêve.

"His grandfather was a handsome man," she said. "I remember dancing with him once at Versailles, but that is all I can recall of the Durieux family. It will be for your half-brother to make the investigations, to discover if they are genuinely wealthy and their breeding unimpeachable."

Rêve was well aware that it was expected that she should marry and the marriage would be arranged in the conventional manner of her country. Yet she had been curiously reluctant to take the step, to leave Valmont, to relinquish the home to which she had so recently returned.

It was therefore with a sense of relief that she realised that it would take some months to contact her brother in Poland and for him to come to Valmont.

It was in fact two months before they had even an answer to the Duchess's letter. France was in a state of unrest and Napoleon was moving his armies about.

There was the war with Russia, and when the messenger finally returned he had more to say of the tribulations he had suffered on his journey than about the Marquis d'Augeron and what he was like.

It seemed that the Marquis had made very little impression on him, although he spoke for some length about a Monsieur de Frémond who had apparently aroused his animosity. Anyway the Duchess's letter had achieved what it had set out to do.

Armand wrote quite pleasantly to say that he understood the position and would proceed to Valmont with all possible speed. They might expect him within the next two months. But the two months had come and gone and still there was no sign of him.

Instead there was another letter from the Comte de Durieux asking that negotiations be put in hand as speedily as possible and hinting that the Emperor himself was interested in the proposed betrothal.

Rêve had felt a sense of panic rise within her. Who was the Comte de Durieux? What did she know of him? Why was he so insistent?

And now after last night, after meeting the man for whom her heart must have been searching ever since she grew up, she knew she could never marry anyone else.

Standing at the window and looking out on to the lake, she realised how little she knew about Monsieur de Ségury. All that she was certain of was that his name was Armand like her half-brother's, that he came from Normandy and that she loved him.

She knew nothing else, and yet did anything else matter? That was all that was of account—that she loved him and he loved her. He might be married for all she knew, he might be penniless or have a price on his head, and yet nothing else was of consequence save that they loved each other.

At the mere thought of him she could feel her whole body tremble.

"My love—my life—*je t'adore!*"

She could hear his voice deep with emotion, she could feel the throb of her heart beneath his hand.

"Mine . . . mine!"

A note of triumph—man, the conqueror! Yet would she ask anything else of life but to be conquered—by him?

When her half-brother eventually arrived, she would have a very different story to tell him from what had been intended when the Duchess first wrote to Poland. She would tell him that she was in love, that the Comte de Durieux must be told that this suit was in vain and that negotiations must start with the family of Armand de Ségury.

And it must be done quickly! Alone, Rêve blushed to herself as she realised how quickly she wanted these negotiations to proceed. She wanted to be married, she wanted to belong in heart, mind and soul. If ever a marriage was made in heaven, theirs would be.

"Armand de Ségury!"

She repeated the name to herself and liked it. Then as she smiled and told herself she would like anything that he was called, however banal, however ordinary it might be, she gave a little sigh and turned from the window.

She must go downstairs, she thought, and take her *petit déjeuner* in her Great-Aunt's bedchamber as she was wont to do.

It would be difficult, she thought, to keep her happiness hidden from the old lady's penetrating eyes, from her shrewdness which guessed at things almost before one was aware of them oneself.

Rêve had half suspicioned that the Duchess had fancied something unusual was occurring when Armand called yesterday. She had said nothing for a few minutes after he had gone from the room.

She appeared to be thinking, her eyes fixed reflectively on the door through which he had departed; then she said quickly:

"A handsome young man indeed! But beneath that attractive visage I sense both character and intelligence. Do you like him, child?"

Rêve had been startled by the question, but with an effort she had made her reply in what she hoped was a disinterested voice.

"I thought him pleasant enough, Madame."

"Doubtless he is thinking in the same extravagant phrases about you," the Duchess said sarcastically, a note of dry humour in her voice which told Rêve she was not deceived by her artlessness. "I wish I could remember a little more about his family, for I like the boy. There is something about him, something which makes me sure that he has both breeding and personality. There are not many young men like that about in these days when counter-jumpers and scullions ape their betters."

Réve had said nothing for fear she might betray herself, and after a moment the old lady had laid her hand on her shoulder and said quietly:

"*Hélas!* Let us hope that your half-brother will soon be here and your future arranged."

Rêve had been certain then that the Duchess had guessed at her feelings and now she half wished that she had confided in her Great-Aunt, for if it had been difficult to keep silent yesterday, it would be even more difficult today.

Her very heart was bursting with happiness, and when she looked in her mirror she felt as if a light were shining from her face, revealing her secret to all who looked at her.

She began to dress, selecting her prettiest gown and taking what was for her a considerable time to arrange her hair. She was humming as she did so the same lilting, light-hearted melody which had been in her mind that night—which now seemed so long ago—when she had come from the Temple to find Armand outside.

She was nearly dressed when there came a knock on the door, and before she could answer, before she could command whoever was outside to enter, the door was burst open and one of the village girls, a big loutish creature with a harelip, came into the room.

"Mam'selle? Oh, Mam'selle!" she cried in an agitated voice, slurring her words more than usual.

Rêve looked up at her in surprise.

"What is the matter, Lili?" she asked, and as the girl struggled for breath she added kindly: "Has something frightened you? You look upset!"

There was no mistaking Lili's agitation. Her hair was tumbling in dark greasy coils from under her white cap, her big red hands were twisting themselves together, and it seemed as if she were about to burst into tears.

"Come at once, Mam'selle, si'l vous plaît. The old lady—the old lady——"

The girls had been told time without number not to refer to the Duchess as "the old lady", but Rêve did not notice the lapse now. She sprang to her feet and before Lili had time to say another word she had rushed from the room and down the wide stairs to the Duchess's apartment.

The door was open, the curtains drawn, and with a fleeting sense of relief Rêve saw that Antoinette was at the bedside. Indeed it must have been Antoinette who sent Lili to find her.

As she sped across the room towards the big four-poster bed draped with oyster-tinted satin she saw the Duchess's face among the pillows and knew what Lili had been afraid to tell her.

She stood arrested half-way across the room, unable to proceed, unable to move.

The Duchess was very old and yet somehow the flame of life had burnt so strongly, so youthfully within her ancient body that it was almost impossible to imagine that the time had come when she would relinquish her hold on the world she had found so amusing.

Rêve's face was stricken as Antoinette turned towards her, and crossing the room, the older woman put her hands about her comfortingly as she had done so often ever since she was born.

"It was a happy death, *ma petite*. You must not grieve. This is the way she would have wished to die."

"But, Antoinette, what shall we do without her?" Rêve said in a small, broken voice.

Antoinette drew her towards the window, her arms still around her.

"Yes, yes, I know, *ma chérie,* but we weep for ourselves. Life will go on! We must only remember we are the richer for having known her."

"Yes, that is true," Rêve said. "We are so much the richer for having known her." She laid her head for a monent on her nurse's shoulder. "How wise you are, Antoinette! You always know the right thing to say, the right thing to do. Sometimes I wish I was as old as Madame and as wise as you."

As she was talking, the tears came to her eyes and began to fall down her cheeks. Understandingly, Antoinette drew her closer, consoling her as if she were a frightened child.

"I know, *ma petite,*" she said. "We all feel like that at times. But for you life is just beginning and you must not waste any of it in useless regrets. Madame la Duchess would not have it. She had lived her life fully. Often she has said to me: 'Antoinette, the only things I regret in my life are the times I said no—and there were not many of them.' "

Rêve smiled through her tears.

"I can hear her say it."

"Always Madame held out her hands towards life. She embraced it, she lived every moment of it in enjoyment, in appreciation and with courage. That is what counts, *ma chérie,* courage."

Rêve raised her head and looked into the face of her nurse. Antoinette was over fifty, but her face was unlined. She was in fact a young-looking woman despite the fact that her hair was almost white. Her expression was one of great sweetness.

It was, Rêve thought sometimes, an expression such as she had seen on the faces of nuns who had devoted their lives to tending the sick and the suffering. It was an expression of dedication and saintliness which came from an inner philosophy of strength and determination.

Antoinette had all these things, and Rêve knew that she had dedicated her life to hers almost from the moment of her birth at Valmont.

Impulsively now she put her arms round the older woman's neck and drew her face down to hers.

"I will try, Antoinette, to be as brave as Madame and as understanding as you."

Antoinette kissed her, then rose to her feet. There was a suspicion of moisture about her eyes as if she were moved by the very simplicity of Rêve's words, but her voice was calm and unemotional as she said:

"We have much to do, my dear. Send Jacques to the village with the news. He will know whom to fetch. You go into the garden and pick what flowers you can to place at Madame's feet as she lies in state in the Great Hall."

Rêve knew she was being dismissed, but she was thankful to accept Antoinette's commands without protestation. She told old Jacques that the Duchess was dead and gave him Antoinette's instructions.

She did not carry the tidings to the kitchen for she knew that Lili would have preceded her there.

Indeed already she could hear the hysterical sobs of the other servants and as she let herself into the garden by a side door she felt for a moment as if she had escaped into the freedom of the sunshine.

But she knew there was no real escape either from this or from anything else. The future had to be faced.

She picked a great armful of flowers. There were roses which once had been cultivated and pruned and which now grew wild, growing as they would in an exotic wildness of their own pattern.

There were too, delphiniums blue as the sky, and flame-coloured gladioli of which her Great-Aunt had been particularly fond.

She would want many more, Rêve decided, but for the moment she had as many as she could carry. She went back to the house with her arms full, and as she did so she heard the sound of a horse's hoofs coming round the sweep of the drive to the front door.

Wondering who it could be, she came from the terrace to the front door of the house and saw to her astonishment a man wearing a coat and waistcoat of light blue with silver lace round the collar, dismounting from a finely harnessed horse. He glanced at the front door as if looking for the bell rope.

Rêve went forward, her arms full of flowers.

"You have a message for someone here?" she inquired.

The man turned at the sound of her voice, saluted her respectfully, and she realised that he wore the livery of the Emperor's personal servants.

"I have a communication, Mademoiselle, for the Comtesse Rêve de Valmont."

"I am the Comtesse," Rêve said. "You may give it to me."

He drew a red-sealed letter from his pocket and handed it over with a bow.

"From the Emperor, Madame," he said reverently.

Rêve realised that to open the letter she must put down her flowers. She turned aside to lay them on the balustrade. It took her a moment or two to balance them securely, then she opened the letter.

For a second she stared at it stupidly as if she

could hardly take in its contents, then slowly the words penetrated her mind.

The Emperor Napoleon Bonaparte presents his compliments to the Comtesse Réve de Valmont and will honour her with his presence on the night of August 16th when he will be passing through St. Benis en route for Paris.

That was all! Réve felt the words dance before her eyes; then she saw that the seal bore the famous 'N' and knew it was no dream. For a moment she could hardly take in the full implications of what she had read.

She could only think of the Duchess lying dead upstairs, the many empty rooms below, the shaking hands of old Jacques, the clumsy loutishness of Lili.

Then she remembered Armand. He would be waiting for her tonight at the Temple by the lake. With a sudden resolution she turned towards the messenger.

"I much regret . . ." she began, but her voice died away.

He had gone—gone while she had been reading the letter and she had not heard him go. There was now no question of a reply.

The Emperor gave his commands and those who received them obeyed.

4

Rêve slipped out of the french windows into the garden. It was not yet eight o'clock and she knew that Armand would not be at the Temple until nine, but she felt as if the house was stifling her and she must escape into the fresh air.

All day she had listened to the wailing and lamentations of the servants, the professional condolences of the layers-out, the conventional soothing sympathy of the priest, and she had managed through it all to keep her own tears in check, her own grief under control.

Now she felt as if she could bear no more.

In the Great Banqueting Hall, which had been stripped of all furniture, the Duchess lay in state. Her thin white hands, which had been kissed so ardently in her youth, were crossed on her withered breast and her face was curiously young again.

The blinds had been drawn, the windows shut and despite the height and size of the room the perfume of the flowers and the smell of the tallow candles arranged round the bier were almost overpowering.

For hours Rêve had knelt at her Great-Aunt's side in prayer but she had felt that it would be wiser to pray for herself. The old lady had escaped from the difficulties, tribulations and uncertainties of life on earth. Those who were left behind would not be so fortunate.

Yet it was impossible to think or wish that the Duchess should be at rest. Despite her age, she had been so vital and alert and she had enjoyed living with a possessive emotion which was at times almost fiercely vehement, as if she were afraid she might miss one second of experience.

Her whole eighty-five years on earth had been an exciting adventure and a turbulent one, and in the afterworld she would—given the choice—ask only more adventures and excitement rather than eternal rest of an uneventual peace.

The Priest had made all the arrangements for the funeral. The Duchess was to be buried in the de Valmont vault situated in the little churchyard which, overgrown and neglected, had once been the treasured pride of the village.

A beautiful grey stone edifice of the Renaissance period, the church had been one of the finest masterpieces of Christian architecture in France; but now it lay half ruined, its stained-glass windows broken, its aisle empty of the elaborately carved oak pews.

The sacred vessels, some of them of great antiquity and almost priceless, had been stolen or smashed. The vestments and altar cloths had been torn into shreds or used for floor covering.

Nevertheless, the doors were tentatively open again, as were the doors of many other churches in France, and the *Curé,* a timid, anxious-faced man who always seemed to be anticipating trouble, spent many weary hours trying to erase from the reredos the words "The Temple of Reason" which had been splashed there in brilliant red paint by the terrorists.

But what was missing more obviously than the treasures stolen or ancient monuments defaced and broken was a congregation.

A few elderly people trickled into the services, occasionally a lovesick girl or a man in trouble with the authorities would sneak in through a side entrance with almost a shamefaced air to kneel in the shadows or hurriedly light a candle before some famed saint.

There was in fact an apologetic, shifty-eyed atmosphere about the church-goers as if they were secretly ashamed of an inner weakness rather than elated by the resuscitation of their religion.

The years when Christianity had been persecuted, laughed at and reviled had taken their toll.

All that remained of a glorious, whole-hearted faith

was the flickering uncertainty of those who had grown to believe that God Himself had forsaken them.

The Duchess's funeral would therefore be a shabby, threadbare service without pomp or many mourners. Rêve would have minded it much more, and indeed it would have hurt her almost unbearably had she not known how indifferent her Great-Aunt would be to such things.

The Duchess had always had a complacent regard for death; indeed she had often joked about it, saying in her inimitable way:

"Death's embrace is the last every woman knows—pray Heaven he proves a charming lover! He is at least an experienced one!"

No, the Duchess would never have trouble herself as to the poorness of the funeral *cortège* or the desolate appearance of the building in which the burial service would be read.

Indeed it was not the Duchess or her funeral that worried Rêve now. As she moved across the green lawns and took the path which went round the lake, she was aware of an emotion within herself which was not connected with sorrow, grief or regret.

It was an aching, empty feeling which she recognised all too clearly, having known it before—it was loneliness.

Never in all the years when she had moved about the country penniless and disguised with Antoinette her only protector had she felt so lonely as she did now.

As a child it had been easy for her to cling to Antoinette, to know that she took the place of both mother and nurse, family and home. But as Rêve grew older she had realised that Antoinette had her limitations.

It was not that she loved her any the less; that would have been impossible, for her love for her old nurse was perhaps the strongest and most unassailable thing in the whole of her life. But she had understood, as she grew to maturity, that there were many parts Antoinette could not play in her life and that she needed the counsel and guidance of someone both of her own blood and of her own social standing.

64

When her Great-Aunt came to chaperon her at Valmont, Rêve knew that part at any rate of what she had sensed instinctively had been missing in her life would be supplied.

Acutely sensitive, she was well aware how sadly her education had been neglected in the years when she had been to all intents and purposes nothing but a gypsy child. But she was equally sure that the Duchess could teach her more than she could have learnt from a dozen governesses or teachers, and she had set herself to learn as quickly as possible all that should have been hers by right of birth.

The Duchess was a hard task-mistress. She expected perfection in deportment, good manners and the traditional behaviour of a *débutante*.

When she was young she had caused a sensation on her presentation at Court; married, her salon in Paris had been the most distinguished and cultured of that time. She had not only been a great beauty, she had also been extremely intelligent, and men of brains—statesmen, writers, poets and diplomats—had thronged her drawing-rooms and listened respectfully while she aired her views on everything and everybody.

Rêve had no idea until her Great-Aunt came to live with her what a wide field of knowledge there was for her to discover or how fascinating such discovery could be.

She often thought to herself that with Antoinette she had learned the fundamental decencies of living—kindness of heart, generosity, sympathy, courage and most important of all—faith in the ultimate purpose of Life.

But with her Great-Aunt she learned the things which matter in the world of fashion.

She discovered how to be sparklingly witty, to be exquisitely graceful, to use one's brain to outwit or to conquer another as a swordsman might fence with an adversary, to be knowledgeable of the correct behaviour of a person of breeding in all possible circumstances, and finally to understand and appreciate all that was worth while in art, literature and music.

It was a vast curriculum for any girl to absorb in a

short space of time, and yet like the ground which has been parched for want of water Rêve soaked up greedily and thirstily into her mind all that the Duchess tried to teach her.

And now the lessons were at an end. The curtain had fallen and the play was over. Somehow Rêve could hardly believe that it could be so, that the old lady who had given her so much had gone from her without a word of farewell, without a last close embrace.

For the first time since the shock of dicovery early that morning Rêve felt the tears well up into her eyes, a sudden constriction in her throat.

And yet she would not let herself cry. Instead, she thought of Armand who would be coming to her in a short while.

It was indeed, whether she realised it or not, the thought of him which had restrained her all day, numbed her sense of loss, mitigated a little the tragedy of her loneliness and her fear of what lay in the future.

Her knowledge of her love for him and his for her was like a sustaining arm which upheld her against her own weakness. More than once she found herself lost in a kind of ecstasy at the thought of him, and then she would chide herself for daring to think of a man in the very hour of her bereavement.

And yet she knew that above all people her Great-Aunt would have understood, and she wished now that she had had the courage to tell her about Armand when he had called at the *Château*.

As she walked towards the wood, Rêve thought that apart from the joy of seeing Armand there were serious things to be considered tonight.

First she must tell him of her Great-Aunt's death, although it was more than likely he would know of this already if he were lodging in the village. Secondly she must discuss with him the Emperor's proposed visit to Valmont. There had been no opportunity as yet to reveal this to anyone else.

Already she was turning to Armand for help and guidance, knowing with an unshakable conviction that

66

he would not fail her and that she could trust him completely and absolutely.

Thirdly, and most important—there was the question of her marriage.

She wanted to marry Armand. The unknown Count in Paris who desired her was but a mythical shadowy figure hardly worth her consideration. It was Armand who mattered, Armand whose dark eyes and hungry lips seemed like magnets to draw her very soul into his keeping.

She was well aware how unconventional, how indeed almost improper was the situation in which she found herself; but she had lived too long in insecurity, in penury and in fear, for the standards and rules of a defeated aristocracy to trouble her unduly.

She had understood how important the conventions were to her Great-Aunt; but the Duchess had indeed been little inconvenienced personally by the "Terror" and the havoc which it had brought to other people's lives had left hers almost untouched.

She had been abroad and all the while that France was rent in twain with horror and bestiality she had lived comfortably among people who were of her own kind and her own class.

No, the Duchess had not lost father, home and all that was familiar within the space of one terrifying, destructive hour.

She had not walked the roads and fields, often barefooted, usually without food and shelter, or known the sharp gnawing pains of hunger, or more agonising still, the pain of fear—fear which followed one like a shadow, wherever one went.

She had not learned to tremble at the sound of every strange voice, of every footfall on the stairs, at every tap on the window. She had not known what it was to have to disguise one's face, to be forced to conceal one's hands lest their delicacy should betray her blood.

She had not known what it was to lie and lie convincingly lest the truth should forfeit life itself.

After such things the dicta of society seemed trivial. Rêve had to learn the right way to curtsy, the number of fingers one should extend in greeting, the exact inclination of the head when bowing, the conventional reply to an introduction, the procedure at the dinner table, the number of cards which should be left and the proper space of time which must elapse before a courtesy call could be returned.

If the Revolution had done nothing else, it had cast away many such ridiculous rules and regulations; and yet, as unfortunately it had nothing to put in their place, they were gradually creeping back one by one, even into the entourage of the Emperor himself.

Rêve felt that where she was concerned she could not be influenced by them.

While her heart was free she was prepared to agree with the Duchess that her marriage must be arranged in a conventional manner.

In a marriage of convenience, the male members of the family discussed at length and without emotion or sentiment the dowries and settlements and the legal aspect of the affair as if the two people concerned were nothing but inanimate sticks of furniture or animals without proper feelings.

But now with her head throbbing with love, Rêve knew that she could never agree to such a proceeding. It was one thing to consider marriage in the abstract, but it was an entirely different matter when one was in love and one's whole being throbbed with desire for another man.

If Armand de Ségury wanted her, she was his, and all the traditions in the world would not make her accept the Comte Giles de Durieux.

As she reached the wood she made her way by a secret, twisting path, known only to herself, to the lower water and the little Temple.

It had been her favourite place of concealment as a child, and when she returned to the *Château* she had found that it was the one spot left where she could recapture the sense of being home and at peace within herself.

Perhaps it was the mirrored beauty of the trees in

the silent water, perhaps the Temple with its classic loveliness and atmosphere of ageless imperturbability.

The moon was rising in the sky, but it was as yet a pale ghost of itself. The stars were coming out one by one. In the east there was still the last dying glow of the setting sun. The wood pigeons had not yet settled themselves for the night.

They were cooing to one another as they roosted in the trees. Every now and then there was a faint splash on the still waters of the lake and the ever widening ripples showed that a fish had risen.

Rêve drew a sigh of relief. It was as if a healing hand had been placed upon her and she felt the burden and misery of the past hours fall away from her shoulders.

She whispered a little prayer as she reached the Temple and felt it was more acceptable than all the formal prayers and responses she had made during the day in the Great Banqueting Hall.

Here in the silence of the evening it was easy to understand that there was a pattern in all things, and that however lonely one might feel within oneself God was still there and that one was in fact never alone.

Rêve entered the Temple and brought out from it several cushions which she put on the steps between the pillars. She sat down and realised that she was tired, though her body was tense and alert, waiting for Armand to come to her.

She remembered the night before last when she had stood in the very place on which she now sat and had looked down to meet his eyes. She had been frightened then, frightened with that horrible paralysing fear which had pursued her since her childhood and which still overwhelmed her at unaccountable moments.

But when he had spoken and had drawn near, she had known instinctively that she need not be physically afraid.

He was a gentleman and she could trust him. She had known that, even in her overwhelming humiliation and shame that he had seen her nakedness. And then like the soft strains of music coming from a violin there had come a throbbing within her heart which gradually invaded her whole senses.

She had felt as if her spirit was winged with light and her whole being was being lifted upwards taut and tense in expectation.

She felt herself quiver and come to life within her very self. She heard her breath quicken and knew a sudden ecstasy which swept over her like a tempestuous wind giving her neither the choice nor the chance to resist it.

That had been love, she knew it now; a love not growing softly and gently in the warm sunshine of friendship, but a love coming as a conqueror—as an eagle strong and determined to secure his prey.

Rêve leant her head back against the cushions and closed her eyes for a moment. She could recapture Armand's words as she had lain in his arms last night.

"You are so lovely," he had whispered against her lips. "I did not believe that such perfection existed in any woman."

"Then you must have known very few," she teased, happiness welling within her, making her want to laugh with a sheer unbridled joy at hearing him praise her, of seeing the look of admiration in his eyes.

"On the contrary," he replied. "I have known many women, but until this moment there has never been one that mattered. Now I cannot even remember them. Their faces are but empty masks; your face, your beauty fills my entire vision."

"They at least taught you to say pretty things," Rêve answered, jealous for a moment of those women who must indeed have loved him.

"They taught me nothing," he replied, "save to mistrust their whole sex and to find the repetition of meaningless compliments a most tedious occupation."

His voice had altered as she spoke. He had suddenly begun to drawl his words and even the expression on his face seemed to change. It seemed to Rêve for a moment that he was a stranger and not the man who had held her in his arms and whispered urgently and with such eagerness of his love.

70

Then as she stared at him, half alarmed, he swept her back into his arms and his mouth sought hers impatiently and hungrily.

"Why do we talk of anything but you?" he asked impatiently. " 'Tis you that I want—that I love—that I worship! You are mine! You were meant for me!"

She knew that he spoke the truth, but it was impossible to answer him for his mouth was on hers and his arms held her so tightly that he seemed to squeeze the very breath from her.

She had been content to rest her head against his shoulder, to feel his passion sweep over her like a flood-tide, leaving her limp, exhausted and happy beyond expression.

But now she found herself wondering about him. Where had he lived? What had he done? Whom did he know?

It was not that she was curious in any social sense, as the Duchess might have been. It mattered not whether Armand de Ségury's father was a blacksmith or a prince, she would still love him.

If she was curious, it was because everything about him was dear and precious to her. There was nothing too trivial that she would not treasure about him, there was nothing too great or too important that she would not want to share it.

Suddenly there was a snapping of a twig as if a foot had stepped on it, the rustle of someone approaching, and instantly the colour came to Rêve's cheeks as she was on her feet, her heart beating wildly.

Armand was coming to her. Her eyes searched the shadows of the trees along the narrow path by which he had come to the Temple the two previous evenings. But there was no one in sight.

Then, as she looked for him, believing that any second would reveal his tall figure, a voice spoke from behind her. Startled, she turned round and to her astonishment saw that it was not Armand who stood there but another man.

He was young and fashionably dressed, and in his own way was not without good looks, but to Rêve, disconcerted and half alarmed by his unexpected appearance, he appeared both evil and menacing.

"Rêve de Valmont?" the stranger inquired, and she noted that he had bold dark eyes which looked her over appraisingly.

Although she was taken by surprise, her voice was perfectly cool and steady as she replied coldly:

"I am the Comtesse Rêve de Valmont."

"I was told at the *Château* I should find you here," the newcomer said, "but let me introduce myself. I am Paul de Frémond."

"Indeed! And you desired to see me?"

Rêve had for the moment no recollection of having heard the name before. She was wondering what she should do. At any moment Armand might arrive and find this unexpected visitor.

"Indeed I had an urgent desire to see you, little Rêve."

Rêve raised her eyebrows.

"Might I inquire, Monsieur, why you presume to address me in such familiar terms?"

"You may indeed," Paul de Frémond replied, "and when you hear my answer you will understand. I have heard you spoken of so often that I feel I have known you for a long time."

"Spoken of by whom?" Rêve inquired, bewildered.

"By your step-brother, Armand d'Augeron."

"My brother! Then he has arrived at the *Château*?"

Paul de Frémond shook his head.

"Let us sit down, for I have a long story to tell you."

"Perhaps, Monsieur, it would be wise to return to the *Château,*" Rêve suggested, but the stranger answered quickly:

"No, I would rather talk here. I need no audience for what I have to impart."

Rêve would have protested, the words were on her lips, then she decided to be silent. Perhaps this newcomer would say what he had to say quickly and go. She disliked and distrusted him on sight and her instinct warned her to be careful.

He had a bumptious, almost buccaneer air about

him; and his eyes wandered from her face to her low-cut evening gown, she felt as if she were mentally undressed, and she flushed at his impertinence.

She seated herself on the cushion which she had just vacated, and he sat down beside her, stretching out his legs in a manner which proclaimed him to be irritatingly at his ease.

Indeed there was, Rêve felt, almost an insolence in the way he made himself comfortable, in the bold manner in which his eyes appraised her and in the faint smile on his thick lips.

The very tone of familiarity in which he addressed her was an insult, and yet there was nothing she could say, nothing she could do but wait until he revealed the reason for his visit.

"A charming spot," he said at length condescendingly.

"You have something to tell me, Monsieur," Rêve prompted.

"A lot, my dear," he replied, "but first let me explain who I am. I am your brother's greatest friend and his companion these past five years. We have lived together, hunted together, drunk together, and if any man knew your brother, it is I."

"Then my brother sent you ahead to tell us of his arrival?" Rêve asked. "We have been expecting him these past two months."

Paul de Frémond looked away from her for a moment, then once again his eyes sought hers.

"Your half-brother is dead, little Rêve."

"Dead!"

Rêve repeated the word almost tonelessly. For the moment she could hardly take in the meaning of what he said. It was so unexpected. Almost with a sense of relief she realised that she felt nothing, not even a sense of shock at this announcement.

"Yes, dead," Paul de Frémond repeated. "He died a fortnight ago in Amsterdam. We were staying there for a few days while our horses rested. We have taken, I must admit, a somewhat long time to reach here, but your half-brother had a considerable zest for life. He denied himself little, and if a place was amusing and its women pretty, he saw no reason to hurry his departure."

Rêve's lips tightened for a moment and she said quietly:

"Kindly tell me exactly what happened and the cause of my brother's death."

"If you are not too squeamish to hear it."

Paul de Frémond gave a short vulgar laugh which echoed across the lake, seeming to shatter the peace like a violent blow.

"I would like to hear the truth," Rêve said steadily.

"Well, I was never one to mince words," he replied. "We were staying in Amsterdam and your brother became enamoured with a certain lady whose name would mean nothing to you. She was, in fact, the wife of a respected Burgomaster. She was pretty enough, but hardly to my taste.

"Anyway, your half-brother courted her and I can assure you she was not loth to be courted, very much to the contrary. Her husband was away on business, so she told us, supplying Napoleon's army with boots. In his absence we gave a party in his house.

"An excellent party it was while it lasted; but unfortunately, when the merry-making was at its height and your brother in a somewhat compromising position with the lady of his choice, the doors were flung open and the Burgomaster returned.

"He had with him a friend and a couple of burly serving men who were only too ready to do his bidding. There was a fight in which unfortunately the majority of the guests were too incapacitated by the food and wine to take a very active part.

"Your brother fought gallantly, but he was caught at a disadvantage. The Burgomaster, who had apparently armed himself with a sword-stick on his travels, ran him through before he could adequately defend himself.

"We were all flung into the street and it was on the dirty cobblestones wet with recent rain that I found your brother was dead."

"Dead in somewhat unfortunate circumstances, to say the least of it," Rêve said, her voice hard.

Paul de Frémond shrugged his shoulders.

"Your brother was a man who enjoyed life, my dear; and why not? He was rich, unmarried, and not without a certain charm of his own. If women surrendered easily to him, it is surely not for us to blame him or them."

"He knew that I was waiting here, anxiously awaiting his arrival to make arrangements for my marriage."

"He spoke of that; in fact we discussed it often," Paul de Frémond replied. "Everything is decided."

"As my brother is dead the question does not arise."

"On the contrary you will want to obey his last wishes in the matter."

"How can he have known they were his last if he died as you say without repentance or priest?"

"I was in your brother's confidence," Paul de Frémond replied. "He trusted me, confided in me. When your Great-Aunt's letter came asking him to journey here to arrange your marriage, we discussed the whole matter. Finally your brother decided that the person you should marry would be me."

Rêve started to her feet.

"You!" she ejaculated. "Are you mad?"

Paul de Frémond looked up at her, but made no attempt to rise.

"On the contrary, I am very sane," he said. "You are attractive, as I anticipated you would be, but even I was not prepared for anyone quite so pretty. I can assure you that even on such short acquaintance I am utterly content with the arrangement."

"I think, Monsieur, that you are being insulting," Rêve said coldly.

She was frightened, but there was no sign of it in the proud carriage of her head.

"You will not speak of such intimate matters which do not concern you."

She continued. "With regard to the news you bring of my brother's death I must ask you, what I should have

75

asked you sooner, to produce your credentials that I may have something by which I can judge whether or not what you tell me is the truth."

Paul de Frémond smiled.

"I like your spirit," he said, "but there is no reason for me to give you chapter and verse for what I say. You know as well as I do that it is the truth. Armand is dead, but he wished me to marry you and marry you I shall. Incidentally, my dear, he made you his heir—the papers are lodged with a notary on his estate. We can send for them at our leisure."

"His heir!"

Rêve hardly breathed the words, then her eyes were dark with anger as she said:

"So that is why you wish to marry me. My brother was wealthy, I know that, and if I am his heiress you wish to get your hands on his money."

Paul de Frémond continued to smile.

"Pray do not be hasty, do not say things which later we shall both regret. But let us by all means be frank with each other. I, my dear Rêve, am penniless. I always have been. I was an *émigré* to England—an orphan of the Revolution they called me!

"My pathetic state brought tears to the eyes of a Nobleman who had known my father in our more affluent days. He had me educated and brought me up with his own family in considerable comfort.

"Then unfortunately he took a dislike to me—or shall I say to certain actions of mine?—and cast me out into the world without a penny to my name. I was forced to leave England for reasons I need not enumerate. Your brother took me in. But if he was my benefactor, I equally was his.

"I amused him, I made life appreciably more enjoyable for him. I have a way of getting what I want in this world. Your brother was an ineffective person in many ways and he found me useful.

"It was I who persuaded him to make a will in your favour before he left home. I am nothing if not practical, and with the world so full of perils and dangers as it is today one can never be too careful."

"I wonder you did not decide to murder him yourself," Rêve said bitterly. "It is obvious that if you planned to marry me, then his death must be to your advantage."

"That is being unnecessarily suspicious," Paul de Frémond said suavely. "Your brother was just as useful to me alive as dead. I had the handling of his money, I had authority to order what I wished. I was major-domo, aide-de-camp, companion, wife and nurse to him all at the same time. But I am not saying that I didn't make it worth my while. A workman, my dear, is worthy of his hire."

His mocking voice ceased for a moment and as Rêve did not speak he continued after a few seconds.

"Actually it was Armand who thought we should be man and wife. He was telling me how indispensable I was to him and bewailing the fact that he had to look after a young half-sister.

"You will have to take her on as well as me, Paul," he said; and then as if a sudden thought struck him, he added:

"You had best marry her. It would simplify everything."

"I promise you that until that moment the idea had not entered my head, but afterwards I saw how sensible it was; and now that Armand is dead, it is imperative that his wishes be carried out."

"So that you may be rich!" Rêve finished sarcastically. "I will arrange that you are paid for your services."

"That is most generous of you," Paul de Frémond said, "but unfortunately in my efforts to safeguard your interests I arranged that the money should not be yours to handle until you were married or twenty-one. I was afraid, you see, that you might feel inclined to give some of it away to your friends. I did not anticipate that I might be the recipient of your bounty. No, my dear, there is no alternative. You will have to marry me and make the best of it."

"I think, Monsieur, you have said quite enough," Rêve said quietly. "You will return to the *Château* and collect your horse or carriage and leave. I should like, later, to receive a formal announcement of my brother's death; but if you cannot arrange this, I will see to it myself. There is, otherwise, no reason for us to have further communication with each other."

Paul de Frémond got slowly to his feet.

"I said before," he remarked softly, "that I admired your spirit. I like my women to have a bit of fire in them, it makes them a deal more entertaining. But as to going away, you have quite the wrong idea, my dear. You cannot get rid of me. I am here to stay."

There was something menacing in his tone, and as she looked up at him Rêve was desperately afraid.

"It is obviously useless to argue with you, Monsieur, but I assure you that I shall find a way to rid myself of you and that quickly."

"Brave words!" Paul de Frémond sneered, "but without substance. Your Great-Aunt lies dead in the *Château*; your half-brother is under the ground in Amsterdam, and your other relations do not exist. I know everything about your family, you see. I know how your father died at the guillotine, how your uncles were killed by the terrorists.

"Armand had quarrelled with his side of the family, what remained of them. They disapproved of him and they are not likely to be interested in his half-sister whom they have never seen. No, there is no one you can turn to except me, and I am the obvious person to look after you.

"Besides, Armand made me the Executor of his will. I am your guardian, therefore, my most charming little Rêve, until such time as you come of age or until you marry. Don't forget that—until you marry."

There was something in the horrible way he spoke which broke through Rêve's control.

"I will never marry you—never," she said, and for a moment her voice was almost hysterical.

"I should not be too sure of that. Besides, a large number of women have found me quite attractive, so why not you? But what is more important, you attract me."

78

As he spoke Paul de Frémond crossed with one step the space between them. Rêve gave a little cry as she saw the sudden lust in his eyes and realised what was his intention. But it was too late.

He put out his arms, gripped her and drawing her close to him. Then with one hand he tipped back her chin so that he could look down into her face.

As he did so, he laughed softly as if at her very impotency.

"Let me go!" Rêve cried.

She would have shouted the words, but her voice seemed to die in her throat.

"By our Lady you're curst pretty," Paul de Frémond said, and then his thick lips were on hers.

She felt a sudden nausea rise within her at his touch and then a darkness and horror encompassed her so that she felt she was sinking into a bottomless pit.

Suddenly, when she felt she must faint beneath the sheer bestiality of his embrace, she was free. She felt his arms release their pressure and realised with an almost intolerable sense of relief that her assailant was being dragged away from her.

As she gasped for breath and her fingers went up to her bruised mouth, she saw that Armand was there— Armand looking like an avenging St. Michael, his hands gripping Paul de Frémond by the collar, his eyes dark with anger.

"What is this swine doing to you?" he asked.

But before she could speak Paul de Frémond had regained his balance and, twisting himself free, he turned towards Armand, whose face was full in the light of the rising moon.

For a moment he stared, obviously startled and astonished. Then he cried out in English:

"Faith, if it isn't Sheringham! Sheringham, the Seducer! What the hell are you doing here?"

"That is just what I am asking you, de Frémond," Armand replied coldly, "and you had better answer quickly before I kill you."

His voice was so menacing that Paul de Frémond instinctively took a step backwards.

"I was not doing anything other than you would have done yourself if you had been here earlier," he said with an effort to appear at his ease.

Armand's hand slashed him across the mouth. He staggered, but did not fall. Slipping his hand quickly into the breast pocket of his coat, he said furiously:

"You'll die for that!"

But Armand with an unexpectedly swift movement knocked his arm upwards before his hand could grasp whatever weapon lay hidden within his coat. Then as the two men confronted each other Armand brought out a pistol.

"If it's duelling you are looking for," he said, "I am only too eager to blow a hole through you, but in the meantime I would have you explain how you dare to come here and threaten this lady."

"So you have been listening, have you?" Paul de Frémond said, and as he spoke he too brought a pistol from the pocket of his coat but not from the one at his breast. *"Tiens,* but I can so easily understand that you should choose to eavesdrop, for it's obvious, my former schoolmate and colleague, why you are in France. You are a spy, an English spy! What a strange pastime for the son of the Prime Minister of England!"

Armand sighed.

"I shall have to kill you, de Frémond. It is unfortunate, but it would really have been better if I had done so years ago at Oxford. You were always an outsider and a commoner, but we treated you with toleration both there and at Eton simply because you were a foreigner and knew no better."

Paul de Frémond's face was suddenly diffused with anger.

"If you thought I wanted to be any different, you were mistaken. You and your stuck-up set of English aristocrats. I hated you then and I hate you now. But England will be defeated and then we will see who survives when the guillotine is set up in Parliament Square."

"At least you will not be there to see it," Armand said. "If I had any sense I would shoot you down as I

80

would shoot a mad dog, but because you've had a gentleman's education I will give you a sporting chance. Prime your pistol! We will fire at ten paces."

Paul de Frémond smiled unpleasantly.

"I was a good shot at Oxford," he boasted. "Do you remember your friend Dewsbury discovered that? But now I am infinitely better. I have had a lot of practice. If you still mumble your Protestant prayers, you had best say them now."

"You murdered Dewsbury," Armand said quietly. "That was one of the reasons why we should have killed you before you had the chance to do more harm in the world; but because we were stupidly magnanimous we let you go. Sent down for duelling with a boy who was too drunk to hold a weapon! I have not forgotten the episode."

"It was not 'cricket', I suppose?" Paul de Frémond asked, and his voice was raw. "Blast you English with your idiotic rules of behaviour, your intolerable air of superiority, your insane belief in your invulnerability. Napoleon will conquer you and nothing you can do, Sheringham, with your puling ideas of 'fair play' can stop him."

Armand suddenly put back his head and laughed.

"Blister it, but you are just the same, de Frémond—you've never grown up! Still the scrubby, dirty-minded little schoolboy you were at Eton, cocking a snook at your betters because you are envious of them."

"Damn your soul in hell," Paul de Frémond shouted, his face crimson with passion. "But for once you are at a disadvantage, Sheringham. An Englishman! A spy on French soil! Do you know what they do to spies, my dandy Viscount?"

"Exactly what I am going to do to you," Armand said softly. "We shoot vermin in England—France will be a cleaner place without you."

"So cocksure! I always loathed your arrogance, m'lord, but when you're dying dead at my feet, I shall be 'top dog' for once."

Again Armand laughed a sound of sheer unforced amusement. For a moment it seemed as if Paul de

Frémond would strike him, then he shrugged his shoulders and bent to the priming of his pistol.

For the first time since the heated and angry exchange of words between the two men Rêve intervened. She had been leaning against the pillar, her eyes wide and dark, her fingers still on her lips. Now she went to Armand's side and put her hand on his arm.

"Oh, Armand, my very dear," she whispered.

He looked down at her and his eyes were gentle and understanding.

"Do not be afraid, my love," he said softly.

"But he is evil," she whispered.

She would have said more, but as if to silence her he raised her hand and kissed it, then he turned towards de Frémond.

"Are you ready?" he asked. "We will stand back to back, walk five paces, each, counting as we go, then turn and fire."

"Have you said your prayers?" Paul de Frémond asked mockingly. "Or is Rêve saying them for you? When I hold her in my arms again I will teach her what love means. You will be dead, but she shall suffer all the insults and humiliations I have endured because of you.

"Her body shall be bruised as my feelings were bruised when you laughed at me at Eton. Her cries for mercy will go unheard, for I shall remember it is you I am punishing. Yes, you, Sheringham, who will have died unmourned on foreign soil!"

"Be silent!"

Armand's voice rang out on a note of command; and Paul de Frémond's jeering words died into silence.

The space between the body of the Temple and its pillars was narrow, but there was just room for two men to walk five paces and turn.

The light was not good but it was bright enough and both men were wearing white cravats which were easy to distinguish in the shadows. Pistols in hand, they stood for a moment back to back.

Each felt the other move and take a forward pace,

and their voices in unison echoed amongst the stone-work.

"One—two—three—four——"

It was not only instinct which told Armand that his opponent would fire before the agreed moment. He remembered the scandal that had succeeded the duel with Lord Dewsbury at Oxford.

Only one frightened and drunken undergraduate had been present, but he had sworn that de Frémond had fired before the signal and that Dewsbury had not even had the chance of letting off his pistol.

As Paul de Frémond's voice shouted 'Four' Armand looked over his shoulder.

He did not turn and would not have done so until the next step had not he seen his opponent wheel and heard the shattering blast of his pistol. With a super-human effort and with a movement which could only be attained by a trained athlete he sprang to one side.

Then his shot rang out and Paul de Frémond staggered with the impact of the shot, then crumpled up and fell sideways on to the stone floor.

Armand was conscious that he was breathing quickly, that Rêve was repeating his name aloud over and over again as if it were a prayer.

He crossed to where de Frémond lay, his legs doubled under him. The bullet had passed into the body just above the heart and already a patch of scarlet was spreading over his white shirt.

Armand went down on one knee beside the fallen man. He put his hand over his heart and felt it beating. Still kneeling at de Frémond's side he turned towards Rêve.

"We shall have to fetch a doctor," he said.

Her eyes were wide as they met his and he saw that for a moment she was incapable of understanding what he asked. For one split part of a second he was tempted to leave de Frémond where he was, to let him die.

Then he put the temptation from him so swiftly that it was hard to remember it had ever been there. It had been a duel between gentlemen, and the loser, if he survived, was entitled to medical aid.

"Yes, a doctor," Armand repeated as much to himself as to Rêve.

She was very lovely in the light of the moon, her eyes wide and dark with anxiety, her face white and strained, but already a little colour was returning to her cheeks, and Armand knew she was breathing again now that the danger was past and he was alive.

Then as he was about to smile at her reassuringly, he saw her face change and an expression of horror cross it.

He had not seen, as Rêve saw, Paul de Frémond make a sudden movement, had not seen his right hand slip into the breast pocket of his coat and draw out something that was concealed there.

Only Rêve saw the flash of steel as de Frémond, with a last almost superhuman spurt of energy and hatred drove the dagger full at Armand's breast.

Armand turned and made a desperate convulsive movement to avoid the blow, but he was too late; the dagger caught him on the side of the head.

He put up his hands as if to defend himself, then a stream of blood spurted over his face blinding him, and slowly he toppled forward over the body of his adversary.

5

Rêve stood for an instant as if frozen to the ground. She felt as if she were in some terrible nightmare from which she could not awake.

Then in the passing of a second her wits returned to her and she sprang forward to kneel at Armand's side, raising him from where he lay across de Frémond's body.

A girl of a different nationality might have swooned or screamed at the sight of blood, but French women—both young and old—had grown used to blood and violence in the years which had passed since the outbreak of the Revolution.

When Rêve first touched Armand he was conscious; but as she exerted all her strength to raise him, his eyelids closed and she knew from the pallor of his face that he had fainted.

With a terrified anxiety which was as if a sword had been plunged into her own heart she wondered if he were dead; but as she tenderly drew his head upwards until it rested in her lap, she was almost sure that he still breathed.

Blood was still pouring from his wound, seeping through his dark hair, dripping from his forehead on to her white dress; yet for the moment she was concerned only with whether he was alive or dead.

She put her hand beneath his coat, feeling for his heart. His body was warm and that in itself gave her courage to face one agonising moment when she could feel nothing.

Then surely and unmistakably she found his heartbeat, and though she was unaware of it, the colour returned to her face in very relief.

Now reassured, she knew that she must attend to his wound. It was gaping wide open, the ragged edges red and raw, the blood oozing now more slowly, but nevertheless in a frightening and continuous flow. Deftly, and with as little movement of her body as possible so as not to disturb Armand's head in her lap, Rêve removed from her shoulders the light silk scarf which matched her evening gown.

With gentle, but skilled fingers she wound it round his head, drawing it tighter and still tighter until the edges of the wound were closed and the flow of blood ceased completely for the moment.

She knotted the ends together and then with the utmost gentleness and care she moved his head from her lap on to the ground.

Relieved of her burden, she went to the steps and picking up one of the cushions which she had arrayed there, she put it beneath Armand's head.

When she had done this, she stood up and for a moment her heart contracted at the colour of his face, at the splashes of blood on his white shirt and the crimson stain already beginning to show through the delicacy of her scarf.

For a moment his face swam mistily before her eyes and she had an almost overwhelming desire to throw herself down on her knees beside him, to press her lips to his, to call his name, to force him to return to consciousness by the very magnetism of her love for him.

Then sharply she told herself that, if she would save Armand's life, there was no time to be lost. His wound must be attended to by a doctor and at once, before he was weakened by further loss of blood.

With a little convulsive gesture Rêve turned away and for the first time looked at de Frémond sprawled on the stone pavement, with the blood-stained dagger he had used so treacherously lying beside him.

Afterwards she would often wonder whether at that moment she might not have cursed him, have reviled him, wounded though he was, for his murderous action; but she saw that he was already dead.

There was no mistaking the colour of his skin, the open eyes staring upwards, the slack horror of his parted lips.

De Frémond was dead! But Armand still lived! That was what mattered; that was all that was of consequence.

Running faster than she had ever run before in the whole of her life, Rêve took the path through the woodland which would bring her to the *Château*.

She lifted the skirt of her gown high in both hands so that unimpeded by its silken folds she could move freely, and only when she reached the front door of the *Château* itself did she pause for a moment to get her breath.

She was conscious then of a tearing pain in her side, but her mind was too concerned with Armand to give much attention to her physical disabilities.

She did not even realise that, moving with such speed through the brambles which abounded beside the wild unkept paths of the wood, she had torn both her stockings and her legs, or that a low-hanging branch of a tree had left a dark red weal against her white forehead.

She was not aware of any of these things; she knew only that Armand's life was in danger and that in the effort to save him every second was precious.

She thrust open the door of the *Château* and entered the hall. It was half in darkness, two candles only flickering in a crystal sconce; then in the distance she heard a murmur of voices and knew whence it came.

Running once again, she sped down the passage which led to the Great Banqueting Hall. The door was ajar and she flung it open with an imperious, almost defiant gesture.

As she had expected, the household was kneeling in prayer, and Rêve saw the scene with an almost visionary clarity.

The Duchess's features were clean-cut against the satin cushion on which her head was laid, her hands clasped on her breast, her body covered with a shroud of royal purple velvet. Banked around her were dozens and dozens of flowers.

None of them were very elaborate or expensive wreaths such as she might have received in the olden days when she was a fashionable figure in a rich and fashionable world. These were flowers that had come from small cottage gardens, from hedgerows and from fields.

Flowers brought by people who had come in the last two years to have not only a respect for the indomitable old lady, but a pride in her eccentricity.

Yes, flowers encircled the Duchess and beyond the flowers was another circle—of mourners who, kneeling with bowed heads, repeated the prayers they had learned from the village Priest in their infancy, prayers which had so often been forgotten in the past few years.

The only light in the Banqueting Hall came from the four great candles set in gold candlesticks, and the shadows on the vast roof and in the corners of the room seemed deep and mysterious, so that the Duchess appeared to be in a little island of light in the midst of a great darkness.

The Duchess was dead, but Rêve was concerned with the living, and her voice at the door rang out strong and compellingly:

"Stop!"

With a little gasp the kneelers turned with one accord to see who interrupted them. She saw on their faces astonishment and recognised without consciously thinking of it not only the household staff but also many familiar faces from the village.

There was the baker, the grocer, the woman who came to the *Château* to do the washing, the cobbler, the old woman who sold cheese in the market-place, the butcher and the advocate.

They were all there, and their first expression of astonishment on their faces was replaced by one of consternation as Rêve moved towards them and they took in the details of her appearance—her white, strained face and dishevelled hair hanging half-unbound over her white shoulders, and the blood on the front of her gown.

It was Antoinette who spoke first, rising hastily to her feet and saying in a voice that was low and yet which in its intensity penetrated every corner of that vast roof:

"What has happened, *ma petite?* Have you been hurt?"

"No, no, I am all right," Rêve answered quickly.

She knew only too well the anxiety and horror underlying Antoinette's question. How often had they been in danger, how often had they known the fear which comes from suspecting an injury!

"It is not for myself that I ask your help," Rêve said, speaking not only to Antoinette but to all those who were assembled there. "It is for a man—a gentleman who is dying. There has been a duel—there is no time to explain now—but he must be brought to the *Château* immediately, and one of you run with all possible speed to the doctor and bid him hurry if he would save a life."

The assembled company got slowly and awkwardly to their feet and as they rose, a buzz of conversation broke out. There were questions on everybody's lips:

"What has happened?"

"Who is it?"

"What can we do?"

"Where will the doctor be at this hour?"

"Be silent!"

Rêve's voice rang out again, her anxiety for Armand making her more autocratic than she had ever been in her whole life before.

"Four men—you—you—you—and you," she said, choosing those nearest to her, "go at once to the little Temple by the lake. Take with you a gate or a door on which to carry the injured men.

"And you," she said, turning to point to a tall, long-legged youth, who gave the impression that he might be able to use his long legs to advantage, "run as swiftly as you can and bring the doctor here."

89

She paused for a moment as if to draw her breath, then continued:

"Antoinette, you and Lili prepare a bedroom, the best in the house, and get towels and bandages and hot water, for we shall need them all."

"The best room is not aired," Antoinette said quietly.

"Then he must be put in the Duchess's room," Rêve said.

"In the Duchess's room!"

For a moment there was a little gasp and fiercely as a tigress might turn in defence of her young, Rêve retorted:

"And why not? Would the Duchess of all people refuse her bed to a wounded man? Her room is open and empty, and she has no further use for it. He shall be taken there! See that it is prepared! And now go, all of you—what are you waiting for?"

They scampered like rabbits at her imperiousness, and only as the four men she had commanded to obey her instructions were leaving did she cry out after them:

"Be careful to bring the right man. There is another there, but he is dead. Leave him! I will tell you later how to deal with his body."

"A dead man!" someone breathed.

But it seemed as if the information she gave them took their very breath away. There was no retort, no further questioning. They hurried away on the errands to which she had appointed them.

The other people in the hall, a few old women and children, seemed to vanish into the great shadows and suddenly Rêve found herself alone with her Great-Aunt.

For a moment she was still. The fragrance of the incense mingled with the heavy scent of the flowers; then, as strange thoughts come to us in moments of crisis, Rêve thought how small the Duchess's body was.

It was so tiny that it might indeed have been the corpse of a child which lay there rather than that of an elderly woman. And yet in life one had never noticed her lack of inches because one had been so overwhelmed by the strength and the formidability of her character.

Suddenly there came to Rêve the most overwhelming conviction that death was not something to be feared, it was indeed but the shedding of an outworn body just as one might discard a dress which was threadbare and no longer useful.

Death was not important! It was living that counted and the strength and courage which one brought to it.

Rêve was certain of this now, if she had not been certain of it before. For one moment she felt as if her Great-Aunt stood beside her. She could almost hear her strange cackling laugh and see the twinkle in her shrewd eyes as she seemed to say:

"Yes, you are learning, child!"

The moment passed and Rêve felt she must have imagined it. Now she had nothing to do but to wait for Armand to be brought to her.

Slowly she left the Banqueting Hall and moved towards the front door. As she went, she prayed with an almost savage intensity that Armand might be saved and his life spared:

"Save him, dear God!" she whispered. "Save him, because I love him so—love him with all my heart and soul—with my whole being."

Surely a love such as hers could not have been conjured to life for nothing? There must be a use for it. But if Armand died, she might just as well die too, for the future would hold nothing but loneliness.

"Oh, God, help me and hear my prayer! Save Armand!" Rêve again whispered.

She linked her fingers so tightly together as she prayed that her knuckles were white and lifeless as she finished; but when she raised her eyes, she realised that she had reached the front door and that the courtyard outside was empty. There was no sign of anyone.

She stood there waiting, tense and watchful, and slowly and insidiously the events of the past half-hour came flooding into her consciousness—de Frémond's unexpected arrival at the Temple, the news he had brought her of her half-brother's death, the unpleasant way he behaved—they all passed like a pageant before her eyes.

91

Then came Armand's arrival and de Frémond's astonishment at the sight of him.

They had spoken together in English, but Rêve had been able to understand them. During her travels with Antoinette they had hidden for six months in a farm on the outskirts of Rouen.

There had been a man also lodging in the farm, which was a poor place, but those who owned it were loyal and trustworthy.

He was an Englishman who had been groom to an aristocrat who had been taken to the guillotine. His horses had been destroyed or stolen, and the groom, because he was a foreigner, had had the greatest difficulty in escaping with his life.

Penniless and therefore unable to return to England, he worked on the farm in return for his board and lodging. It amused him to teach Rêve English and she learnt easily because she liked him for his cheeky good humour and because his love for animals was only equalled by her own.

By the time that Antoinette felt it best to move elsewhere Rêve could speak English fluently.

She had the chance to practise her new accomplishment two years later when in search of Rêve's de Valmont relatives Antoinette took rooms in the suburbs of Paris. Their lodgings were over a small shop which was kept by a Frenchman and his English wife.

The latter had been personal maid to an English Nobleman's wife who had toured the Continent ten years earlier and settled for a short time in Paris.

The English maid had fallen in love with the *concierge* at the hotel at which they had been staying and m'lady had returned to England alone.

Rêve's English was quite proficient by the time she had discovered the de Valmont cousins and they left their lodgings over the store. But it was not until the Duchess came to Valmont that she realised that her knowledge of English was lacking in quality.

When the Duchess first heard her speak, she lay back in her chair and laughed until the tears came into

92

her eyes. Rêve had regarded her with curiosity and then with some sense of resentment.

"What amuses you so greatly, Madame?" she asked.

"Your English, child, your English!" the Duchess said, wiping her eyes.

"I am delighted if it amuses you, Madame," Rêve said a little stiffly, "but I would also be glad if I might share the joke."

The Duchess laughed again, then composed herself with difficulty.

"Your English, my dear," she said at length. "It is fluent, very fluent, but it is the English of the stable, of the servants' hall! And your accent! *Mon Dieu! Mon Dieu!*"

She raised her hands in horror, and then at the sight of Rêve's mortified expression she apologised with a charm which was all her own.

"Forgive me, my dear, I am being unkind, but it took me by surprise. I had not expected you to speak any other language but your own, seeing you had not the opportunity of being well educated, and to hear you speaking English with what is known to them as a "cockney" accent was too much for my sense of humour.

"You must pardon my laughter, and now to make amends I will polish your vocabulary and improve your pronunciation until you will not be ashamed to talk to anyone, even at the Court of St. James's itself. It is a bargain, but first tell me that I am forgiven."

Rêve smiled her forgiveness and the Duchess kept her part of the bargain well.

She herself spoke English perfectly for the Duke de Malessene had for a short while been Ambassador to the Court of St. James's and the Duchess had caused a sensation in England and proved herself as popular a figure in London as she was in Paris.

In a few months Rêve was speaking as perfectly and with as pure an accent as the Duchess herself; and through a friend of the old lady they had maanged to procure a number of books, novels and more serious words in English which she read and enjoyed.

It had therefore been very easy for her to follow what de Frémond and Armand were saying to each other. She even understood the insults which de Frémond had thrown at his former schoolmate in that sneering voice which was an added insult in itself.

But what was of importance, Rêve knew, was the revelation de Frémond had made as to Armand's real identity.

He had referred to him as the Viscount Sheringham, son of the Prime Minister of England, and Armand had not denied it.

As she stood waiting at the door of the *Château*, Rêve put her fingers to her eyes with a gesture almost of despair. Could anything be more dangerous than that Armand, with such a position and rank, should be in France and wounded desperately, almost unto death?

She was well aware that the danger to him lay not only from the authorities and that Napoleon's men made short work of spies, but also from everyone with whom he came in contact.

The years of the Revolution had made every man wary of his own skin. They might, if appealed to, hide their own countrymen and protect them, but it would be difficult indeed to persuade a Frenchman who had lived under the shadow of fear for his own safety for so long to risk both his life and his livelihood in protecting a foreign spy.

How dare Armand venture here! How dare he disguise himself, knowing the penalty of being discovered!

As she thought of the risks he had taken, Rêve was filled with admiration and her love, if anything, was deepened by this new knowledge. Only a really brave man, she thought, would undertake to come to France under the present conditions.

Napoleon hated the whole British race with an almost savage ferocity because his plans for the invasion of their little island had been frustrated and they alone of all Europe continued to ignore his sovereignty and to mock at his conquests.

The Battle of Trafalgar had left France astonished and not a little apprehensive. Before that they had begun to believe that not only Napoleon but they themselves were invincible, and yet the English had defeated and destroyed their navy with a completeness which made any excuse or explanation impossible.

And yet the son of the British Prime Minister had crossed the Channel to become an English spy on French territory! How could Armand do anything so foolhardy, so crazy? Had de Frémond been making it up? Had she been mistaken in what she had overheard?

Rêve's thoughts seemed to go round in circles, madly seeking a way of escape. But she knew the truth. Armand was indeed the Viscount Sheringham.

She thought now that she might have detected from the very beginning little differences between him and the average Frenchman. There was nothing tangible, nothing one could really put into words, and yet the difference was there; a difference which she admired, liked—no, the right word was loved.

Now she felt almost sick with fear lest someone besides herself should notice it too.

What was she to say to the men when they returned? What was she to tell them? But before she had come to any decision, while she stood in the doorway, trembling with the very intensity of her own feelings, she heard footsteps and voices. Eagerly she ran out into the courtyard.

Yes the men were coming back. They were carrying a gate which they must have taken from its hinges, and lying on it, his body supported by cushions from the Temple, was Armand.

The light of the moon was on his face and his pallor was so ghastly that instinctively Rêve glanced towards one of the men carrying him, and her look in itself was an interrogation. He answered her unspoken inquiry.

"Monsieur is alive, Mademoiselle. Is the doctor here yet?"

"Not yet!" Rêve answered, and she was surprised

how calm and cool her own voice sounded. "Will you bring him upstairs?"

She led the way through the door. Fortunately the wide staircase, designed for the panniers and hoops of Rêve's forbears, was easy to negotiate. Antoinette waited at the top of the staircase outside the door of the Duchess's bedchamber.

They carried Armand in and with a gentleness that was surprising in four rough men they lifted him from the gate on to the bed. His body sank weakly into the softness of the feathers and the silken cushions in which the Duchess had delighted to luxuriate.

Tapers were alight in the chandelier and in the candelabra on either side of the dressing-table. Their bright light gleamed against the oyster satin of the hangings and on the Duchess's intimate possessions which were still lying about.

There were her gold-backed hair brushes, the diamond-studded miniatures, the vases of Sèvres china, the collection of snuff-boxes which had been used by her late husband and which in themselves were reputed to be worth a small fortune.

It was a strange setting indeed for a man with a blood-stained head and still wearing his riding boots.

Rêve's eyes came to rest on the faces of the men who had carried Armand from the wood. They were moving towards the door, but slowly, and she knew that they were waiting for her to speak to them, to give them some explanation of what had occurred.

Yet for a moment she could not think of anything to say. Her voice was choked in her throat, her lips were dry, and she could remember de Frémond's mocking voice saying:

"Sheringham! What the hell are you doing here?"

Sheringham! Sheringham! Sheringham! An English spy! The son of the English Prime Minister! He was lying here in her Great-Aunt's bed, while those who had brought him were waiting, waiting for her to speak.

At length, as if they could stand her silence no longer, one of the men, a fat, jovial man whom Rêve recognised as being the Patron of the local inn, said:

"This gentleman has been staying with us, Mademoiselle. He has been there these last two nights. Would you have me bring his clothes up to the *Château?*"

Rêve was well aware, as he finished speaking, of the curiosity and speculation which lay behind the bland inquiry on the other three faces watching her. She was aware, too, that Antoinette, busying herself at Armand's bedside, was listening too.

Yes, they were all listening, waiting for her to speak, waiting for an explanation as to why she should behave in this way and what had happened at the Temple.

Suddenly into the fog which seemed to obscure her brain as if it were wrapped in cotton-wool there came a gleam of intelligence.

Before she had time really to think of it, to puzzle it out, to formulate it into a proper tale, the story was there in her mind ready to be spoken and her lips were moving almost before she was ready for them to do so.

"Yes, the gentleman has been staying with you, Monsieur Bouvert," she said to the Innkeeper. "And he had a reason for doing so—the reason being the destruction of the man you have seen lying dead in the wood near the Temple for he was a traitor."

"And who is he, Mademoiselle, if we may make so bold?" the Innkeeper asked. "He is a stranger to these parts, I'll bet my boots on that score."

"The man who is dead," Rêve said, "is a Monsieur de Frémond. He was at one time the confidant and friend of my half-brother, the Marquis d'Augeron, but he abused that trust. He was, my brother discovered, involved in a plot to assassinate the Emperor."

"The Emperor!"

"Yes, the Emperor's life was in danger," Rêve said. "My brother learnt of this and for that reason he came here to Valmont in disguise. It was not Monsieur Armand de Ségury who stayed at your inn, Monsieur Bouvert, but my half-brother, Monsieur le Marquis d'Augeron, who has but recently arrived in this country from Poland."

"The Marquis!"

There was awe and respect in the exclamation and Rêve heard behind her Antoinette say softly:

"So this is your half-brother!"

"Yes," she repeated, "my half-brother, and he was waiting to catch those treacherous assailants who were plotting to assassinate our beloved Emperor. But unfortunately, before the plot was ready to be denounced, Monsieur de Frémond arrived here and finding me alone by the Temple insulted me.

"My half-brother overheard him. He came to my rescue and as you can see for yourselves shots were exchanged. De Frémond's bullet went wide, but Monsieur's found its mark. As he lay on the ground de Frémond drew a dagger from his breast pocket and stabbed my brother in the head.

"It was a cowardly, treacherous act of a man who strikes to kill whether it be someone who has befriended him for many years or the Emperor to whom as a Frenchman his allegiance and devotion should be given."

There was sudden silence as Rêve finished speaking. The four men at the door glanced towards the bed with a new respect and something like admiration in their eyes, and then one man with a dark wizened face said:

"But why should Monsieur le Marquis have come to St. Benis to find a plot against our Emperor? Why did he not go to Paris to warn His Majesty of what these scoundrels intended?"

To Rêve there was just the faintest hint of suspicion in his tones, and it was with an air of superiority that she gave him the right answer:

"Monsieur did not go to Paris to find the Emperor because the Emperor himself is coming here."

"Here!"

The word burst from the four lips simultaneously.

"Yes, here. I had the communication today. The *Château* will be honoured with His Majesty's presence on the night of Wednesday, August 16th."

"Mademoiselle! It is incredible and wonderful! The Emperor here in Valmont!"

The four men stared at Rêve as if she had given them

98

news of the visitation of angels; and then, thankful not only for Armand's sake but for her own, she heard a step on the stairs which told her that the doctor was approaching.

He came hurrying to the room. Fat, jovial old Dr. Maurel, who had brought Rêve into the world and had tended her family from the days when he was old enough to take his father's place.

He was nearing sixty and was sweating profusely from the haste with which he had come from the village.

His shirt was stained with wine and his coat had not been cleaned or pressed since the day he had inherited it from his father along with the little black bag of instruments which he carried in his left hand. But his good humour and kindly sympathetic face were more welcome at that moment to Rêve than anything else in the whole world.

There was a twinkle in his brown eyes which he never lost even in the most serious moment of death and disaster, and his big hand with its nails broken from working in his garden was familiarly comforting.

Léon Maurel looked what he was—the best-humoured, kindest and most considerate man on earth. But what was not obvious on first acquaintance, but which Rêve knew as did everyone else in the village, was the fact that he was a natural healer.

His methods were haphazard and at times none too clean, but if gardeners have green fingers when they plant things in the earth, Léon Maurel had green fingers when he dealt with the health of human beings.

There was something in his vitality, some magnetism about him which made his patients live, made them want to get well, and it was the visit to the doctor which cured the inhabitants of St. Benis rather than the obnoxious pills which he made up for them in his dispensary.

But Léon Maurel's patients recovered. He made them live, he made them realise that the world was a good place and that one could afford to laugh at it and in it. And so they lived!

There was not a man or a woman in St. Benis who would not have given a snap of the fingers for all the doctors with big reputations who had been called into the service of Napoleon and who were having honours and distinctions heaped upon them for their various achievements.

"Your servant, Mademoiselle," Dr. Maurel said to Rêve, and she clung to his hand as a drowning man might cling to a piece of driftwood.

"Please, Doctor, save him," she said, the words bursting almost involuntarily from her lips.

"We shall do that if it is humanly possible," Dr. Maurel replied.

He glanced from Rêve to the men still standing open mouthed in the doorway.

"Haven't you boys anything to do?" he asked, and sheepishly but smilingly they shuffled from the room.

"Now, let's see what is wrong," he said approaching the bed, waves of heat and vitality seeming to radiate from him.

"It is his head," Rêve exclaimed quickly. "A dagger thrust just above the eyebrows. I bound it together."

"Good girl!"

The Doctor put his bag down on the table beside the bed with what seemed to Rêve almost intolerable slowness, then glanced at Antoinette.

"Have you got what I shall require?" he asked. "Towels, hot water, bandages?"

"Everything," Antoinette answered.

"*Bon!* I might have guessed you would have. You're the most efficient woman I know," he said, and for a moment his big laugh echoed strangely in the big bedroom.

"Oh, Doctor, please hurry!" Rêve said. "His wound is so deep and he had bled so much. I know that every minute is of account."

The Doctor looked at her.

"So this young man is of importance," he said.

Rêve did not answer, but her eyes besought him eloquently to make haste. He looked at her quivering face and put one of his hands on her shoulder.

100

"Go and sit down by the window," he said. "If I want you, I will call you."

Obediently she did as she was told. As she did so, she heard his voice with its usual, half humorous, half sympathetic note in it say to Antoinette:

"It is the heart of that little one which suffers!"

Rêve waited apprehensively for Antoinette's answer, but she did not reply.

6

Rêve sat at the open window, looking out on to the lake, as she had sat hour after hour for the last three days.

She did not see the glittering silver water or the brilliance of the flowers growing by the water's edge, nor did she hear the song of the birds or the humming of the bees among the roses, but all her thoughts and feelings were fixed in a concentrated tenseness upon Armand.

He lay in the bed in the room behind her, his face almost as pale as the pillows on which his head was supported, his body still and immobile as if already the hand of Death was upon him.

Sometimes he was so quiet that in an agony of fear Rêve would rise from the window and cross the room to stand beside the bed, looking down at him, listening for the soft motion of his breathing which would tell her that he was still alive.

Sometimes she would imagine she could hear nothing, and in a terror which was more painful than any emotion she had ever experienced in her life before, she would run to the door and fetch Antoinette, to be reassured that he was still alive until the next moment of horror and uncertainty came to terrify her afresh.

At other times Armand was not so quiet. In a high fever he would toss from side to side, crying out deliriously in a thick, almost incoherent voice; and at these moments Rêve was desperately afraid lest he should betray himself.

She insisted on nursing him herself with the help of Antoinette and fiercely opposed Doctor Maurel's suggestion that he should get further help from the village.

"We can manage," she said firmly; and then, as she saw the incredulity in the doctor's eyes, she added: "Do you think that Antoinette and I are so helpless that we cannot look after one sick man? If so, you must have a very poor opinion of us, Doctor."

"It is not that, Mademoiselle," Dr. Maurel replied. "People make the best nurses when their own feelings are not involved. You appear to care so deeply for this brother of yours that I thought at first the relationship must be a very different one. But it is good to see warm family affection and God knows, poor child, you have little family left."

"That is true," Rêve said, "and if for no other reason you must save Armand's life."

"My dear, I have done all that I can. It is only a question of time now—time, the great healer, helped by a man's youth and vigour, which I swear are better medicines than anything a physician can prescribe."

"You think—you are certain that he will—live?" Rêve's lips hardly dared to breathe the words.

Her eyes scrutinised the doctor's face as if she would tear the truth from him, however much he might wish to spare her from knowing it.

"I can tell you nothing more than I have told you already," Dr. Maurel replied quietly. "We can only hope and pray."

"Yes, we can do that."

Rêve almost whispered the words. She wondered if the doctor had any idea how passionately she prayed both night and day for Armand's recovery.

Indeed she prayed until at times she felt as if her spirit left her body, as if it winged itself to the very gates of Heaven in supplication for the life of the man she loved.

And now three days had passed and Armand was still unconscious.

Suddenly Rêve thought she heard a movement; but when she turned her head, he was lying still and quiet, his eyes closed, his hands limp against the softness of the linen sheets.

"Oh, Armand, my darling," her heart cried out to

him. "Come back to me from that strange land where you are dwelling at the moment—a land of oblivion between this world and the next, where you are unaware of my love and yet not enfolded in the mercy and love of God. Come back to me! I want you, I need you! Come back to me!"

Again and again her heart cried out to him. Still there was no sign from the bed, only a deep unbroken silence in the room, while from everywhere else outside and in the house there came the muffled sound of movement.

It seemed to Rêve that an army of people had descended on the *Château* since, to save Armand, she had told the men of the village that his wound was due to an attempt to save the Emperor's life and had added that the Emperor himself was coming to Valmont.

From that moment a transformation had taken place in the village of St. Benis. Had Rêve not been so consumed by her anxiety for Armand, she would have been amused at what had taken place immediately after her revelation.

If the villagers and workmen of St. Benis had thought the *Château* adequately repaired and decorated for its legal and traditional owner, they certainly did not consider it good enough for their beloved Emperor.

There were painters working inside the house and outside, without orders and without payment, and without even asking permission to work.

There were glaziers and stone-masons, polishers and joiners, carpenters and cabinet makers. They had all found themselves a task of some sort, even to unpacking the furniture which had belonged to the Duchess and which had lain for so long in its packing cases in the big empty rooms.

Rêve was surprised, too, to find that the staff at the *Château* had been very considerably augmented by bright-faced girls and even a footman or two, but she made no comment.

Indeed, she felt as if she moved in another world herself. She could think of one thing and one thing

104

only, and the visit of a thousand Emperors would have left her unmoved at this moment while Armand's life hung in the balance.

But when she was not worrying about his chance of survival, she was worrying about his saefty. So far he had been amazingly lucky.

That first night after the doctor had sewn up the gash in Armand's head, had given Antoinette and herself instructions as to how to nurse him, and had gone from the *Château,* suddenly a terrifying thought had come to Rêve.

It was a thought which had made her stand paralysed with horror and then sent her hand fluttering to her breast as if in a sudden stabbing pain. It was a very innocent remark of Antoinette's which caused this consternation. She had said:

"I must undress the poor young gentleman. Will you go and tell Jacques to have his luggage brought up here so that I can find a nightshirt for him?"

It was then that Rêve remembered that de Frémond would have come to the *Château* with both his luggage and his servants. There lay the danger!

If the servants talked, if they said that the Marquis d'Augeron was dead, killed in a drunken brawl in Amsterdam, what chance had she of saving Armand's life, of succeeding in her subterfuge of pretending that he was her half-brother?

Without a word to Antoinette she rushed from the room, down the stairs and into the hall. The first thing she saw was a pile of luggage. Leather trunks of all sizes and shapes were piled there, obviously waiting for some strong arms to carry them upstairs.

At least half of them, Rêve saw, bore a Marquis's coronet over her brother's monogram.

She realised that Paul de Frémond had brought her half-brother's luggage with his to the *Château* and for a moment she felt almost faint with fear. But at last, summoning all her courage, she went in search of Jacques.

She found him in the pantry, polishing a piece of silver and grumbling to himself as he usually did. He glanced up as Rêve entered and rose respectfully, if slowly to his feet, his face twisting a little with the pain of his rheumatism as he did so.

"Where are the servants who brought the luggage which is waiting in the hall?" Rêve inquired.

"Out in the stables, Mademoiselle, and a cheeky lot they be, too, a-shouting for their money. I tells them that I have no money and no instructions to give them any."

"I will see to it," Rêve said.

She went down the long passage which led through the kitchen quarters directly out to the stables. It was getting late, but as she anticipated, the men were making no effort to retire for the night.

They were sitting on the mounting block and the steps of the stable, talking and laughing. Some of them had bottles in their hands, and one man was playing a merry jig on a fiddle. The music came to an end as she walked towards them.

The moonlight illuminated her white shoulders, her proudly held head. She came to a stop near them and then waited a moment before speaking. As she did so, one man came forward, an elderly man with a heavy grey moustache and shifty, calculating eyes.

"Are you in charge here?" Rêve asked.

"Yes, Mademoiselle."

"You brought Monsieur de Frémond here from Amsterdam?"

"Yes, Mademoiselle."

"And from Poland?"

The question came faintly.

"No, Mademoiselle. We understand Monsieur had trouble with his own servants and they returned to their own country. The gentleman was cursing good and plenty when he engaged us."

There was a little twitter amongst the men as he said this, and Rêve felt her spirits rise.

"All Monsieur de Frémond's servants returned home?" she inquired.

"As far as I know, Mademoiselle, for we are from Amsterdam. You won't find any foreigners amongst us."

Rêve felt the relief spreading over her whole body like a soothing balm. She could understand what had happened. The servants had been ready to serve her half-brother, but they had not liked de Frémond.

While her brother lived, they must obey his orders; but on his death they had made it quite clear that they would no longer accept de Frémond's commands or call him master.

They had returned home and he had been forced to engage a strange staff for the last part of his journey.

Rêve took a deep breath.

"Monsieur de Frémond will have no further need of you," she said, and again that little twitter came from among the men. "If you will tell me what is owing, I will give it to you, and you can leave as early as you like in the morning."

"Thank you, Mademoiselle. We will do what you suggest," the elderly man said.

"And the sum that you require for your services?" Rêve said.

He named a sum which staggered her. For a moment she thought that her hearing must be mistaken, but something in the look in his eye, the crafty expression in his face told her all to clearly that he had doubled, if not trebled the original figure.

Because de Frémond was dead, there was no one to relate what was the sum agreed. And yet so thankful was Rêve at the thought of getting rid of these men that she would not argue with them. She was determined to pay the money so that they could go. The question was how to find so much gold?

"You will have the sum you ask before you leave in the morning," she said curtly and turned and walked away through the moonlight to the house.

As she went she heard a man's laugh, and it was followed by a buzz of voices.

She had been tricked, she knew that but she did not care. Anything to know that one more danger to Armand was eliminated.

But where was she to find the money? She knew that there was no possibility of Antoinette having such a

107

large sum in her possession, even though she always had a little cash available to pay the housekeeping accounts.

There might be some gold amongst her Great-Aunt's possessions, and yet she doubted it. The Duchess had had a horror of robbers and most of her money had been placed for safety in a bank in Paris. Where, where could she obtain it?

Suddenly Rêve thought of de Frémond's luggage. There might be gold in that. Neither he nor her half-brother would have travelled without carrying a considerable fortune between them. She reached the hall and stood looking at the luggage.

Out of the vast pile she finally picked out one box. It was of tooled leather and heavily padlocked, and she was certain that it contained something of value. The difficulty now was to find the keys.

With a sense of relief she saw two of the men who had carried Armand from the Temple coming back into the house.

For a moment she wondered why they were there, and then she guessed that they had fetched de Frémond's body from the Temple and placed it somewhere to await burial. She called them and asked them to carry the luggage upstairs.

They obeyed her without question, the heavy trunks resting on their broad shoulders, their big hands making light work of the many boxes.

There was an ante-room to the Duchess's bedroom, where her clothes had always been kept for it was lined with cupboards, all of them smelling sweetly of lavender which Antoinette picked in the garden every year and sewed into muslin bags tied with purple ribbon.

As the last trunk went upstairs, Rêve followed them and found that Antoinette had already begun to unpack, two cupboards having been cleared of the Duchess's elaborate gowns. Antoinette glanced up as the men entered the room with their last burden.

"Is that a coroneted box?" she asked. "If not put it over there. Those are the ones which will not be needed. They can be disposed of later."

The men did as they were told. Antoinette drew from the trunk that she had opened a coat of green velvet embroidered with silver and ornamented with diamond buttons which flashed in the candlelight.

"Supposing these clothes don't fit Armand," Rêve thought suddenly.

She had no idea what had been the height of her half-brother, Armand; the Armand whom she loved was tall, but not so fleshily built as de Frémond.

She began to see the many pitfalls and snares which surrounded her now that she had lied and must go on lying. But even as a feeling of shame and depression swept over her, she asked herself what would be her position at this moment had it been Armand who had been killed.

She remembered Paul de Frémond's plans for their marriage and felt again the lustful brutality of his hot lips.

The colour flamed into Rêve's cheeks at the memory and she turned to Antoinette quickly.

"Have you found any keys? I think there must be some gold in the box that is padlocked. I need it for the coachmen."

"How much?" Antoinette asked briefly, busy with the unpacking.

Rêve told her and she sat back on her heels in sheer astonishment.

"But it is incredible, ridiculous! The men are robbing you. I will speak with them."

"No, no," Rêve said quickly. "Let us pay them and they can go. We don't want them here. There is no time for argument. My brother is a rich man. We don't know what arrangements he had made and it is impossible to ask him."

"Yes, it is indeed impossible to do that, the poor soul. The doctor says it may be some days before he will regain consciousness. A blow like that on the head can affect the brain. I remember a cousin of mine——"

Rêve realised that Antoinette was going to talk about her family and before she could get too involved in the story she said:

"The keys, Antoinette, that is what I need."

"Most gentlemen keep their keys on them when they travel," Antoinette replied. "I will look in Monsieur's coat."

She rose and went from the ante-room and into the bedroom. Armand's coat was lying over the chair, Rêve saw her put her hand into the pockets and then saw her do the same with his breeches pockets.

"There are no keys here," Antoinette said.

Rêve drew a deep breath. She had suddenly realised where the keys would be. In de Frémond's possession, of course! He would have taken them when her half-brother was killed, even if he had not kept them before in his position of secretary, major-domo or whatever position he had held as companion to the Marquis d'Augeron.

"We shall doubtless find them amongst the luggage," Antoinette said, confidently returning to the open trunk. "I will look as I unpack."

She bent to lift a pair of white satin breeches from the folds of white paper, but Rêve had left the room. She ran downstairs, through the hall and past the door of the Great Banqueting Hall where the Duchess lay in state. She had an idea where the men would have placed de Frémond's body.

There was a small unused room in the front of the house which was furnished only with a big oak table which had proved too big and too ugly to be put elsewhere in the *Château*. It was a room used on formal occasions for village meetings when there was a gathering which could not be comfortably accommodated in the smaller houses of those in authority.

It was a tall, dark room which always smelt slightly musty, and as Rêve opened the door now she felt an almost overwhelming sense of dislike both for the room and for what it held.

The tapers on the mantelpiece had been lit and by their light Rêve could see that de Frémond's body lay on the long oak table.

Someone had crossed his hands on his breast in

the approved fashion and had closed his eyes, putting a sou on each of them to keep his eyelids down.

The draught from the door caused the candles to flicker and for the moment as she entered the room she thought that de Frémond was smiling at her, jeering at her as if he knew what she had said and done.

It was with an effort that Rêve made herself close the door behind her and go forward. As the candles ceased flickering, she saw that de Frémond was not smiling, but even in death his lips were somehow lewd and bestial.

Steeling herself for what she must do, she approached the table. It took her but a few seconds to discover the keys in the left-hand pocket of his coat. She drew them out with a hand that trembled.

It was a big bunch, and she found herself staring down at them, wondering exactly what they had meant to de Frémond. Power for one thing, she thought, power over her half-brother, and power to get what he wanted.

She shivered. The cold steel of the keys was somehow as horrible as the man who had owned them. She glanced at de Frémond's face and suddenly her nerve snapped so that she could bear it no longer.

With an exclamation of fear and horror she ran across the room, wrenched open the door and heard it slam behind her as she ran down the corridor which led to the hall.

Only when she reached the very door of the anteroom to the Duchess's bedroom did she stop for a moment to get her breath and remember that Antoinette must not suspect anything.

For one moment Rêve had played with the idea of telling Antoinette the truth, and then, as she had sat in the window seat of the room while Dr. Maurel was attending to Armand's wound and Antoinette was beside him helping, she had known that it would not be wise.

Antoinette loved her, she knew that, loved her with all her heart and with all her being. She had risked her life for her, cared for her and tended her. She had

111

done as much as any mother would do for her own child during the long years when Rêve had been orphaned and penniless.

But because of that very love and because of the fear which had been their daily attendant for so long, Antoinette would not allow her to take any more risks. It would seem to her entirely wrong for Rêve to hide and succour an English spy, however much she loved him.

The risk was too great, and Rêve knew that Antoinette would oppose her taking it by every means in her power. No, Antoinette must never know. Of that she was certain.

With an effort to appear normal and unperturbed she entered the ante-room. Antoinette was still busy.

"Never have I seen a gentleman with so many clothes," she said. "You would have thought that he would have brought a valet with him to care for his things."

"I understand there was some trouble at Amsterdam and his own servants returned to Poland," Rêve said.

"Oh, that accounts for it, then," Antoinette said. "But he will have to have someone, for old Jacques will never manage to valet all these clothes, that's as sure as I'm sitting here."

"But of course we must find my brother a valet," Rêve said quickly. "We can send to Paris to one of the bureaux. I am told that they provide excellent servants."

"I am sure they do," Antoinette said sarcastically, "but at what price? Have you come into a fortune, *ma petite,* that you can talk in that high-handed manner?"

Rêve would have answered her, but at that moment the lock in which she had been trying the keys which she had taken from de Frémond flew open. She raised the lid and gave a gasp at which Antoinette turned; then it was her turn to exclaim.

"Mon Dieu, are they real?"

Antoinette might well ask the same question, for the coroneted box which Rêve had thought contained valuables, because of its heavy padlock was filled to the brim with gold—gold louis shining dully in the light

112

of the candles. A veritable fortune lay there before their eyes.

And yet Rêve wondered many times in the past few days, what use such money was if it could not buy the only thing she wanted.

How often in the years of her penury had she thought how wonderful it would be to be rich, to be able to pay gold for everything she wanted! And yet now she knew with an absolute certainty—as really as she had always known it—that money could not buy the things that mattered.

There was only one thing that she wanted—that Armand should live, and no amount of money could ensure that.

Almost instinctively, because her thoughts had taken her in a full circle, Rêve began to pray again:

"Oh, God, let him live—Please, God, let him live."

She repeated the words over and over again, and then suddenly there came a sound from the bed. Quickly she got to her feet and moved to Armand's side. He was moving his head restlessly from side to side and she wondered if the fever was rising again.

She touched his hand to see if it was hot, but even as she did so the door opened and Antoinette came in, followed by Dr. Maurel.

"Well, and how is our patient today?" Dr. Maurel inquired very quietly.

He seldom raised his voice in the sick-room, and it seemed to Rêve an ominous thing that he often spoke almost in a whisper when he was near Armand.

"He made a sound," Rêve replied. "I was wondering if the fever——"

She stopped, the words dying on her lips, for Armand was speaking. He murmured something and with her invariable quick sense of relief at such moments Rêve realised that he spoke in French. It was something about the fields and the trees.

Then quite unexpectedly, while they all stood looking at him, he opened his eyes. Rêve felt as if her heart had stopped beating:

"Where am I?" he asked, and his voice was clear and distinct, if weak.

The doctor moved forward, his big fingers searching for Armand's pulse.

"You are at Valmont," he replied. "You are quite safe. Do not worry yourself."

"At—at Valmont?"

Armand repeated the word, and Rêve saw that his eyes were puzzled. Afraid of what he might say, terrified that he might reveal himself to Antoinette and Dr. Maurel, she bent forward.

"You are here with me, Armand," she said. "Don't talk now. We are going to get you well."

Her voice, soft and soothing, seemed to satisfy him. He gave a little sigh, closed his eyes and appeared to drop off into an easy sleep.

Rêve looked up to meet the doctor's smile.

"He will be all right," he said quietly. "When he wakens again, give him a little chicken broth with a few drops of cognac in it, but not too much, you understand. Just a few spoonfuls every hour. I congratulate you, Mademoiselle Nurse."

"You mean—that he is—really better," Rêve stammered.

"I mean just that," Dr. Maurel said quietly.

"Thank God!"

Rêve's ejaculation came straight from the heart. She could not prevent herself from showing the wonderful relief the doctor's words brought her. She realised that Antoinette looked at her curiously.

Dr. Maurel patted her shoulder and Antoinette hurried to open the door for him to leave the room.

After a moment, Rêve crossed to her seat in the window.

"I must be careful," she told herself.

She did not think that Antoinette was really suspicious, but she obviously thought it odd that Rêve should care so deeply about a half-brother whom she had never seen before and about whom, until his arrival, she had been to all intents and purposes extremely indifferent.

But Antoinette, Rêve remembered uncomfortably, had an unfortunate way of knowing as a child when she was lying. When she grew up, she had not wanted to lie, but even so, Antoinette would have known it if she had.

But her love and her fear for Armand's safety had made her not only lie, but create a whole structure of falsehood and pretence.

And undoubtedly Antoinette might be a very real danger to Armand. She had dedicated her life to Rêve as a nun might dedicate her service to God. She had been young, barely sixteen, when she had first known suffering and unhappiness.

One of a large family, she had fallen in love with a man who was affianced to her eldest sister, and he had loved her. Under the apple blossom in the orchard, hidden from the old farm-house by the gnarled branches of the heavily laden trees, they had sped into each other's arms with the sure intensity of two homing pigeons.

They had not meant it to happen. Indeed, love had come upon them so gradually that it was there long before they were aware of it.

Only after Laurent had been coming to the farm to court Antoinette's sister for over a year, did Antoinette awaken to the fact that she loved him not as a brother, but as something deeper and more intimate.

She had thought her secret was hers and hers alone, that it was hidden away in the very depth of her heart, until with that instinct sharpened by love she had realised that Laurent was avoiding her.

He would turn his head away as she entered the room, would studiously stand aside from contact with her, seeming at times almost rude in his indifference to what she said or to her presence at meal times.

One day, quite inadvertently, in passing him some food their fingers had touched and she had known. Known when the slow colour flooded into his weather-beaten face, known from the startled glance that he gave her, from the suffocation in her own throat—that he loved her too.

She had gone down to the apple orchard after him because she could not help herself. She had seen him slip away alone while her sister was changing into her best clothes so that she and Laurent could go to church together.

Without thinking, compelled by some age-old instinct stronger than herself, Antoinette followed him into the orchard.

It must have been about in the centre of the field that he heard her footsteps and turned to see who was following him.

It was then, as their eyes met, when all pretence was impossible and no words mattered, that Antoinette had rushed into his arms with the pink and white blossom falling around them like confetti.

Their lips had met in one long kiss, but they had both realised, even as they cling together, that it was hopeless.

Laurent was affianced to Antoinette's sister and the marriage would take place when her dowry, which had been steadily increasing throughout the year, was big enough to warrant the ceremony.

There was no possible appeal which either of them could make. Antoinette was the youngest of the family. It was not her turn to marry, and even if she wanted to, there would be no money for her. Besides, they both knew that love had little to do with marriage.

Marriage was a sensible, legal contract made between two families and entered into with financial advantage to both parties. Love had nothing to do with such arrangements and both Antoinette and Laurent knew that there was only heartbreak and unhappiness left for both of them.

Antoinette was only sixteen in years, but she was far older in wisdom. She approached her father that evening and told him that she intended to leave the farm and go into service.

"I wish to better myself," she said proudly, then felt ashamed when he was pleased with what he imagined were her ambitious ideas.

He took her up to the *Château* the next day. He had

116

a friend there, a herdsman who had occasionally purchased a pig from the farm or brought a cow over for service.

There was much drinking of wine and exchanging of compliments. Antoinette had her cheek pinched, was told she was a pretty girl and if she worked as well as she looked, the "big house" was sure to employ her.

The upshot of it all had been with within three days Antoinette entered the *Château* as a sewing maid.

It was then that she had fallen in love for the second time with one of the loveliest people she had ever seen—a tall, graceful woman, whose limbs seemed to move with a grace that was like the wind blowing over the cornfields and whose smile made the sun less golden in comparison.

"If you sew as well as your father says," she had told the wide-eyed Antoinette, "you shall help my good Marie with my clothes. If your stitches are too big, you will have to go into the kitchen, for I am very particular, am I not, Marie?"

"And rightly, Madame," the old maid said sourly.

The lovely lady laughed.

"Marie is jealous," she told Antoinette, "because her eyes are getting dim and she cannot see as well as she did. But no one in the world will ever sew as beautifully as Marie could when she was younger. You will have to work very hard to be even half as good as she was; but you can help her, and if she is too cross with you, come and tell me and I will protect you."

She laughed again, and putting out a hand glittering with diamond rings, she laid it on her old maid's arm.

"We must let the young ones have a chance, Marie," she said consolingly. "Let this child help you instead of sitting up half the night making your poor old eyes blood-shot with the strain of trying to see when you know you can't."

"It is, of course, as Madame wishes," Marie said stiffly.

The Countess had turned to Antoinette. She put her hand under her chin and turned her eager young face up to hers.

"Be kind and helpful to Marie," she said. "We all have to get old and it will be your turn one day. Don't forget that."

Antoinette had not forgotten it, and in a few years' time when old Marie's weakening eyes had made her almost completely blind, she had maided the Countess and looked after the old woman at the same time, striving out of the kindness of her heart not to let Marie realise how helpless she was or how little she could do for her beloved mistress.

After Antoinette had been at the *Château* for many years, a third love had come to her.

Laurent had married her sister by this time and she had almost ceased to think of him; but sometimes, when the apple blossom stood on the trees, her heart would ache a little and she would work harder as if in an effort to forget her thoughts.

She had a lot to do. Old Marie died, the Countess grew ill and her lovely face altered and sharpened with pain. When she died, it was Antoinette's hand she held until the last moment when her spirit leapt free of her tortured body.

Then Antoinette expected there would be changes in the *Château* and wondered if she would have to return home; but the Count asked her to stay on with him, which she did until he too died; finding life empty and his heart inconsolable without his beloved wife.

After that there were changes indeed, but not for Antoinette. The new Comte de Valmont, son of the previous holder of the title, came from Paris and brought with him his bride.

Antoinette liked the new Countess from the moment when she stepped from the coach and looked up at the *Château* exclaimed:

"*Mon cher,* you did not tell me what an enchanting Palace you owned!"

The new Countess brought her own maid with her, but the girl pined for the gaiety and excitements of Paris and soon she was sent away and Antoinette took her place.

It was with a happiness lovely to see that two years

later the Countess told Antoinette that she was to have a child.

"My husband and I have wanted a baby so much," she said. "I had a son when I was very young, but he was taken from me by his relatives and always some part of me has felt incomplete, because, happy as I am with my husband, every woman wants a baby. And now God has heard my prayers and in the spring my little child will be born."

Once again the apple blossom was in bloom when Rêve came into the world, but this time Antoinette had no time to remember Laurent.

She could think only of the small pink and white cherub which she was told was to be christened Rêve because she was a dream come true.

"You must look after her, Antoinette," the Countess had murmured, "because you are the only person I would trust her with in the whole world. My little Rêve, my little dream; the little daughter I have wanted so much."

That then had been Antoinette's life. Devotion to three people.

It was not a very large number by some people's standards, and yet how rich, how varied, how immensely precious was the fact that in loving she had been loved in return and that none of those she had loved had ever failed her.

Never in her whole life had Rêve had secrets from Antoinette. She had told her everything for two reasons —firstly, because at one time there had been no one else to talk to, and secondly because Antoinette's sympathy and devotion made her the ideal listener as well as the ideal counsellor.

Yet now she must keep from her the greatest secret of all. It made Rêve sad, but she knew that to every woman there comes that moment when a man supplants everything else in her life.

It was not that in being loyal to Armand she was being disloyal to Antoinette. It was only that her love was such a fundamental part of herself that it must take precedence over everything, however important it had seemed before he came.

She would tell Armand all about Antoinette, she thought, and perhaps, if he thought it best, they would ultimately confide in her, at least before they took the important step of being married. But first, before they thought of such things, Armand must be got to safety.

It was difficult to guess why he had come to France. De Frémond had accused him of spying and to Rêve there was something very horrible in the word.

A spy, an informer, a man who betrayed the confidences of those who trusted him! And yet she supposed that in war anything was possible; and was not France at war with England?

For the first time since she had heard them other of de Frémond's words returned to her mind.

"Faith!" he had exclaimed, "if it isn't Sheringham! Sheringham, the seducer!"

Rêve remembered the jeering innuendo in his voice as he spoke the last words. What did it mean? She knew, of course, the actual meaning of the word, even though it was spoken in English.

Now she wondered for one split second if Armand had deceived her, if his love for her had not been the real love she had believed it to be but merely the lust of the hunter, the desire of a man for an attractive woman.

And then, even as such thoughts came to her mind, she put them from her, knowing that they were base and dishonourable. Armand was not like that.

She was as sure of that as if his arms were around her and he was telling her to trust her instinct where he was concerned.

If he had seduced women in the past—as undoubtedly he might have done—it was but the virility of an attractive, well-built young man with red blood coursing through his veins. Where she was concerned things were very different.

He had made no attempt to seduce her, had merely told her of his love and drawn from her a love as sacred and beautiful as if they had stood together in the presence of God himself.

Their love, it was true, had meant that their hearts had beaten together in unison, that a flame had risen within each of them, their pulses had throbbed together and their lips had sought each other's. And yet was not that as God had intended man and woman to be—mutually attracted one to the other.

Yet their desire had been infused with that Divine fire which seemed to lift them from the bestiality of animals into the glory and beauty of the Godhead.

What did it matter what de Frémond had said? The evil had spent itself uselessly, for she knew with all certainty the truth of Armand's love for her and hers for him.

All that mattered now was to keep him safe, to save him from himself, from a misjudged word, a slip which might mean discovery and the penalty extracted from all those who fought against the Emperor.

At the very thought Rêve clenched her hands together. She must warn him, she must tell him what she had heard, make certain that he took up the part assigned to him without fear of discovery.

She crossed the room to his side. He was asleep, and yet she felt that it was not a heavy sleep. Impulsively, without thinking, she bent forward and whispered his name.

"Armand! Armand! Can you hear me?"

She felt him stir and knew that his consciousness was returning to him slowly, and with difficulty. She knew it was wrong to waken him, yet at the same time she was afraid that he might awake at another time when she was not in the room.

"Armand! Armand!" she said again.

Slowly he opened his eyes. They were clear, and she saw that there was no fever in them. They rested on her face and she smiled a little tumultuously at him, feeling very near to tears in knowing that he was seeing her once again.

"Oh, Armand," she whispered, and her lips quivered. She restrained an impulse to bend forward and kiss him. There would be time for that later. She must tell him first who he was supposed to be, warn him of the dangers which lay ahead.

But before she could speak, before she could force even a word to her trembling lips, he spoke:

"Who are you?" he asked.

7

"How long will he be like this?" Rêve asked.

Watching her expressive face, Dr. Maurel thought he had never seen anyone look so attractive when desperately worried.

For a moment he did not answer and then, as she waited, he shrugged his shoulders, making an impressive gesture which was more eloquent than any words.

"Who can tell?" he said at length. "It may be a few days, six months, a year, or perhaps—for ever."

"For ever!"

Rêve hardly seemed to breathe the words.

"I remember a man once who fell off his horse when riding along a dark road on a stormy night," Dr. Maurel went on. "He pitched on his head and lost his memory completely. He had no idea who he was or where he had come from. Fortunately his relatives claimed him, and after a while he began to think that he remembered things because of what they told him about the past.

"But actually he had no memory for anything that had happened before his accident. One night, ten years later, he was going along the same road. There was a flash of lightning, his horse stumbled, and his memory returned to him completely and in an instant."

"Is that how it happens usually?" Rêve asked.

Dr. Maurel shook his head.

"No, indeed, that was an exception. Uusally the memory returns slowly. Little things seem to cause an echo in the patient's mind—a note of music, a book or a poem he has read before, a familiar face. It is rather like the dawn breaking. Gradually the darkness goes and the world is light."

"And you think in Armand's case that will happen?" Rêve questioned.

Dr. Maurel smiled and putting out his big hand, laid it on her arm.

"My child, if I could answer questions like that, I should not be a country doctor. Who can possibly forecast the workings of Providence, for it is Providence who decides these things? Your brother's memory may return in a flash; it may come to him slowly, or not at all. At the moment he tells me he remembers nothing—nothing at all.

"He does not even recall how he got the wound which caused all this damage. But perhaps in a week or so, as he gets stronger, something may revive that stunned consciousness. When he is really better, perhaps in several months' time, a visit to his own estates might prove beneficial.

"In the meantime our chief concern must be to get the wound healed and not to let him be worried. Does it matter so very much that he cannot remember his journey here? Who knows what the past may have held for him, but at least at present he is happy and content."

Rêve smiled automatically in response to the lightness in Dr. Maurel's tone. When he had left her, she stood for a long time in the Silver Salon looking out over the lake. Was there ever such a tangle?

Armand, with complete loss of memory so that she dared not warn him of the danger in which he stood!

At first she had been inclined to believe that he was hiding the truth from her because in his weakness he was not certain whether she was friend or foe; then gradually she had come to realise that he was not acting, not pretending.

He was in truth behaving absolutely naturally because he did not remember anything. What made it even more difficult was the fact that he accepted all she told him with the innocence and credulity of a trusting child.

"I am Armand d'Augeron, you tell me," he said to her. "I like the sound of the name. It is distinguished."

"Yes, your name is Armand," Rêve said, a slight emphasis on the word.

"A nice name, don't you think?" he asked dreamily. "There are many things that I should have hated to be called."

"What, for instance?" Rêve asked, thinking that perhaps the reply might be illuminating.

"Oh, I cannot recollect them at the moment," Armand replied lazily. "And I suppose that names don't really matter a fig. It is the people who bear them that make them memorable. Your name is as charming as you are yourself. But I expect a lot of people have told you that."

His voice was so impersonal, so casual that Rêve could have cried out at the very tone of it. Sometimes she felt she could hardly bear the fact that Armand had accepted, without comment or suspicion, the fact that she was his half-sister.

"I am glad," he had said.

She knew that he was pleased, although there was no warmth, no urgency in his tone, none of that fierce intensity with which he had addressed her when they were together in the Temple.

How long ago it seemed now! Sometimes Rêve wondered to herself whether it was her memory which was at fault, not Armand's, and if indeed she had but dreamt the whole thing.

But there was Paul de Frémond's grave in the churchyard to tell her that it was true. She had seen it when she went to take flowers to place in the family vault where the Duchess had been interred.

She had stood there looking down at the newly turned earth, devoid of any flowers or markings; then with an effort she had forced herself to say a prayer for de Frémond's soul.

From that very first return to consciousness when Armand had looked at her in the face and asked: "Who are you?" she had felt as if she were caught in some snare from which she would never be able to escape.

It was almost inconceivable that the Armand whom she loved and who had loved her with a fierce, passionate intensity, should now speak to her courteously and with the pleasant, easy affection of a brother.

It was only the fact that Antoinette had come into the room while she was still answering his question which had prevented her from telling him there and then exactly who she was and what she believed she meant in his life.

Sometimes Rêve regretted bitterly that she had been forced to lie to Armand, and that, having lied, she had felt it both politic and sensible to carry on the pretence while he was still so ill.

But she had never thought for one moment that anything so tragic or so fantastic would happen as that he should lose his memory.

"Who are you?" he had asked, and with the soft, half-smile on her lips of a woman who loves, she had answered him.

"I am Rêve! Do you not remember me? Rêve!"

Her eyes held his, but she saw no gleam of recognition in them; yet she was certain now that there had been something else—admiration, perhaps, or something deeper, she was not quite certain.

And then Antoinette had come into the room.

"You are Rêve," Armand had repeated with difficulty, and hastily, because she was afraid, Rêve had said the fatal words:

"Yes, surely, you remember? I am your half-sister, Rêve de Valmont."

"My half-sister!" Armand repeated slowly, and Rêve had looked round to find Antoinette standing beside her.

"You must not talk too much, Monsieur," the latter said quietly and added to Rêve: "Let him sleep, poor man."

Antoinette had smoothed the pillows and drawn Rêve away from the bedside; then seated beside her on the window seat, she had said what seemed to Rêve now to have been prophetic words:

"He may lose his memory for a few months, for a

blow on the head sometimes causes that. If he asks many questions, do not hurry him. Just answer them and try not to appear surprised that many obvious things escape him."

"He may lose his memory!" Rêve echoed stupidly.

"It is but to be expected," Antoinette answered. "The doctor was saying to me that such a deep head wound was bound to have a bad repercussion of some sort on the system. Some people might become semi-paralysed with such a blow, but there is nothing like that about Monsieur. He must have what we call 'a charmed life'."

"You are quite sure nothing like that has happened to him?"

The words burst from Rêve's lips and her face was white. Antoinette took her hand in hers.

"No, no, of course not, you stupid child. Would I have mentioned it if I had thought there was the slightest chance of such a thing? Why, I have really disturbed you! It is indeed silly of me, but I had no idea you would be so upset."

"I am all right," Rêve said hastily. "It was just the shock of thinking that so strong a young man might not be able to walk or move."

"Antoinette patted her hand reassuringly.

"Forget that I suggested anything so horrid. Monsieur will be all right, and already you are very fond of him. That is good! For too long, *ma petite,* you have been without a family."

"Yes, that is why I care so deeply," Rêve said, not daring to look at Antoinette for fear she should notice that she lied.

"Yes, of course that is it," Antoinette answered. "He is indeed handsome, your brother; and I am quite certain very charming. What a pity you did not get to know each other before that villain attacked him."

"A pity indeed!" Rêve agreed. "When he is well again, we must make up for lost time."

"Of course," Antoinette smiled. "And now that Monsieur is here, he will be able to deal with all the negotiations regarding your mrariage."

127

"Yes—yes, he—can do that——"

Rêve's words were slow and slightly tremulous.

"I am very glad," Antoinette said. "I have worried about you, *ma petite*. Let us be frank and admit that is is *your* well-being, your future which is of more importance than anything else. I want to see you happy and settled."

"Yes—my future," Rêve repeated, but she had known then how careful she must be where Antoinette was concerned.

Antoinette must never suspect, must never know who Armand was. If she did, she would not hesitate to betray him if she believed it was for the ultimate good of Rêve herself.

And so the farce had begun and continued. Only there was no question of acting on Armand's part because he had no idea that he was not who Rêve told him he was.

Things were all the easier in that neither she nor any of the other persons in the *Château* could answer questions about his past life in Poland. They could only tell him about themselves, and that in itself made the situation far less dangerous than it might have been.

Now the Emperor was arriving that night, and while Rêve shivered at the thought, she need not be afraid of anything that Armand might say or do, for he was in fact completely convinced that he was the Marquis d'Augeron and was looking forward to Napoleon Bonaparte's visit with the same interest and supercilious curiosity that any French aristocrat might have shown in the circumstances.

Feelings in the *Château* were indeed mixed regarding the Emperor's arrival. Rêve was beset with anxiety and terror lest Armand should betray himself; Antoinette, imbued as she was with the Duchess's opinions, which were those of the old régime towards the first Empire, looked on the Emperor as an upstart who was aping his betters.

But for the rest of the household and for those who lived in the village it was a moment of ecstasy, excitement and almost hysterical adoration.

The *Château* itself had been transformed so that Rêve hardly recognised her own home. Everywhere there was the faint smell of paint, but the rooms indeed looked beautiful and even more elaborate, if possible, then in the days when her father had lived there in all his grandeur.

The Duchess's fine tapestries, velvet hangings and valuable furniture had been displayed to their best advantage, and everywhere there were flowers.

Flowers arranged in great banks of colour in the hall, in cut crystal and valuable china vases in the salons, while in the Great Banqueting Hall garlands were wreathed along every wall and entwined round the minstrel's gallery until the room was veritably a bower of blossom.

Would they have done as much for any of their former kings? Rêve wondered and knew that it was the people's desire to hero-worship which gave them this almost fanatical adoration of Napoleon.

He had soared into prominence and his victories had made him seem almost divinely omnipotent so that France had risen like a phoenix from the fire of the Revolution, to the glories and success of a fame she had never achieved before.

The citizens of St. Benis, typical of the people of France, believed in Napoleon as their forefathers had believed in God. Would their faith prove justified or would he eventually fail them?

Rêve asked the question as she turned from the window to move restlessly over the soft carpet of the Silver Salon. She caught sight of herself in the glass as she moved and knew that she looked her best to greet the Emperor.

Her gown was of hyacinth blue satin with a sash of rose-pink velvet embroidered with moonstones which Antoinette had fashioned from some of the exquisite materials that the Duchess had brought with her from Italy.

Armand was not to come down to dinner. The doctor had permitted him to rise from his bed and sit in his room, but he had forbidden him to cross the threshold.

The wound, he said, had knit and healed quicker than he had dared to hope for, but any excitement might cause it to open again. Besides, Armand was still very weak.

Yet never had there been a more difficult patient. Armand declared he was bored, and Rêve could well believe it from the expression on his face. He wanted to be out again, he wanted to look at the house, to see the gardens, to take up life as he had left it.

At first Rêve had been perturbed and half afraid at his restless, nervous energy; then she had understood. Subconsciously he knew there was something for him to do, but he could not remember what it was.

At the back of his mind was the sense of urgency, of something to be accomplished; but while he could not remember the details, its impetus gave him a frustrated sense of irritation that he must be treated as an invalid.

"Napoleon coming here?" he said, when Rêve told him. "I want to see him."

"Why?" Rêve asked.

Armand knit his brows for a moment in concentration.

"But of course I want to see him," he said after a moment's pause. " 'Boney' the terrible, the 'Nappy' who has got all Europe cowed. Yes, naturally I want to see him. Don't you?"

"I have seen him," Rêve said quietly.

"Yes, I remember. Antoinette told me that you went to Paris, bearded the lion in his den and demanded that your estates should be given back to you. That was brave of you. What should you have done if he had said no?"

Rêve laughed.

"Persisted, I suppose, until he changed his mind."

"Napoleon Bonaparte!" Armand said reflectively. "I seem to know a deuce of a lot about him and yet somehow there seem to be things I can't remember. There is

a song about him I used to hear the children sing—
how did it go?

> 'This little Boney says he'll come
> At merry Christmas time;
> But that, I say, is all a hum
> Or I no more will rhyme.'

"Now why do I remember that? Where was he coming and why?"

"I've no idea!" Rêve replied. "It's a silly verse anyway."

She moved restlessly across the room as she spoke and picked up her guitar and struck a chord, hoping Armand's attention would be distracted by her action. She dared not whisper the truth, dared not say:

"Napoleon is the man you have doubtless come from England to see. He is the man who threatened to invade your country and the verse you repeated referred to that. He failed in that project, but he means to conquer Britain.

"He is your deadly enemy, the man of whom the whole world is afraid. Watch him, for if he learns who you are, he will not hesitate to destroy you. And yet you must have known the risk when you crossed the Channel which divides our two countries."

How could she say that to Armand when he looked so pale and weak with dark lines under his eyes and his head still swathed in bandages? No, she dared not say it. And yet who knew what tonight might bring forth, what drama might not be enacted here in the *Château?*

At a sudden clatter of hoofs outside, Rêve went to a side window from which she could overlook the courtyard. Soldiers in the uniform of the Royal Guard were riding up to the front door.

Behind them came officers in blue embroidered with gold, their scarlet cuffs and scarlet collars vivid splashes of colour, and riding behind them was a small man inconspicuously dressed in dark blue, a black unlaced hat pulled low over his forehead, his face unsmiling, expressionless as if he did not hear the ringing cheers and cries of elation which had followed him all the way from St. Benis up the long drive to the *Château*.

The guards were dismounting. Rêve turned from the window and very slowly descended the staircase.

She was waiting in the Great Hall as two officers came marching in, bowed to her, and turning smartly, stood aside for the entry of the Emperor.

He walked quickly with an air of impatience, and Rêve rising from a deep curtsy, met his eyes for the second time in her life and knew that, whatever his enemies might say of him, Napoleon Bonaparte was a great man.

One had only to look into his face to forget how short he was; one had only to see that high peaked nose, cropped hair and intent, searching eyes to understand how the force that had galvanised France into action had emanated from this plainly dressed, unpretentious little Corsican.

"May I welcome you to Valmont, Sire?" Rêve said.

"I am glad to be here," Napoleon replied. "I have heard a lot about the beauties of your *Château*. They are not exaggerated."

He spoke in a quick, staccato manner, and then glanced about him as Rêve led the way to the Silver Salon. There was wine waiting for him, but Napoleon waved old Jacques aside with an imperious hand.

"I am not thirsty," he said.

He strode to the window and looked out on to the lake.

"A fine place," he said. "Very fine indeed. I am taking it from you. I need it for one of my Generals."

"Taking it from me, Sire?"

Rêve hardly recognised her own voice, and she felt herself shake all over with the sudden shock.

"Yes! You will be paid, of course," he said testily as if the details were of no consequence.

Then turning he saw her face. "It upsets you?" he asked. "But why? You would not be able to live here, for you are to be married."

132

Rêve's hand crept to her throat as if she felt she was being strangled.

"But, Sire——" she began.

"Giles de Durieux is waiting for you," the Emperor said. "Indeed he is getting impatient. I have promised him that your marriage shall be expedited as soon as possible. I am on my way to Fontainebleau. You must come there with me, you and your half-brother, who I understand is to arrange the marriage. Durieux is an old friend of mine and I would not see him disconsolate. I assure you that you will find him charming—yes, charming."

"But, Sire, I do not wish to be married. My brother is ill. He could not leave here as yet."

"Yes, yes, I understand that he was wounded by an assailant who was seeking my life rather than his. It was very creditable of him to discover the plot and he shall not go unrewarded. What is more, he shall see my own doctor. If Corvisart cannot put him right, nobody can.

"It will all be arranged at Fontainebleau. You must pack your prettiest gowns, Comtesse, for you will find many rivals to your beauty at my Palace."

It seemed to Rêve that there was nothing she could say. She felt the room swim before her eyes and wondered for a moment if she might faint, then knew with a desperation born of despair that she must do what was required of her and that this was not the moment to try to escape from the toils of a net which was closing around her with a relentlessness terrifying beyond words.

The Emperor asked to see the rest of the *Château* and she escorted him through the State rooms. He approved of the furnishings and the pictures. He liked everything, in fact, and appeared to be entirely oblivious of her feelings, for he said not once but many times:

"This will do for Junot. He has done well for me and I am pleased with him. He will like this place, for he is fond of the country."

"So am I, Sire," Rêve said pathetically, but he seemed not to have heard her.

133

It was only when they returned again to the Silver Salon that she summoned up enough courage to say in a voice which was unsteady through sheer nervousness:

"I have no desire to be married, Sire. Could not the Count de Durieux be persuaded to look elsewhere, or at least to have the arrangements postponed for another year or so?"

For the first time Napoleon's searching eyes seemed to see her as an individual, and he scrutinised her so intently that she felt as if he searched out the very secrets of her soul

"You have no wish to be married," he said. "But why? All young women should be married and in your particular position it is a necessity. Besides, the Count de Durieux is a wealthy, distinguished man. Have you seen him?"

"No, I know nothing about the Count," Rêve replied.

"Ah, when you have seen him you will ask me no longer to postpone the ceremony but to hurry up the formalities. A clever man and one in whom I have great trust. You will be happy, my dear. I am assured of that, so let us have no more girlish vapourings."

He rose abruptly to his feet as he spoke.

"We will meet at dinner," he said.

There was nothing Rêve could do but sink into a deep curtsy as he went to the suite at the end of the corridor which had been reserved for his use.

Alone, she sped like a startled fawn towards Armand's bedroom. He was sitting in a chair as she entered and she saw that his face was drawn and grey. She guessed it was from the effort of dressing.

He was wearing knee breeches of white satin and a coat of blue velvet which Rêve remembered seeing Antoinette unpack from the luggage that de Frémond had brought from Amsterdam. She had been afraid ever since this morning, when Armand had said he would dress to meet the Emperor, that the clothes would not fit.

It would be one more thing which might throw suspicion upon Armand in the role he had assumed so easily and without question.

She had thought, but had been by no means certain that the coats looked about the right size, but for all she knew the breeches might be impossible. Yet Armand was wearing them, and she felt a wave of relief sweep over her.

"Oh, you are dressed," she exclaimed.

He looked up with a frown between his eyes.

"Yes, I am dressed," he said grumpily, "and curst difficult it was too. This blasted head of mine makes me reel about as if I were a seasick sailor. Damn it all, the valets had to hold me up as if I were a baby, and drop me into my clothes."

"But you got them on," Rêve said unnecessarily.

"Yes, and confoundedly uncomfortable they are too." Armand replied. "I thought one was supposed to lose weight in bed, but this coat cuts me under the arms and it is too narrow across the back. Who is my tailor? I shall tell the fool what I think of him."

"You bought your clothes in Poland," Rêve replied, "but you will be able to order more when we go to Paris. The Emperor wishes us to go immediately to Fontainebleau."

"Fontainebleau! That sounds interesting."

"Perhaps it will be for you, but he desires the arrangements to be made immediately for my marriage."

Her eyes searched Armand's face as she spoke. Surely, surely he would show some sign that he minded this if nothing else; but his expression did not change.

"I wish to God I didn't feel such a fool being as weak as a kitten and hardly able to stand on my own two feet. Pour me out a brandy, there's a good girl. It is in that decanter on the far table."

Rêve hurried to do his bidding. She saw that there was blueness round his mouth and guessed that he was feeling faint. She was certain that the exertion of getting out of bed had been too much for him, but he had insisted on rising, and had she not sent two footmen to assist him, she knew that he would have attempted it alone.

She poured him the brandy, which he sipped and after a moment the strained look vanished from his face.

"That is better," he said at length. "Now tell me what you were saying again. It sounded as if you were talking through a thick fog about ten miles away."

"I was telling you that the Emperor wishes us to go to Fontainebleau, that my marriage is to take place with the Count Giles de Durieux as quickly as possible, and that you are to arrange it. And oh, Armand, the Emperor is taking Valmont from me."

"The devil he is!" Armand exclaimed. "But why?"

"He wants to give it to one of his Generals. He is rewarding them all with titles and vast estates, but I had never believed that, having given me back Valmont, he would take it away again."

Rêve's voice broke and there were tears in her eyes.

"But you won't be able to live here if you are married," Armand said.

Rêve stamped her foot in a sudden burst of anger.

"You are as bad as the Emperor," she said. "Why cannot I live here? I have no intention of being wed to the Count de Durieux. Not all the Emperors in the world will make me marry him."

Armand looked up at her in surprise. Her outburst had come in the very moment he was sipping his brandy, and now he looked at her over the rim of his glass. It was a long second before he spoke.

"You are very pretty when you are angry," he said at length, "I had not realised until now how pretty you are. I have been thinking you were someone very kind, someone who was nursing me back to health. You might have been a nun, for I had forgotten you were a woman.

"But now I see you are very much a woman; and if you don't want to marry this man, I see no reason why you should. I will tell the Emperor. I will say that we have decided not to go through with the arrangements. You can leave it all to me."

Now Rêve's anger had all gone. With a sound that was half a sob she turned towards Armand, and suddenly knelt down at his feet, her arms resting on his knees.

"No, Armand you cannot do that," she said. "We dare not offend the Emperor. It would be dangerous, very dangerous for you to cross him in any way, so say nothing which will displease His Majesty. You must promise me, here and now, Armand, that you will agree to anything he suggests."

Armand set down his glass of brandy on the table beside him.

"Why should I?" he asked. "I am not afraid of Napoleon Bonaparte. After all, who is he? A little——"

Rêve put up her fingers and laid them against his lips.

"Anyone might overhear what you are saying," she said. "You do not understand, but I beg you to do what I wish. We will go to Fontainebleau together as the Emperor desires and you may make arrangements for my marriage. I will agree to that, I will agree to anything, so long as you are careful. Promise me you will say nothing which might be misconstrued or held against you."

"Curse it, why are you so frightened?" Armand asked. "You are trembling, Rêve, what has upset you? Come, I want the truth."

"It is nothing, nothing," Rêve cried. "If I am trembling, it is because it has been rather an ordeal meeting the Emperor by myself and to be told that he wants Valmont for someone else!"

She paused for a moment, and then continued:

"But of course he is right, I will not be living here, I shall be married. I am just making a fuss about nothing. Oh, Armand, promise me that you will agree to whatever the Emperor says."

"You are upsetting yourself needlessly," Armand said. "Nappy cannot be such a bogy as all that. If the fellow has got to come in here ordering us about, I may as well feel strong enough to tackle him."

"Oh, Armand, Armand," Rêve cried in a kind of fever. "You must not speak about the Emperor like that. You must be respectful, you must be humble. Everyone says the same. He has to have exactly what he wants or he makes like unbearable for those who offend him."

"Blister it, I can promise you that I am not afraid of him," Armand said, when suddenly a voice from the door said, making them both jump:

"And of whom are you not afraid?"

Armand and Rêve got to their feet, Rêve to stand white-faced and trembling, while Armand seemed completely composed, a faint smile on his lips as he bowed.

"Your servant, Sire.'

The Emperor shut the door behind him and came farther into the room.

"I am glad to see that you have left your bed of sickness, Monsieur le Marquis; but tell me, for I am curious, of whom were you speaking when I entered the room?"

"You, Sire, Armand answered quietly.

Rêve gave a little exclamation, but Napoleons eyes were on Armand. He advanced until they were close together and he was forced to look up at Armand be cause of his height.

"Sit down," he said. "You are obviously not well enough to stand. The wound in the head has healed?"

"Yes, Sire, it is very much better. I am suffering only from weakness at being kept in bed and fed with gruel and pap by a lot of fussy women."

A faint smile touched the Emperor's lips. With a gesture of his hand he indicated the chair which Armand had vacated and seated himself in another high-backed one in the room. Rêve sank on to the sofa, her fingers clasped together, her eyes very dark in a white face, roving from one man to the other.

"And now," the Emperor said, "tell me, young man, why you are not afraid of me?"

"I have made it a practice, Sire, never to be afraid of anything which I have not seen or actually encountered."

"A good principle," the Emperor said, "and one which I hope will not be adopted by my enemies. I have been making inquiries about you, Marquis, and I find that you are one of our subjects whom we could ill afford to have living in other lands. You are a linguist, I believe. You have also travelled a great deal, having an intimate knowledge of England amongst other places."

Rêve felt her heart beat so loudly that she wondered that the two men had not heard it. Where, she wondered, could the Emperor have got his information?

She knew, of course, that he had spies everywhere, and for a moment she wondered if by any chance he was playing with them, whether he had discovered that the real Marquis d'Augeron had been killed in Amsterdam, and if he were merely inciting Armand further to incriminate himself before he denounced him for the imposter that he was.

In terror she watched Armand, sitting perfectly at his ease, knit his brow for a moment and then say:

"You have doubtless been told, Sire, of the tiresome disability this recent wound has inflicted upon me. My memory is so bad that at times I wonder if I am indeed myself. You speak to me of England, yet all that I can recall is that it is a pleasant country, with great trees and green parks, and that there was excellent trout fishing in one place I must have visited and yet I cannot remember where."

"You will able to visit England again, Marquis, when I have brought her to her knees in defeat," Napoleon said grimly, and for a moment his mouth was set tightly.

"*If* England is defeated," Armand said with a question in his voice, "it will not be on her knees. She will die as a good soldier should—standing up."

For a moment Rêve closed her eyes. This was the end. This was the moment when Armand betrayed himself. She was past praying, past doing anything. She could only suffer with a physical agony as he signed his own death warrant.

To her astonishment she heard the Emperor laugh. She could hardly believe it was true, could hardly believe that she had heard aright. She opened her eyes. Yes, he was laughing, actually laughing.

"That is good, Marquis, very good indeed," he exclaimed. "I must remember that. All good soldiers should die standing up. Yes, that may well serve as a message to my victorous armies."

He glanced at the clock on the mantelpiece and rose.

"Dinner should be ready," he said. "May I offer you my arm, Comtesse, to the dining hall? As for you, Marquis, we shall meet at Fontainebleau. You will bring your sister to the Palace, and when you are well enough to decide her future, I would like to talk to you about your own. I have always a place around me for young men with ideas and with courage."

Armand rose to his feet; but before he could speak, the Emperor had offered his arm with a flourish to Rêve. Side by side they left the room and the door closed behind them.

For a long moment Armand stood staring after them; then as he sank back in the chair, he put his fingers to his head and said aloud:

"Now why did I say that? Why did I feel so strongly that I must say that about England?"

8

Imogène de Monestier stepped from her green marble bath and stood regarding her naked body in an oval mirror surrounded by plump cupids.

There was every justification for the satisfaction in her eyes. Her body was perfect, high-breasted, narrow-hipped and her skin, white and unblemished, had that soft flush which is only found in the most perfect pearls.

Yes, she was lovely, from the crown of her proud, poised little head to the soles of her pink-toed feet.

With a gesture Imogène indicated that her maid might now wrap her in the big, warm, scented bath-towel, and when she had seated herself on a low, gilt-framed chair which matched the gilt-covered walls of her bathroom, a second maid hurried forward to wipe her feet; while yet another stood by with a tray on which were powders, perfumes and lotions of every possible description.

There were many people who criticised and derided Imogène de Monesteir's extravagant way of living. But Imogène herself had long ceased to pay the slightest attention to what her critics said of her.

She had flouted convention since, as a very young girl, she had run away from the convent in which her parents had left her to be educated and found her way to Paris, riding pillion on the pack-horse of a handsome pedlar.

It was the first of her escapades, but by no means the last. Exquisitely beautiful, clever and hard-hearted as the most determined adventurer, she succeeded in enjoying life simply because she was utterly and completely indifferent to everything save her own inclinations and unbridled physical desires.

Affection and tenderness were words which had little place in Imogène's vocabulary. She had no affinity for anything that was soft, gentle or gracious in life. Women as a whole bored her except that like all persons of her type she would occasionally envelop one of her sex in an emotional, possessive friendship.

But, having elevated the favoured woman to a place of importance in the social sphere, she would drop her equally as quickly and with an absolute disregard for hurt feelings, injured pride or loss of kudos.

It was men round whom Imogène's life was centred, men who found her beauty irresistible and who became—far too easily—her adoring slaves until she tired of them.

Then she would discard a lover without a second thought and with no consideration of the misery and heart-break she caused in the process.

The trouble was that Imogène had so many assets with which to dazzle and fascinate the world. To begin with, she had been born into one of the most distinguished and blue-blooded of the Bourbon families.

She had, it is true, flouted their consideration and their recognition, and had betrayed her own class by marrying one of Napoleon's upstart Generals. But this could not erase the fact that she was herself an aristocrat without question. She was also clever, witty and extremely talented.

All this might have been forgiven her had she not been so beautiful. It was impossible to ignore her loveliness when she entered a room with an inborn dignity and grace which further enhanced her exquisite features and sculptured body.

There were enough beautiful women in Paris and in Fontainebleau for her to have her rivals, and yet in the whole of the Emperor's entourage there was no one with quite Imogène's quality of both beauty and breeding.

Her enemies were legion. Her own people of the

ancien régime—the aristocratic Bourbons—hated her for having, in their opinion, gone over to the enemy.

The new society, the recently created nobility, were uncomfortable and ill at ease in Imogène's presence, fancying that she laughed at them—which she did—and feeling that their naturally gauche vulgarity was accentuated by the contrast with Imogène's impeccable taste and a culture which came from a centuries-old line of ancestors.

Yet no feeling of animosity, jealousy or hatred could isolate Imogène or make her anything but a courted woman where men were concerned.

Her beauty, her wit, and, what was more, the position she held in the Imperial Court were enough to turn the head of the most practical and experienced courtier; and the men in Napoleon's palaces were often neither.

The recently created Duke de Monestier, who was one of Napoleon's favourite Generals, was a large, ugly man whose father had been a well-to-do corn-chandler at Amiens. Fabien de Monestier had, however, no inclination to follow in his father's footsteps.

He was a born soldier; from the time that he could first think or talk, his thoughts had been concentrated on soldiers and armies, on fights and battles. He actually enjoyed the most brutal and bloodiest attacks by his enemies.

His courage in battle was fabulous, and his men, who idolised him, recounted his deeds of valour with a pride which left him glowing with a warm satisfaction and pleased him more than all the decorations with which Napoleon loaded him.

But his triumphs seemed unimportant and his victories but ineffectual skirmishes under the cold eye of his wife. Blunt, insensitive and stupid where women were concerned, Fabien de Monestier could never understand why the most beautiful woman in France had condescended to marry him.

He had become her lover after a very short acquaintance; but that, as he well knew, was nothing extraordinary where Imogène was concerned; he had merely

143

followed where many had trodden before him, and he was now supplanted by many others.

He felt murderously jealous when he thought of it and yet he had learned by bitter experience that his rage and passionate accusations evoked nothing from Imogène but a smile and the question whether he would prefer her to leave him once and for all.

Angry or jealous as he might be, he knew that his life would be insufferable without her.

Unversed as he was in the ways of women, Imogène had him completely in her power, and the man who made foreign armies shake at the *mention of his name* must, in his turn, tremble and sweat because a woman's eyes rested on him in quiet irony.

"I shall kill you one day," he had told Imogène more than once.

Yet when she flung back her lovely head and asked in a tone of utter sweetness

"Why not now?"

He had known that his big hands would never encircle her white neck except with the passion of a lover and that merely to touch her was to turn his strength into a hungry weakness which made him remember only that she was the most desirable woman he had ever known—and his wife.

Paris had never ceased to marvel at Imogène's marriage, and when, as time went on, it was not dissolved, they still continued to talk and speculate as to what the eventual outcome would be.

Imogène's behaviour during her husband's long absences on the battlefield provided an unending source for scandal and gossip, and yet she sailed serenely through their midst, taking lover after lover, causing heart-break and misery, preventing marriages and destroying those that had already been made, without apparently any just retribution overtaking her.

"If only she could be unhappy just for once," Napoleon's youngest sister, the Princess Pauline Borghese, had been heard to say.

She herself was as beautiful as a Greek goddess and usually as naked, but her charms paled as the moon before the sun when Imogène was around, and she hated the Duchess with a ferocity which appeared only to amuse Imogène when she was told of it.

Nothing was too extravagant, nothing was too exotic or luxurious as a background for Imogène's beauty. Fabien de Monestier would receive urgent messages on the very eve of a battle or even on the battlefield itself to send his wife more money, more jewels, more loot from the countries he was conquering in Napoleon's name.

At first he was appalled by his wife's demands, but when she had threatened him, quietly and effectively, that if he did not obey her she would leave him, he capitulated.

Every week he sent messengers to Paris with sealed packages or dispatched conveyances with heavy loads of pictures, furniture, tapestries and sculptures from the cities he conquered.

The Emperor's countenance of such flagrant behaviour was explained, according to local gossips, by the fact that he himself was enamoured by Imogène. This was actually untrue. Napoleon had never been Imogène's lover; and as it happened, her beauty left him unmoved.

But there was something which drew them together, some point of contact in that they were both equally hard-headed, both exorbitantly ambitious, both when the occasion arose utterly and completely ruthless.

There was also, as far as the Emperor was concerned, some satisfaction in having at his court as the wife of one of his most distinguished generals a woman who by right of birth should have taken her place amongst those who were working against him.

He found Imogène useful in that she had a personal knowledge of those who were being most formidable and aggressive among the *ancien régime*.

"Tell me about this person," he would say to her, naming a Duke who was known to be the centre of some infamous intrigue against him.

"Oh, that is cousin Gérard," Imogène would explain with a lilting laugh. "You need not be frightened of him. He has a passion for the 'macabre', but his life is a model of good works. He is the usual example of frustrated sex which expends itself in ineffective intrigue. Throw that report you have about him from Fouché into the wastepaper basket."

Fouché, a little foxy man with a small dark face and slit eyes, was Napoleon's Minister of the Interior and Head of the Police.

He was another of Imogène's enemies because she so often mocked at him; and yet, try as he would, he could find nothing which would destroy Napoleon's interest in her.

His spies watched her for months on end, but they discovered nothing except a succession of infidelities which Imogène made no effort to conceal. And he blushed with anger when Imogène at a State Ball asked him in front of everyone if he intended adding his own name to the list of lovers which he was compiling so arduously.

Napoleon's laugh had made the insult almost unbearable. Fouché's spies were traditionally so well taught that it was a generally accepted idea that people had no idea they were being spied on until it was too late to do anything about it.

"I have no secrets, Monsieur Fouché." Imogène continued, "but if you do not believe me, I will give you a seat behind a curtain in my bedroom. What you would hear would certainly be educative, but not informative."

Fouché left her alone after that—an ominous gesture everyone said; but Imogène was supremely unafraid. She was in fact afraid of nothing save perhaps of old age and the gradual destruction of her beauty.

But that was a long way off, she decided as, dried and powdered, she stood once more naked before the looking-glass while her maid held ready a soft transparent chemise of Indian muslin.

A few minutes later, wearing a peignoir of white velvet trimmed with priceless lace from a conquered royalty, Imogène moved from her bathroom into her bedroom where several people were waiting to talk to her.

She dismissed two of them with a wave of her hand, but told the third to stay.

Count Metternich, the Austrian Ambassador, did not seem surprised at the favour. Tall and slender, with a supercilious smile upon his lips, he was one of the most interesting men in Paris and undoubtedly the most sought-after by the fair sex.

He and Imogène had been lovers a long time ago, but now they had other uses for each other. The Ambassador's letters to his own country were invariably full of information which he had culled from Imogène's more intimate knowledge of personalities and events at Court.

"You got my message, Clemens?" Imogène asked the Count.

He kissed her hand and murmured some extravagant compliments with his lips while his eyes rested on her lovely face without emotion.

"Yes, I received it," Count Metternich replied, "but I have no information regarding the young man in question."

"But Fouché says he is quite certain that he was in Austria three of four years ago."

"He may have been," Count Metternich replied, "but I was not there myself. Yet now you speak of it, I do remember the name. Wait a minute, something comes back to me, something connected with my own family."

"Yes, yes, tell me," Imogène said impatiently.

"It had to do with my cousin, Camille. A pretty girl, whose father owns one of the big estates north of Vienna—Yes, I remember now. There was a scandal—not a big one, for it was hushed up. What was it now? . . . She was in love with some young man who seduced her but did not propose marriage. Yes, that was it. The whole story returns to me now."

"And his name?" Imogène said breathlessly.

"His name," Count Metternich repeated. "Yes, I am certain almost completely certain, that it was Armand d'Augeron. But I will find out more for you. I will write today at once, to a member of my family, Camille's grandmother, who is at this moment living at

Chantilly. She will tell me all I wish to know, all you wish to hear about this young man. But tell me why he interests you so greatly?"

"Need you ask that question?" Imogène inquired.

"He is good-looking, I admit it," the Count answered, "but hardly, I should have thought, your type."

"Have I a type?" Imogène inquired.

"Every woman—every man for that matter—has in their mind's eye a certain ideal in the opposite sex, and those to whom they give their love, even as a passing amusement, must always have some of this ideal reflected within them."

"And what is my ideal?" Imogène said mockingly. "Fabien—or you?"

"Neither!" Count Metternich replied, "and yet in a way there is some resemblance between us. We are both honest men who make no secret of our desires and we want what we desire with a fervour which comes from an undivided concentration."

Imogène flung back her head and laughed. As she did so her robe flew open to her waist revealing the lovely curves of her breasts.

"Oh, but that is too amusing!" she said. "That you should imagine yourself undivided, you, the master of intrigue!"

"I was speaking of myself as a man, not as a diplomat," the Count said.

"And both are combined to make—Clemens?" Imogène inquired. "No, no, my friend, you and Fabien have nothing in common, and neither of you in the slightest resembles Armand d'Augeron."

"You have still not answered my question," the Count said. "Why are you so interested in him?"

Imogène made a little grimace in the mirror, yet managed to make it charming, and said with a smile:

"Perhaps because he is not interested in me."

"That cannot be true," the Count said.

"I assure you it is indeed a fact," Imogène said. "I have smiled at him, I have even—if we must put it vulgarly—exerted my wiles, and he remains utterly unmoved."

"He cannot then be right in the head."

"That is a fact, for his wound is a fresh one," Imogène said, "but I would not have thought it would have affected his virility. His sister is obviously hostile to me, but that is to be expected for women seldom find me compatible."

It was the Count's turn to laugh.

"Imogène, you are incorrigible. Leave the young man alone. If he has been ill, he obviously finds the pomposities of the palace overwhelmingly tedious and is doubtless itching to return to the rustication of his estates in Poland."

"I refuse to believe it," Imogène said. "But all the same I would know more about him. You will see to it?"

"I shall do, of course, whatever you command me," the Count said. "The details of my cousin's seduction shall be yours as quickly as it is possible for a messenger to ride to Chantilly and bring an answer to my inquiries, though what good the information will do you I cannot pretend to imagine."

"You were never very imaginative, my dear Clemens, except in moments of great ardency," Imogène said complacently. "I remember one occasion——"

The Count held up his hand to stop her.

"Spare my blushes," he said. "Besides, I must go. I have to call on the Grand Duchess of Cleve and Berg."

"Caroline Murat? Imogène said. "And how is our Emperor's sister at the moment? Heavens, but that woman has love affairs with the ponderous solemnity of an elephant about to give birth."

Count Metternich frowned.

"It would be wise to guard your tongue where the Grand Duchess is concerned. She is dangerous and she is no friend of yours."

"I should be astounded if she expressed any other emotion where I am concerned," Imogène said lightly. "Tell her you have called on me first, it will annoy her."

"I shall do nothing of the sort," Count Metternich replied, and raised Imogène fingers to his lips, he kissed them.

"As you go," Imogène said, "tell them I will see no further callers this morning. I have a slight headache."

"But surely that is extremely unkind to young Jules de Méry? He has been waiting, I understand, for nearly three hours. The boy suffers, Imogène, and one has only to watch him as you enter a room to see a soul in torture."

"Do not speak of him," Imogène said with a little shudder. "He bores me—bores me to distraction. I have told him not to come here, but he is fool enough to disobey my orders."

"And yet you loved him long enough to devour him body and soul, as you have devoured so many," the Count said.

Imogène's laugh rang out, spontaneous and lovely.

"Loved him! My dear, how stupid you are! Have you not realised by now that I have never loved anyone, except of course myself?"

"I am a great admirer of the truth," Count Metternich said, "but sometimes it appals me."

He kissed Imogène's hand again and turned towards the door. She watched him go, and then turned back to the dressing-table, a smile on her lips, her eyes sparkling as if with hidden laughter.

How pompous Clemens was getting, she thought; and yet in some ways she was fond of him. It was rumoured that he was secretly the lover of the lovely Duchess d'Abrantes, but one never knew with Clemens. He was too polished, too suave ever to betray himself where a woman or anything else was concerned.

Imogène stretched her hands above her head, yawned, and saw her reflection in the mirror. The robe had fallen open once again. Her breasts were caught against the transparent lace of her chemise and she thought it a pity that so much liveliness should go unseen.

It was still early and she had no appointments until the afternoon. Imogène yawned again and touched the gilt bell which stood on her dressing-table. Almost instantly her maid was by her side.

"Tell Comte Jules de Méry that I will receive him,"

Imogène said, "and see that we are not disturbed until I ring for you."

She glanced into the mirror as she spoke, but this time she saw not her own face but that of a young man with bored, grey eyes and a dark head swathed in bandages.

No one would have accused Armand of looking bored at that particular moment. He was sitting on a sofa in the window of Rêve's apartment and listening to the gossip she had been told the night before.

"They say that Comte Louis de Narbonne is rumoured to have been Marie Antoinette's last lover. Do you think it is true?"

"Why not ask him?" Armand replied.

"Now you are ridiculous!" Rêve retorted. "I am only telling you what the Princess Pauline told me. There was no one about whom she had not got some fantastic anecdote, but at the same time she was very gracious and kind to me and I felt honoured that she should single me out."

"I cannot quite see why," Armand replied. "She may be the Emperor's sister, but his family owe their position entirely to him. The airs and graces they give themselves are amusing if one considers who they were and where they were brought up."

"You are as bad as my Great Aunt," Rêve expostulated. "Do you remember . . . ?"

She stopped suddenly. Armand would not remember meeting the old Duchess. As the Marquis d'Augeron he was supposed never to have seen her. To cover her lapse she said quickly:

"Oh, but I forgot. What did the Emperor want to see you about last night?"

"He asked me if, when I am well, I will become one of his personal Aides-de-camp," Armand replied.

Rêve jumped up in sheer astonishment from the chair in which she had been sitting.

"Armand! And you never told me."

"I am telling you now."

"But what are you going to do?"

151

"Do I have a choice in the matter?" Armand said. "I thought those things were an Imperial command, that one must obey or die."

Rêve shuddered suddenly.

"What did you say?" she asked.

"I thanked him for the honour," Armand replied, "and said that, as soon as Doctor Corvisart thought me well enough, I would present myself humbly for his attention. In the meantime, as I pointed out, I would be busy with the arrangements for your marriage."

"Did he say anything to that?" Rêve asked.

"Yes, he reminded me, as we already know, that the Count Giles de Durieux arrives here today. He spoke of him in the most glowing terms and he himself seemed to be very anxious to see him."

"You know why the Emperor is so interested in the Count, don't you, Armand?"

"No," Armand replied. "Is there a special reason?"

"That is another thing the Princess Pauline told me," Rêve said in a low voice. "She asked me why I had come here. I told her that it was at the Emperor's invitation and that my marriage was to be arranged with the Count. 'Oh, but of course, that is my brother's latest and most valued astrologer,' she said and her voice was very scornful."

"An astrologer," Armand said. "That explains it! I have always been told that Napoleon never goes into battle without first consulting the stars and that he even takes his fortune-tellers with him into the thick of the fight. I never entirely believed it, but now I am not so sure. Also, there is something about the way he speaks of the Count which disturbs me. It is almost as if he has a veneration for the man."

"And that means that if, having seen the Count, I refuse to marry him, we shall incur the Emperor's personal anger and animosity."

"Oh, but that is ridiculous," Armand replied. "Boney likes his own way, that is obvious; but surely he cannot go so far as to insist that a girl he has only seen twice in his life must marry a man who dabbles with the planets and such nonsense?"

"Some people do not think it nonsense," Rêve said.

"Well, if you want to know what I think," Armand replied, "I think the whole thing is a lot of rubbish from beginning to end. That Emperor of yours may be great in some ways, but he is damned little in others."

"Why do you say 'that Emperor of yours'?" Rêve asked.

"Did I?" Armand replied. "Oh, I suppose I must have meant that you are always supporting him. I am afraid, if the truth were known, that my sympathies are with the *ancien régime*—not that I think much of the ones I have seen."

"The Duchess de Monestier certainly singled you out for attention last night," Rêve said with a tiny edge to her voice.

Armand did not answer and after a moment she glanced towards him and saw that he was lying with his head against a cushion, his eyes closed, a faint smile on his lips.

"Armand, do you think she is very pretty?" Rêve asked in a very small voice.

Armand opened his eyes.

"Who? The Princess Pauline?"

"No, of course not. You know we are not speaking of her but of the Duchess de Monestier."

"She is good-looking enough," Armand replied, "but I have seen a lot of women like her in my time. To tell the truth, Rêve, this place bores me. I have never been here before and yet somehow everything about it is vaguely familiar. The ceremony, the people, the way they talk, the things they say, their laughter, even the movement of their hands—it makes me yawn. Let us go back to Valmont."

Rêve felt her heart beat and her face was alight; then suddenly like a cloud passing across the sun, the light faded and a look almost of despair came into her face.

"You forget," she said, "that in a few days Valmont will no longer be mine."

"Yes, I had forgotten that," Armand agreed, "but the Emperor had promised to pay you well for it."

153

"A marriage dowry for his pet astrologer," Rêve said bitterly.

At her tone Armand sat up suddenly on the sofa and put out his hand.

"Listen, Rêve," he said. "If this marriage is going to make you unhappy I swear I will prevent it. We will avoid it somehow, whether the Emperor likes it or not. Yet the other night when we talked about it you were so insistent that I should say nothing, that I must agree with Nappy's notion to put a ring on your finger."

"Yes, I know."

Rêve got to her feet and walked to the window, her back towards Armand, to stand looking out on to the fountains and gardens.

Should she tell him now or wait a little longer? It was too soon for him to travel. Dr. Corvisart had said that he must take life as easily as possible for another week or so.

"He must convalesce, Mademoiselle," he said. "No dancing, no riding, and above all, no drinking."

No riding! The word echoed now in Rêve's mind. If Armand was to escape from Fontainebleau, he must ride—ride to the coast with perhaps Napoleon's soldiers at his heels.

No, it was too soon. She dared not speak yet. She could only pray for time, pray that nothing drastic might happen before she could extricate Armand from this mess in which they were both so involved.

With an effort she turned from the window, striving to smile at him as he lay back watching her.

"Let us at least wait until we have seen the Count," she said. "He may not be as bad as we anticipate. And if he is a good astrologer we might ask him to tell our fortunes, yours and mine. It would be interesting to know what is to happen to both of us in the future."

As Rêve spoke, there came into Armand's face a preoccupied look which was becoming increasingly familiar.

She knew what it portended, that he was trying to remember something which eluded him, trying to recall the past, to still that small nagging voice within him

154

which told him that something lay undone. What it was he still had no idea.

"You must rest this afternoon," Rêve said. "I have promised to go for a drive with the Princess Pauline. She is going to show me the strange formation of the rocks in the woods around here."

"That sounds an innocent and quite unexceptionable afternoon's amusement," Armand said. "For my own part, I shall stay here as you suggest and sleep."

"And when I return—" Rêve began.

She was interrupted by a knock on the door.

"Come in," she said, expecting it would be Antoinette.

But it was a page who entered. He was wearing the peacock green livery with scarlet facings which she knew was the private livery of the Duchess de Monestier.

The page presented his note to Armand with a low bow.

"I will await an answer outside, Monsieur," he said, and backed humbly towards the door.

Rêve watched Armand open the note. He read it slowly, his lips curving a little as if what was written amused him, but his eyes were cynical.

Rêve felt an anger rising within her as well as some other emotion which she recognised all too easily as a bitter jealousy which threatened to consume her to the detriment of all caution.

At last she could stand the silence no longer.

"What does she want?" she inquired.

Armand looked up and now his smile had broadened.

"She invites me, dear sister," he said, "to drive with her in the woods to see the curious formation of the rocks round Fontainebleau. Afterwards she suggested that I return to her house in the town for a glass of wine. An innocent—and let us hope—a harmless way of spending the afternoon?"

"But you will not go?" Rêve asked, her voice almost breaking on the words.

"Why not?" Armand inquired. "It should prove amusing, and perhaps, even—instructive. Who knows?"

155

9

Armand drew back the curtains from the window of his bedroom, which overlooked the ornamental lake where the carp swam round and round beneath the splashing fountains.

He had dressed early for dinner and the dying sun glittered on the elegance of his green satin coat, the spotless perfection of his white breeches and the crisp folds of his cravat.

Unlike the majority of other gentlemen who would be at the Palace this evening he wore no jewels. It had become a conceit with him this past week to discard the rings, tie-pins, fobs and sparkling buttons which were so much in vogue in masculine society.

He felt, though he could not explain it, a strange fastidiousness, a desire to simplify everything, not only the clothes of the men and women with whom he associated, but the Palace itself with its ornate salons, over decorated ceilings, ormolu furnishings, tasselled draperies and glittering, gilt-laced flunkeys.

Armand told himself now that it was not only his taste which was affronted by such a display of ostentatious embellishments, but something deeper, something more fundamental.

Yet he did not know what, and as he stared out into the gardens he found himself thinking, as he had thought so frequently of late, that if only his memory would return to him he would find the secret of everything.

He was immeasurably better in health. The doctors had decided that the bandages round his head were no longer necessary.

Now there was nothing left to show of the assault that had been made on him save a long red scar running like a ribbon from above his right eyebrow to be lost in the thickness of his skilfully arranged hair.

If outwardly all was well, Armand knew, however, that inwardly nothing was changed from what it had been when he first came from the oblivion of unconsciousness to ask: "Where am I?" He still could remember nothing.

His head felt as if it were full of clouds. Sometimes for a moment his memory seemed to pierce through them like the sun, and then they would close again to dim and overshadow the light.

The dizzy, overwhelming headaches from which he had suffered at the beginning had gone, but still this numbness remained, this inability to think or to remember what had happened to him in the past.

Armand remembered at school hearing for the first time the famous Greek words: Γνωθι σαυτον—know thyself. And now he asked himself, Who was he? What did he know about himself? What, indeed, did he know about anything or anyone with whom he was in contact?

Occasionally he had been surprised at his own knowledge, as on the evening before last when he had found himself talking fluently to Monsieur Talleyrand, the Foreign Minister, of the complicated politics which existed between England and Ireland.

He had been well launched in the discussion before he wondered why he knew so much about them. They had gone on to speak of the English desire to colonise, of her unfortunate relationship with the States of America.

Armand had waxed quite eloquent on the subject while Talleyrand had sat back with half-closed eyes, his long upper lip tight drawn, his ugly, clawlike hands grasping the golden crook of the ebony stick he habitually carried.

Suddenly, as he talked, Armand remembered quite clearly and unmistakably a conversation in which Talleyrand's name had been mentioned. Where it had taken place or with whom it had been made he could not recall, but he could hear a voice saying:

157

"He is pompous, affected, insolent, a shameless liar with a face llike a decayed corpse hanging over his silk embroidered uniform."

His memory had surprised him so much that his eloquence had dried up and he found himself stammering and faltering, so that Talleyrand had eventually grown bored with him and turned away to speak with someone more interesting.

Armand had been awake long into the night wondering why he should have remembered such a thing and how it could have been said to him of one of Napoleon's most trusted and distinguished ministers.

But that was only one of the many problems which presented themselves to him. Why did he not remember his estates in Poland? Why should the very thought of them bring an almost increased blankness, as if he came up against a brick wall?

The Emperor had told him that he had visited England. His memories of that country were returning quite clearly. He could remember green parklands, stately houses of grey stone circled as by a necklace with their terraces and flower gardens. He could not put a name to them, but he could see them quite clearly.

He could remember a London street which sloped downhill to a battlemented Palace outside which there were red-coated sentries on guard. He could remember the bow window of a famous club—at least he felt it must be that, though he could not put a name to it.

He could also remember driving through the streets in a hurry and entering a door on which the number "10" was written, but whose house it was or where it was situated he had no idea.

Every day it seemed as if scraps of the past returned to him. They came to his mind rather as if they were paintings of some particular spot, of some particular incident. But they remained immobile, disconnected incidents which apparently had no connection one with the other.

He felt there must be some clue or key to them and if once he could find it, everything would fall into shape and create a pattern; but for the moment such memories were in their isolation completely meaningless.

And then there was Rêve. When he thought of her, the expression on his face softened. She was very sweet, and yet strangely enough it surprised him to find that he had a sister.

He had a feeling that in a way she should not be there, that her relationship was somehow unnatural, and yet of course such imaginings were ridiculous.

But it was with Rêve most of all that he had that haunting sense that there was something that he must remember, some action to which he was committed. She had only to come into the room for the impression to leap instantly to his mind.

He had only to look at her lovely face and eloquent eyes for a sense of urgency to arise within him, a feeling that he must force his brain to become his servant rather than be mastered by it.

Sometimes it seemed to Armand as if everything that was happening to him was a long way away and that he stood watching other people move, walk, eat and talk from a great distance.

He felt himself divorced from them, yet what made it so hard was the fact that he could put nothing into words.

The doctors had done their best for him.

"Talk to me of your early life, Monsieur le Marquis," Dr. Corvisart had said to him surprisingly one day; and though he had tried to answer him, there was nothing that he could say.

"Think of your house—your estates—your friends—your employees and servants in Poland," the doctor had insisted. "Surely there is one face that you can remember?"

Armand had put his hands to his eyes.

"All I can see," he said, "is a splodge on the map. I can see myself drawing Poland and colouring it in with pale brown paint. A nicely shaped little country, I thought——"

"Yes, yes," Dr. Corvisart said testily, "but that gets us no further. Think of your possessions. Can you not

159

see yourself riding round the estate, doubtless on a fine piece of horse-flesh? Can you recall entertaining your friends—giving a ball—a dinner party—sitting in your chair at the head of the table——?"

Armand suddenly felt bored.

"If I could remember any of these things, Doctor, I would tell you. As it is, my mind remains a blank."

Dr. Corvisart had looked annoyed, then he hastily changed exasperation to an expression of false encouragement.

"Do not trouble yourself about it, Monsieur. Your memory will return at any time now. Perhaps tonight, perhaps tomorrow! You have but to touch the right spring and, hey presto! everything will fall into place."

"I hope you are right, Doctor," Armand said a little skeptically, and decided there and then not to call in the doctor again.

There was nothing wrong with him now, nothing save that he remained a spectator on the outskirts of life. It was at night that things were worse, when he was unable to sleep. He would walk up and down his bedroom, trying to bring his memory to life and failing dismally until, tired out, in the early hours of the morning he would fling himself down on the bed as petulantly as if he were a child refused some special treat that he most especially desired.

It would all come back to him in time, everyone told him. He could be certain of that. And yet could he be certain of anything? Know thyself!

If only he could say that in all truth, if only he could know just a little bit of what had happened to him before he awoke in a bed hung with oyster satin curtains to see Rêve's face close to his, her eyes dark with anxiety.

As he thought of Rêve, Armand frowned and turned from the window to walk across the room as if in perturbation. She worried him. He was certain that she did not wish to marry Comte Giles de Durieux, certain that she shrank from the man, and yet he could not get her to say so.

The arrangements for the wedding were being made

and the advocates of both parties had been in conference together.

Armand was certain that Rêve was keeping something from him, something he did not know, something she did not intend him to know, but which he instinctively realised lay beneath a deliberate reserve.

It was a secret she carried about with her, and nothing which he could say or do would persuade her to reveal it.

Once or twice he had felt that she was about to confide in him. The words had seemed to tremble on her lips, and then as he had waited she had withdrawn into silence or changed the conversation to something quite different.

He had known that the moment in which she might have confided in him had passed and that he could not force her confidence.

If Rêve would only be frank, he thought, and tell him once and for all that she did not wish to marry the Count, he would prevent the marriage even if the Emperor himself commanded it.

But Rêve would say nothing save that she was willing for the plans for the ceremony to go forward, and though Armand was sure that she was hiding something from him, he could not discover the truth.

He himself could not formulate a definite opinion about the Count. He had been with Rêve in the sitting-room in her apartment when the Count was announced, and he had known, as she moved a little nearer to him and her breath came quicker from between her parted lips, that she was afraid.

"Monsieur le Comte de Durieux," a lackey had announced from the door in stentorian tones, and then there had been a little pause.

Slowly, moving with great dignity, the Count entered the room. He was a tall man, much taller than Armand had expected. He was plainly, almost soberly dressed in a coat of black velvet, embellished only with large buttons set with blood-red rubies.

A huge ruby, the size of a pigeon's egg, which he wore as a ring was his only other jewel, and while

161

it burned with a strange, almost supernatural fire, it also showed to advantage the Count's long white fingers with their skilfully polished nails.

His face was white too, almost bloodless, while his eyes were dark and intensely alive. They glittered and shone beneath his heavy eyelids and seemed to take in everything in the room with one quick, appraising glance.

His hair was dark, unpowdered and touched with grey at the temples. His features were clear cut and aristocratic and there was no doubt that he was a distinctly handsome man. But there was something about him which was curiously repellent, Armand thought.

Perhaps it was his too pale face and his bloodless lips, perhaps the way his eyes seemed to flicker over everything in a manner which reminded one of a snake with a poison-fang on the point of striking.

And yet that was but a first impression, and when the Count spoke it was difficult to remember that one had ever thought anything of the kind.

His voice was caressing, almost hypnotic, except when he was excited, when it rose to a high falsetto, curiously feminine and quite unforgettable in its surprising hysteria.

At other times he had an undeniable charm which made it impossible for one not to feel oneself drawn magnetically towards him as if he had some special attraction which was irresistible.

The Count had crossed the small sitting-room with an unhurried gait and with the utmost composure. He kissed Rêve's hand and had apparently not noticed that her fingers were stiff and cold beneath his touch.

"Mademoiselle, I am very sensible of the honour that you have done me in coming here," he said softly.

Then he had turned to Armand and begun to talk effusively and with an obvious desire to please. After a few minutes the stiffness with which they regarded him seemed to vanish and both Armand and Rêve felt themselves relax and become at their ease.

The Court was amusing, he was witty, he was, too,

almost ingratiatingly humble when he spoke of his and Rêve's intended marriage.

"It is the first time in my life that I have ever wanted to marry anyone," he told Armand, "but your sister captivated me from the very instant that I saw her. She was sitting in the ante-room of this very Palace, waiting to petition the Emperor. I passed through on my way to the throne room and I saw her, so young, so exquisite and in a way so lost. I made inquiries as to who she was.

"When they told me her name, I remembered her father and many of her relatives, and I knew then that she must become my wife or else I must remain a bachelor for the rest of my existence here on earth."

Armand would have liked to think that the Count was talking only for effect, but there was a ring of sincerity in his tone which was undeniable. Yet when he was with Rêve, Armand thought, he did not behave like a man who was overwhelmingly in love.

Perhaps it was because he had a stern control over his emotions, perhaps it was because he was no stripling but a man of nearly middle age. Nevertheless, the fact remained that, while he was amusing, entertaining, courteous and invariably considerate, he did not appear to love Rêve with that ardency or desire that he expressed so eloquently in words.

For one thing he never appeared to wish to be alone with her; and while Armand was well aware that this suited Rêve, for her inclination was apparently to avoid a tête-à-tête with her fiancé at all costs.

It did seem to him that a marriage begun in such a way could never bring real happiness to his lovely little sister. More and more he began to worry about Rêve's future.

She was so sweet, so gentle, that he could not bear to think that she might be hurt, distressed of unhappy, or that any man should treat her badly.

More than that, he found himself beginning to dread the thought of being separated from her, to loathe the idea of her going away with the Count, and of having to make his own way back to Poland alone. He wanted to have Rêve beside him, to share in her laughter, to watch the emotions flicker over her expressive face.

If only she would confide in him, he thought, if only the barrier which lay between them, whatever it might be, could be lifted. It was there, that barrier; he could feel it spoiling their relationship one with the other—an intangible, yet positive thing.

Armand sighed, and as he did so, the clock on the mantelpiece struck the half-hour. There was still plenty of time before dinner and he decided that he would go to Rêve's apartment and wait there until the time came for them to descend to the crowded ante-room where the Emperor's guests waited until he appeared.

Rêve's sitting-room was like all the rooms in the Palace, ornate and very luxurious. The chairs were of crimson velvet laced with gold and matched by curtains of crimson lustrine with gold fringes, while in the middle of the room hung a cluster of English crystals.

There were exquisite pieces of tapestry, a great amount of ormolu furniture and some valuable pictures. Rêve found it beautiful, but to Armand it was overpowering and once again he longed for simplicity, for space and clean, clear-cut lines, for furniture which was not heavily gilded and for draperies which owed their beauty to their colour and texture rather than to their fringes and furbelows.

He had a sudden vision of the kind of room he liked. It was a big room with long high windows looking out on to a green garden, with very little furniture and what there was polished from generations of use, while on the plain panelled walls there were just two or three perfect pictures.

Now where was that room? Armand wondered to himself, and then he forgot what he had been thinking, for the communicating door opened and Rêve came running into the room from her bedchamber.

She was dressed in white, and round her head was a wreath of fresh flowers. She looked lovelier than Armand had ever seen her before.

"Do you like it?" she asked eagerly. "It was Antoinette's idea, but the *coiffeur* is waiting in case you think the flowers look affected, in which case I will put a ribbon or a bandeau of pearls around my head."

"Do not touch it," Armand said firmly; "the wreath is perfect."

"And the dress?" Rêve asked anxiously.

It was of white *crêpe,* almost Grecian in design, the high waist line ending beneath her small, pointed breasts.

"That, too, is perfect."

"I am glad, terribly glad," Rêve whispered, and there was something poignant and breathless in her voice.

Armand looked down at her in surprise, his eyes searching hers.

"Does it matter so much?" he asked.

"Yes, of course it does," Rêve replied.

"Why? So that you shall please the Count?" Armand inquired, and somehow he could not prevent a slight edge to his voice.

"No, of course not," Rêve answered. "It is you I want to please."

Their eyes met and Armand felt something strange and unexpected pass between them, a feeling that he could not explain.

"Listen, Rêve," he said, "I have got to talk to you. There is something you must tell me."

He saw the expression in her eyes and knew that the barrier between them was falling; then the door from her bedroom opened and Antoinette came into the room. It seemed to Armand that Rêve started almost guiltily.

"What is it, Antoinette?" she asked, and surprisingly her voice was sharp.

"The hairdresser waits, *ma petite,*" Antoinette replied.

"Tell him that I am completely satisfied, that I want nothing further done," Rêve answered.

But Antoinette was not dismissed so easily.

"Do you think Mademoiselle looks nice, Monsieur?" she asked Armand. "The wreath was an inspiration."

"It is perfect," he replied almost automatically, his eyes on Rêve's face. "I have already said so."

165

"Then I am very pleased," Antoinette said smiling. "The idea came to me last night. I was thinking of all the ladies I had seen here in the palace, of their magnificent dresses, of the jewels which festoon everything from their necks to their fans, and I was wondering to myself how my little one could compete, how she could stand out among such wealth, such elegance, and then the idea came to me. Something quite simple, I thought, like flowers.

"No one wears flowers on their heads—they carry them in their hands so that the poor things wilt and look tired after a very short while—but a wreath of flowers made by God would be much more effective than anything fashioned by man.

"Now I have put my little idea to the test and you, Monsieur, are pleased. That is good!"

"Yes, yes, I am pleased," Armand said absently.

"And Mademoiselle has told you what we have planned together?" Antoinette inquired.

Rêve looked at her and then back at Armand.

"No, I have not yet had time," she said, "Armand, Antoinette and I think it would be wise if she went to Valmont. There are so many things to be packed up there. We cannot trust the village girls and as far as we know the Emperor, with his impatience, may move the new occupants in at any moment.

"It is only for a few days, and Antoinette has already engaged a maid to take her place if we cannot manage without her. Do you think she should go?"

"But of course," Armand said firmly, then added more graciously: "We shall miss you, of course, Antoinette; but I know that you will return to your mistress as quickly as possible."

"I shall certainly do that, Monsieur," Antoinette said, and coming closer to Armand she looked into his face. "You will look after her while I am away, Monsieur? I have never left her side since she was a little one, not after we escaped from Valmont when the terrorists beat upon the door.

"I trust few people, Monsieur, but I trust you. You

will remember that it is Mademoiselle's safety which counts before everything else?"

There was no mistaking the anxiety in Antoinette's tone or the sincerity with which she spoke. Armand looked at her gentle face and then he held out his hand.

"You can trust me, Antoinette," he said. "My sister shall come to no harm while I am with her."

"If only there was someone else that we could send to Valmont," Antoinette said in worried tones, "but there is no one, Monsieur, and there are many things which must be brought away at once. The Emperor has purchased the furniture with the house, but there are Mademoiselle's personal possessions and many things connected with her family which she will always treasure and preserve.

"There are, too, the belongings of her Great-Aunt, Madame la Duchesse, but who knows which they are but me?"

"It is obvious that no one can go but you, Antoinette," Armand said. "Order the fastest vehicle that you can obtain so that you will not be longer on the way than necessary, and return in the same manner."

"I shall do everything as speedily as I possibly can," Antoinette said. "I go very early in the morning. I shall see Mademoiselle again tonight, but not you, Monsieur. *Au revoir!* Promise me that you will guard Mademoiselle with your very life."

"I have already promised you that," Armand said. "Why are you so worried, Antoinette? There is nothing to fear. Mademoiselle can be in no danger here save perhaps of over-eating at these endless banquets or over-tiring herself by dancing too late. But you speak as if you were afraid of something very different."

Antoinette twisted her fingers together.

"I know not of what I am afraid, Monsieur," she said, "but I am—and that is the truth."

"You worry too much, darling Antoinette," Rêve said, putting her arm round Antoinette's shoulder and laying her cheek for a moment against that of the older woman.

"Yes, I suppose I do," Antoinette said, "and yet I

167

feel as if there was something wrong. It is almost like a premonition. I cannot understand it myself—yet it is there."

"You are imagining such things," Rêve said quickly, almost too quickly, Armand thought. "There is nothing of which you need be afraid. Hurry to Valmont and return as quickly as you can. You will find me safe and sound with Armand guarding me, doubtless with a drawn sword."

She laughed lightly as she spoke and the moment of tension was past. There was no longer any time for conversation, for it was nearly the hour for dinner and the company in all their finery would be assembling in the ante-room.

"We must go," Armand said firmly.

He held out his arm and Rêve laid her fingers on it, then she looked up at him and laughed.

"I feel happy tonight," she said.

"I am glad," he replied, "very glad."

Her eyes fell before his, and a faint flush came to her cheeks. Already they were in the corridor and there were other guests moving in the same direction, laughing, chattering, bowing and curtsying, and making audible criticisms about their enemies.

Rêve recognised some of the people—the Prince de Neufchâtel, a little, ill-looking man with a crop-curled head of dark hair; the second Consul, Jean Jacques Regis de Cambacérès, with his eyes sunk deep in his head, his hair badly dressed, wearing fustian breeches and common turn-down boots.

And, of course, she knew Madame Fouché by sight. No one, having seen her once, would forget her yellow wig over her vulgar, discontented face. There were innumerable jokes in the Palace about her and the fact that her husband, son of a grocer at Nantes, had originally belonged to a religious society called the Oratoriens.

It was at the turn of the stairs that they met the Duchess de Monestier. For a moment both Rêve and Armand forgot their manners to gape at her almost open-mouthed.

Always spectacular, always eclipsing the other women in her originality, Imogène de Monestier had outshone even herself tonight. She wore a dress of silver tissue which moulded her figure so closely that she might just as well have painted her naked body with a coat of silver paint and worn nothing else.

Shimmering as she moved, the ripple of every muscle, every curve, every line of her exquisite limbs revealed, she wore as her only ornamentation a necklace of emeralds, so large, so magnificent that they took the breath away.

Fabien had looted them for her but a few months earlier from a Russian princess, and had sent them, as they were so valuable, under armed guard to Fonçier, the Emperor's jeweller, to have them made up.

They were fabulous and so enormous as to be almost barbaric in their beauty, and yet round Imogène's neck they seemed to take second place to her own loveliness.

Looking at the Duchess, Rêve realised that her eyes were green too, and that there was the same hard light in them which seemed to emanate from the emeralds.

"Armand, *mon brave!*"

Imogène's pronunciation of his name was soft and seductive. She held out her hand and he kissed it. As he did so, her fingers curled round his so that she imprisoned him and he looked up to meet her eyes.

"I shall see you tonight?" she asked.

"But of course," he replied. "I believe that we dance after dinner."

For a moment her lips tightened at his misunderstanding of what she intended, then she smiled.

"I will save you the last waltz, *mon ami,*" she said softly and turned away.

Rêve drew in a deep breath.

"I hate her," she said.

Her tone was so violent that Armand looked at her in surprise. He would have said something but at that moment the Count was at their side.

He wore black, which was the colour he habitually affected, but tonight there was a purple ribbon across

169

his chest and his coat was covered with decorations of all descriptions. There were diamond stars and bursting suns, the Cross of the Holy Sepulchre, the Orders of St. Nicholas, St. Marino and St. Constantine.

He was almost as glittering a figure in his way as Imogène had been in hers. In fact Armand thought he was almost ridiculously over-decorated, and then he noticed in surprise that Rêve was smiling with a faint air of coquetry at him.

The Count raised her hand to his lips. As he released it, he said:

"I am glad to find you both together. I have but a few moments ago left the Emperor. His Majesty expressed surprise that I had not invited you to my Castle. The idea, I admit, had not occurred to me; but as I have to go there tomorrow for a few nights to make some researches, I extend to you both an invitation to come with me to inspect my home and my estate.

Rêve and Armand said nothing, and after a second's pause the Count continued:

"It is not far from Paris, but five miles as the crow flies, although by road, if we take that route, it is slightly longer." He smiled at his joke. "We can leave here in the forenoon and we can be at Creux in time for dinner. Will you honour me by accepting my invitation?"

"Yes, of course," Rêve said, "and thank you very much for asking us. We shall like that, Armand, shall we not?"

She spoke with some enthusiasm, and Armand replied:

"Yes—yes, of course, if it pleases you, and I think I am inclined to agree with the Emperor that you should see the house where you are to live after your marriage."

"That is settled then," Rêve said, and smiling up at the Count she asked: "Is your Castle very large?"

"Large enough to withstand any onslaughts of the enemy in ancient days,' the Count replied. "But I am sure you will find it comfortable. I have spent much money and, what is more important, a great deal of my time in making improvement.

The Emperor honours me by declaring it is one of the finest buildings in the whole length and breadth of France. In fact he is such an admirer of Creux that at times I am afraid he will take it from me."

The Count smiled as he spoke and both Rêve and Armand realised that this was a jest, for everyone knew that the Count basked in the Emperor's favour and had all the privileges of an acknowledged favourite.

Chattering to the Count in an unusually animated way, Rêve moved towards the ante-room and Armand followed her. It was some minutes later, while Giles de Durieux was greeting an old friend, that he was able to whisper in her ear:

"Do you really want to go? You need not accept unless you really wish to see the Castle."

Rêve looked up quickly and he realised there was a veiled expression in her eyes.

"Why should I not want to go?" she asked, and her tone was almost truculent.

"There is no reason on earth why you should not," Armand said. "I was just surprised at your accepting the invitation so eagerly."

"I thought it would do us both good to get away from here," Rêve replied.

"Well, there's something in that," Armand admitted. "I readily admit to finding Palace life a deadly bore. But I thought you were enjoying yourself."

"I was," Rêve replied.

As she spoke she looked across the room at the Duchess de Monestier flaunting herself almost shamelessly among a crowd of courtiers. Anything, she thought passionately, was better than that she should stay here in Fontainebleau and watch Armand being carried off by that horrible woman. It was not only jealousy which made her hate the Duchess, Rêve thought miserably, it was worse than that.

Imogène de Monestier was horrible, there was something utterly ruthless about her, something which told

171

Rêve all too clearly that she would stick at nothing to get her own way, to satisfy her greedy sensual desires.

Yes, she hated her, but Armand could not understand her hatred. Why should he?

She had a sudden idea that, when they got to Creux, it might be easier to escape from there than from Fontainebleau. Once at the castle she would tell Armand the truth—tell him who he was, and warn him of the danger in which he stood.

Yes, that was what she would do. It was no use going on like this, no use waiting any longer. She would tell Armand everything and when he returned to England, she would beg him to take her with him.

She felt almost light-hearted now that the decision was made. All this would be forgotten—the dangers, the subterfuge . . . and Imogène de Monestier. She felt happiness welling up inside her as if already the future was golden.

Then she saw that someone was standing beside Armand. He was an elderly man and she realised that he was a General for he wore the full-dress uniform of blue embroidered with gold and embellished with a monstrous high scarlet collar.

His white pantaloons were flourished all over the front and down the seams with gold thread and his Hessian boots were bound with gold tassels. He was a highly ornate figure, but Rêve had hardly time to notice his appearance for she realised that he was speaking to Armand in low, confidential tones.

"I have good news for you, Monsieur le Marquis," he was saying. "The Emperor has honoured you by appointing you one of his personal aides-de-camp. You are instructed that, when dinner is over, you are to follow His Majesty to the Council room."

Armand drew himself up and bowed.

"Thank you, *mon Général,*" he said. "And what do we do when we get there?"

The General looked surprised at the question.

"The Emperor holds a Council of War most evenings," he said. "It is his custom to invite various people to discuss the military position with him, and tonight General Miollis is here. It is expected that he will receive special instructions of some sort, but what they may be is known at this moment only to the Emperor himself."

"It sounds like an interesting occasion," Armand said. "Thank you, Sir, for bringing me His Majesty's instructions."

"A pleasure, Monsieur," the General replied.

The two men bowed, and at that moment an usher with a gold stick entered the room to arrange the guests in order of precedence prior to the Emperor's arrival.

There was no time for Rêve to say anything more to Armand. She could only give him a despairing glance, which he could not understand, before she was swept away to take her place.

There were only a few minutes to wait now before the women would sink to the ground in the low obeisant curtsy which would herald the arrival of His Imperial Majesty, Napoleon Bonaparte, Emperor of France and King of Italy.

10

Armand sprawled in a chair, his eyelids drooping lazily as with a cynical smile twisting the corners of his lips he regarded Imogène de Monestier.

She was reclining on a couch covered with a rug made of Russian sable, and the only light in the room came from a candelabrum fashioned of twisted gold serpents holding aloft three high unshaded candles.

The light, little though it was, contrived to reveal every line of Imogène's exquisite figure in her silver lamé dress. It glinted, too, on the great emeralds round her throat, and the contrast between their strange serpentine depths and the magnolia skin of her naked shoulders was very pronounced.

Imogène watched Armand for a few moments from beneath her long eyelashes, then she flung back her head in a primitive, seductive movement as old as the Garden of Eden.

"Talk to me," she said softly.

"What about?" Armand inquired.

She looked at him and there was a glint of anger in her dark eyes, but her voice was very sweet as she replied:

"Ourselves, of course. How can one ever get to know anyone among the crowds at the Palace? Besides, I wanted to see what you were like when we were alone —really alone, as we are now."

Armand moved his head lazily and glanced at the shadows in the corners of the room. They were as dark and mysterious as the room itself, which was octagonal and the walls were hung with peacock feathers.

Doors ornamented with green and gold mosaic opened on one side into Imogène's bedchamber, on the other side windows revealed a walled garden. Lanterns, hung discreetly from the branches of exotic trees, lit a pool of black marble in the centre of the garden, and around it were set exquisitely sculptured statues of nude gods and goddesses.

Every flower in the garden was white. There were lilies in great profusion, their scent almost overpowering, and banks of white roses, phlox, gladioli, lupins, and tuber-roses, making a protecting wall of blossom and fragrance around the pool.

It was all perfectly designed and arranged; but it was as artificial, Armand thought, in its perfection as Imogène herself with her deliberate enticements and her tutored voice of dulcet sweetness.

"I hoped we should have been together this afternoon, *mon brave,*" Imogène said softly, "and when you could not come driving with me I went alone—but I thought—about you."

Armand's smile deepened.

"And what did you think?" he asked.

"I thought," Imogène replied, "that you are a very attractive young man and, as I am a very attractive woman, we should get to know each other better."

She ceased speaking and there was a little silence. Now she stretched out her arms as if to yawn, arching her back a little as she did so and revealing the exquisite line from her white rounded throat to her small pointed breasts.

Armand gave a short laugh.

"Every trick!" he said; "and how well I know them all! There was a woman I knew once; she was very lovely. In a way you remind me of her, for her technique was invariably the same. Soft lights, her white skin against the shadows, and the feline grace of a tiger. She had a great success in London, I——"

He stopped suddenly.

"I am remembering things," he said, and there was a touch of excitement in his voice. "What was her name? . . . No, I can't remember that . . . But I knew her in London, I am sure of that. I can see her house now. There were six steps up to the front door, which

175

was opened by a black page and her bedroom windows overlooked the Green Park. Yes, thank God, I can remember that quite clearly."

"And you are forgetting me!" Imogène reminded him.

"You will forgive my preoccupation," Armand said, "but the most absorbing interest in my life just recently has been to try and remember the past."

"There are quite a number of people who are concerned in solving that very problem where you are concerned," Imogène said meaningly.

"How do you know that?" Armand asked quickly.

"I know most things," she replied, "things that would surprise you. Tell me, *mon ami,* what was discussed this evening at the Emperor's Council of War?"

"You can hardly expect me to answer that question," Armand replied.

He got to his feet as he spoke and walked towards the long windows opening into the garden.

"And suppose I entreat you to tell me what was said," a soft voice said at his side.

He had not heard Imogène rise from the couch, and now he looked down to find her at his elbow. He was conscious of the heady oriental perfume she used. She was very lovely, there was no denying that. Her eyes were gleaming beneath her long eyelashes, her red lips curved invitingly over her tiny white teeth.

As he looked down at her, she swayed a little nearer towards him, one of her slender hands reaching up to catch the lapel of his evening coat.

"What was decided?" she asked. "I am a woman and curious. It amuses me to talk of wars and armies as well as of love."

"What was said in the Council Room was secret," Armand replied. "You know that, and you know quite well that I would not repeat to you or anyone else the decisions that were taken or the plans that were discussed."

"So loyal! So honourable!" Imogène said a little mockingly; then she laughed a tantalising sound of sheer merriment. *"Mon cher* Armand, do you really imagine that to learn the truth I have to entice them from the latest and most raw recruit to the War Council? Instead I will tell you what was decided tonight. It was that General Moillis should take six thousand troops, invade Tuscany and confiscate all the British goods there. Am I not right?"

Armand looked astonished.

"But how do you know this?" he asked.

"The way I know most things at the Palace," she replied. "If you are really curious, General Miollis is an old love of mine. He would not leave Fontainebleau without saying good-bye."

Armand gave an expressive shrug of his shoulders.

"Cherchez la femme," he said almost under his breath.

"As all good Frenchmen should," Imogène completed for him.

"When women are told secrets—they are no longer secrets," Armand said scathingly.

Imogène sighed and drew a little closer to him.

"They say that even the Emperor himself talks when he lays his head against a white shoulder," she said, "and at this moment I can think of a better thing to do than talking!"

Armand moved suddenly and gripped Imogène's arms hard just above the elbows. He held her at arm's length from him and looked down into her face.

"What exactly are you trying to do?" he said. "Ferret out what secrets I may know, or are you trying to seduce me because your body burns for mine? Answer me and truthfully?"

The strength of Armand's fingers bruised Imogène's arms, but her smile was more enigmatic than ever.

"I like strong men," she said. "Hurt me! I would like you to hurt me."

He released her as unexpectedly as he had laid his hands upon her.

"I had no desire to come here tonight," he said. "I knew what to expect, and frankly I am not in the mood for making love. I want to remember about myself, I want to ponder over my new position in the

177

entourage of the Emperor, and I want to think about my sister and her problems.

"But you waited for me, you captured me and brought me here virtually as your prisoner, and now you must accept me for what I am—a man who has many things to consider, and making love is not amongst them."

Imogène gave a little sigh.

"I do not understand you," she said. "Perhaps that is why you attract me. So many men have loved me, so many men have sought desperately and with an insatiable hunger for the favours which I am offering you. I am wondering if it is my hearing that is at fault, or if for once I have been mistaken and you are not the man I thought you to be."

There was a bitter taunt in the last few words, but Armand merely smiled at her.

"Is that meant to put me on my mettle?" he said. "Then you are indeed mistaken in your man. In the past I have known many women— Yes, I can remember that, even if I cannot remember their names—but I am sure of one thing. I have pursued them. I am the hunter, not the hunted."

Imogène's body stiffened.

"Are you conceited enough to think that I am pursuing you?" she asked.

"Aren't you?" Armand inquired.

Her eyes narrowed and it seemed as if she would turn and revile him, would let the whole force of her anger burst out at him. Then with an amazing effort at self-control she constrained herself.

Instead she crossed the room to his side and with a swift movement put both her arms round his neck and drew down his head.

"You are tired and worried," she said. "But I want you, Armand d'Augeron. You attract me more than any man I have ever known. I want you! Love me and let me show you what a love such as mine can mean to a man."

"Do you think that if I am drugged with love you

178

will be able to obtain from me the secrets that you wish to hear?" Armand said.

Imogène took her arms from around his neck and stepped back as if he had struck her.

"Fool!" she said. "Do you think that I am a spy, or that you could tell me anything that I do not know already? I was but testing you, testing your loyalty, and if you insist on hearing the truth, General Miollis himself asked me to do so, because he suspected you."

"Suspected me?" Armand questioned.

"That surprises you, does it not? People do not trust you as easily as you think, young man. General Miollis thought there was something strange about you. He was not certain what it was, but the suspicion was there and he asked me to make sure of your loyalty and your integrity. Now are you satisfied?"

"But I do not understand," Armand said. "He was suspicious of what? That I might betray the Emperor? To whom?"

"To his enemies," Imogène answered. "The Emperor has enemies everywhere. They are not only in foreign nations, but here in our very midst."

"Yet the Emperor himself trusts me."

"You saved his life," Imogène replied. "Napoleon Bonaparte is a brave man, but he values his safety very highly. He is also superstitious and one of his soothsayers told him that someone would come into his life who would be very fortunate to him. He believes that person to be you.

"He may be right, he may be wrong; only time can tell. But many of his Generals are not so credulous of what the stars foretell."

"Suppose I am a traitor, suppose General Miollis is right and there is something strange about me, do you imagine that you would have discovered it here, to-night?"

"Of course," Imogène said with quiet confidence.

Armand laughed.

"So the stage was set," he said, "with lights, a couch, and a woman's inviting lips. Well, the play is over, Madame. Have I your permission to retire?"

"No!"

Imogène's reply was emphatic.

Armand raised his eyebrows.

"No?" he echoed.

"No! I do not wish you to go. I have been frank and told you one of the reasons why I invited you here tonight, but not the real reason, the reason why I asked you to come driving with me this afternoon, the reason why we are alone here without even my maid within call."

She came a little nearer to him, and now her face in the light of the candles was soft and for a moment young and simple in its very sincerity.

"I wanted you to come here tonight, *mon brave*," she said, "because from the moment I first saw you walk across the ballroom you seemed different to me, different from any other man.

"Something in my heart awoke at the very sight of you, something which has grown steadily stronger until now I feel I can hide it no longer from you but must tell you what I feel. I love you, Armand; I love you, and I want your love."

Imogène's voice rang out passionately; then she flung wide her arms in a gesture of abject surrender, and yet there was nothing humble, nothing supplicating in her attitude. Instead it was the action of a woman, triumphant and confident, of a woman utterly sure of her invincible charm.

Yet the lure was there, the lure of enticement as compelling as when the goddesses sped from Olympus to reveal themselves in all their beauty to some wandering shepherd boy who had attracted their attention.

For the moment it seemed to Armand as if the whole room swam around him, the thick cloud within his head seemed intensified; Imogène's perfume was in his nostrils, the softness of her body lay within reach of his arms.

But an arrogant, inbred pride within himself kept him from capitulating. There was something which jarred upon him, something which kept his self-control rigid so that he could say in an apparently unmoved voice:

"Is this another trick at seduction?"

He expected Imogène to be angry at his question, expected the fury he had already sensed once or twice that evening behind the smiling mask of her face to break over him. Instead she laughed lightly and replied:

"If tricks are what you want, I will give you one, and a new one since you are so satiated with those which are old."

She glided away from him towards the candelabrum and reached out her hand, snuffed the candles. They were now in darkness save for the light of the lanterns coming softly through the windows and flooding the white garden.

Then, as Armand waited, he heard a soft movement and into the lantern-light from the shadows came Imogène. For a moment he could only stare at her.

Slowly, with an exquisite grace she moved into the garden and down towards the marble pool. Her body was as white as the flowers, for she wore nothing save the great necklace of emeralds around her neck.

As Imogène moved away from Armand, she glanced back over her shoulder and in her eyes and on her lips there was an invitation for him to follow her.

Hardly knowing that he did so, Armand took a few steps forward; and then, as he watched her go down the steps towards the marble pool and as the perfume of the lilies came up towards him in a fragrant wave which was almost overpowering, he felt at one and the same time that there was something familiar, yet something wrong, with the whole scene.

Once again it was no longer part of the world in which he moved.

He was a stranger, an outsider, watching a play taking place on a stage—the actress, a lovely naked woman with a wealth of jewels around her neck, the scene a secret garden with the water in the pool stirring as she descended into it and the lantern-light on her face, her breasts, her thighs, and on her little hand, which fluttered out invitingly towards him as she turned.

He stood at the window, his fingers grasping the peacock hangings so fiercely that he almost tore them down from the pole on which they were hung.

It seemed to him that an eternity passed as he stood there, an eternity in which the waves of memory seemed to recede and then advance, to advance and then recede; yet he knew no more save that this had happened before. But where and when, and why?

He could not find the answer; but he knew that something was wrong, that something was missing, something which should have been there, but which was lost and forgotten.

Because of that thing which he could not remember, Armand felt himself tortured almost unbearably with a longing and a yearning more intense and more powerful than anything else he had ever known.

He must remember; he must. . . .

But while he strove against the density of his own mind, Imogène was waiting. She advanced no farther into the pool, only stood there on the first black marble step, the water lapping her ankles.

As she waited, the smile slowly vanished from her face and her teeth bit hard into her lower lip, for Armand had turned from the window and disappeared into the darkness of the room.

She heard his footsteps cross the floor, heard a door open and close again, and she knew that she had lost him. All her tricks, as he had called them, had failed.

For a moment she could hardly believe it possible, could hardly credit her own eyes and ears. Then slowly she came from the pool, her feet leaving wet patches on the marble steps as she walked from the garden into the darkness of the empty room.

She passed through it into her bedchamber, where two candles were burning on the dressing-table. She went towards them, and lifting one high in her hand she held it close to her face so that she could see herself in the mirror.

The light revealed her eyes wide and dark in her white face, but for her mouth there was only a thin line—the lips tight pressed until they were bloodless.

Imogène stared at herself for a long time. Then she

rang the bell for her maid and the sound was sharp, imperious and infinitely foreboding.

Rêve found Armand strangely silent as they set off the following day for Creux Castle. There were dark lines under his eyes and he did not look as well as he did the day before.

She had meant to be angry with him, for she too had been awake thinking of Imogène de Monestier and hating her bitterly with all the misery of a gentle heart which until then had never known hatred or jealousy.

But when Armand appeared, looking wan, his scar unusually livid against the pallor of his forehead, Rêve's heart melted within her and she could think no longer of her own unhappiness, but only of his health.

She took a lot of trouble to arrange the cushions behind him in the coach, and commanded him to put his feet up on one of the little seats facing them.

"It is not a long way," she said, "but the jolting is not good for you. You know Dr. Corvisart said how careful you must be."

"I am well enough," Armand replied ungraciously and somewhat impatiently.

But Rêve was not hurt. She understood that like most men he disliked being fussed over, and if he felt ill, he would rather die than admit it.

Yet, worried as she was about him, she could not prevent her natural curiosity from asking him one question after they had been journeying a little while from the Palace of Fontainebleau.

"Did you stay late with the Duchess de Monestier last night?" she inquired.

"How did you know I was with the Duchess?" Armand countered.

"She told me so herself," Rêve replied a little bitterly, remembering all too well Imogène's superior voice saying:

"Run along to bed, child. I will look after your brother for you."

Rêve had not known what to reply. The ball was over

183

and most of the guests were either leaving the Palace
or retiring to their apartments there.

Armand was, as she knew, still closeted with the Emperor in the Council Room, and she had gone along
the passage in that direction, hoping that he would
appear and that she could tell him that the dancing
had finished and that she wished to retire.

But she had met Imogène, and the mere sight of that
glittering, splendid figure contrived to make her feel
badly dressed and unattractive, so that to Imogène's
command that she should go to bed she had no reply.

She would have liked to be defiant, to have remained there, to have forced Armand to choose between them—the older woman in her dress of shimmering silver or herself, so young and unsophisticated
in her plain white gown. But she had been afraid—
afraid of what Armand's decision might be.

What chance had she beside Imogène de Monestier
—a notorious beauty, a woman who was famed throughout France for her love affairs and for the adoration
she received as her rightful due from every man
she encountered,

Rêve had crept away to her own apartment and flung
herself face downwards on the bed to cry bitterly and
broken-heartedly into her pillow.

When she had wept until she could weep no longer,
she had stayed awake in the dark, torturing herself
at the thought of Armand and Imogène together, of
Imogène lying in Armand's arms as she had once done,
of his lips seeking hers, of his voice murmuring the sweet
unforgettable things which had opened to Rêve the
gates of paradise.

How long ago those two wonderful nights in the garden at Valmont seemed now! So much had happened,
and it was hard to remember that it was weeks rather
than years since they had first met, since she had first
awoken to the magic in Armand's voice.

As she sat beside him in the coach now, she thought
how different he looked from the way he had looked
then.

The eagerness had gone from his face; he looked

tired and dispirited; and even when Imogène de Monestier was talking to him, the expression of boredom had not for long been missing from his eyes and mouth.

"Suppose I tell him now who he is and why he is here?" Rêve thought.

But, as always, something within her shrank from the thought.

She was afraid, afraid for so many reasons that she could hardly bear to enumerate them. First of all there was Armand's health, his incompletely healed wound, the cautions that Dr. Corvisart had insisted on his taking, and the difficulties in the way of escape from the Palace of Fontainebleau and the environs of Paris.

And there were other reasons too, reasons that Rêve hardly dared express to herself.

Suppose Armand did not believe her, suppose he thought she was merely deranged and that her brain was affected rather than his own?

Rêve could almost hear him laughing at the tale. There was that to be considered, that and a thousand other difficulties which might arise and with which at the moment she felt she was quite incapable of coping.

"You are very silent," Armand said as the coach rumbled its way over the dusty, uneven roads.

"I thought you were tired and did not want to talk," Rêve replied.

He smiled and took up her hand which lay on the seat beside him.

"Are you always so considerate of my feelings?" he asked as he took up her fingers. "What pretty hands you have!"

"Thank you," Rêve replied.

"Most women have ugly hands," Armand said, "but yours are so small and soft and gentle. When my head aches, I like to feel them on my forehead."

"Is it aching now?" Rêve asked.

"No, not now," Armand replied.

Turning her hand over, he looked at the palm.

"A long life line and that is all I know about palmistry. Doubtless the worthy Count will be able to tell us more."

"He is not a palmist but an astrologer," Rêve corrected.

"Has he spoken to you about this little hobby of his?" Armand asked.

Rêve shook her head.

"No, he had never mentioned it, and somehow I have not liked to bring up the subject. It makes me uncomfortable to think that he might be able to read my thoughts."

"Would you mind if he could?"

"No, but he would not be complimented."

Armand laughed.

"That is frank at any rate."

His fingers closed over Rêve's with a sudden fierceness.

"If you do not wish to marry him after you have seen the Castle, then you must tell me so. Let us make this very clear. I will not have you made unhappy, I will not have you attached to anyone whom you dislike. I am not afraid of the Emperor and we are not his slaves, even if we all have to acknowledge him our Imperial Master."

Rêve felt herself tremble, not so much at his words but at the touch of his hands, at the pressure of his fingers upon hers, at the sudden note of possession in his voice.

If only he would be jealous of her, she thought, if only he would think of her not as a sister but as a woman, someone who might belong to him.

While she waited, without answering his statement, her whole being quivered with her love and her need for him, Armand released her hand and his eyelids closed wearily.

"Wake me up when we arrive," he said, and proceeded to go to sleep.

She watched him for the rest of the journey, watched him while he slept peacefully, quite unconscious of her nearness and unaware of the love which shone unguarded in her face.

Then as the horses turned in through two magnificent iron gates and she saw ahead of her the vast turrets and towers of the Castle of Creux, Rêve put her hand on Armand's arm.

"We are nearly there, Armand," she said softly.

But he was fast asleep and did not hear her. She shook him.

"Wake up, Armand."

"What is it? What do you want?" he asked.

As the words left his lips Rêve gave a little cry, for he had spoken in English.

He opened his eyes and stared at her.

"What is the matter?" he asked, and this time he spoke in French.

She would have told him the reason for her exclamation, but it was too late. The horses were already clattering over the drawbridge and into the courtyard. The high walls of the Castle loomed above them, grooms were running from all directions to the horses' heads, and innumerable lackeys in purple livery were standing in an open doorway.

"We are here," Rêve said in a low voice.

"As I see," Armand replied, yawning a little and picking up his hat from the floor of the coach.

Rêve saw that he had no idea that he had done anything unusual or that his words on waking were significant. There was nothing she could say, nothing she could do at this moment, for the coach door was being opened and the steps were being let down.

At the top of the steps leading to the Castle door the Count was waiting.

For one moment Rêve thought he looked like a hooded hawk standing there in his sombre black clothes; and then as he advanced down the steps to welcome them, she forced herself to smile, to take his hand of welcome in what she hoped was an entirely natural manner.

"Welcome to Creux, Mademoiselle," he said, "and you too, Monsieur le Marquis d'Augeron. Welcome to a house which will always accord you a place of honour when it is the home of your best-beloved sister."

187

Armand bowed.

"Thank you, Sir. My sister and I are very glad to be here. I have heard many stories about the magnificence of Creux, and I see they are not exaggerated."

"I thought you would not be disappointed," the Count said complacently, leading the way through the great, arched front door into the richly decorated marble hall.

"You will need wine and food after your journey," he said. "They are waiting for us in the tapestry room."

Rêve found herself in an enormous salon hung with tapestry and decorated with a collection of furniture which she knew at a glance was both unique and valuable; yet there was a stiffness and formality about the place which struck a chill through her whole body.

She could not explain the impression even to herself save that its very formality seemed somehow awe-inspiring and vaguely repressive.

Wine and food were put before them and after a little while the Count suggested that Rêve might like to see her rooms.

"I have given you what is known as the Queen's Bedchamber," he said. "It is part of the State apartments which are used by Royal visitors. But it is also a tradition in my family that the bride of the reigning Count shall sleep there for a year after her marriage. I thought, therefore, that as this is our betrothal visit, you would like to use the room which will be yours for at least a year after our marriage has taken place."

"It is kind of you to think of it," Rêve said.

She felt her heart sink and knew that the moment was steadily drawing nearer when she must tell Armand the truth and escape as best she could from the net which was drawing tighter and tighter around them both.

The Queen's Bedroom was magnificent, but once again Rêve felt herself repulsed and somehow antagonised by the atmosphere.

Despite the luxurious hangings, the great bed, ornamented with painted cupids, the curtains of exquisite needlework, the furniture of carved silver, the mirrors which decorated every panel on the walls, there was something chill and unwelcoming about the room. She had a sudden premonition as if of evil.

It was a warm day, but she felt as cold as if an icy wind was blowing through the room. She forced words of appreciation to her trembling lips.

"It is a magnificent room! What splendid furnishings! What treasures you have in this lovely castle."

The Count was smiling as he withdrew to leave her alone, and only then did Rêve run instinctively to the window and fling it wide as if the fresh air from outside would disperse the atmosphere within.

"I am being imaginative and stupid," she said aloud. "It is Armand who is in danger—not myself."

And yet the feeling persisted, the feeling that something terrifying and hateful was waiting for her, but she did not know what.

Maids came hurrying into the room with her luggage. Soon everything was unpacked and Rêve had changed from her travelling-dress into an evening gown.

More than once, as she dressed, she felt herself shiver; but the maids who helped her had cheeks pink with heat and exertion, and there was not a breath of wind outside to account for her chillness.

She was dressed and ready a good half-hour before there was any necessity to descend the stairs to the Crimson Salon where they were to meet before dinner. Rêve dismissed the maids, thinking that she would sit for a while at the window and compose herself for the ordeal which lay ahead of her.

Either tonight or tomorrow she must tell Armand the truth. The opportunity would present itself some way or another; and whatever difficulties lay in the way, she must not hesitate, must prevaricate no longer.

She wished now that she had had the strength of mind to tell him when they were at Fontainebleau.

There was something about the Castle and indeed about the Count himself which frightened her, and every second it seemed as if she was growing more frightened, more apprehensive rather than more reassured.

She stared out of the window at the formal gardens

189

colourful with flowers, at the swallows which winged their way low across the still moat, at the deer grazing in the park under the overhanging trees.

There was nothing which could frighten her here, it was but a childish fancy. What was haunting her, making her feel ghost-ridden and eerie in this peaceful place?

What was it more likely to be than her own guilty conscience which was creating bogies out of the most simple things. She tried to pray, but the words would not come.

Impatient with her own stupidity, Rêve got to her feet and decided that she would go downstairs and wait in the Crimson Salon. Armand might be down early and they could have a few words together before the Count appeared.

She moved towards the door and, as she did so, there was a click from the other side of the room. She turned and to her astonishment saw one of the panels, which was covered by a looking-glass, swing slowly forward.

Rêve stared, paralysed with fear, her heart beating quickly. Into the room stepped a woman. Her hair was dark and tied in an untidy, dishevelled manner with a dirty unpressed ribbon of blood-red satin.

Her face was very thin and deeply lined beneath eyes which seemed too tired and listless to be alive, and her mouth drooped at the corners in a way which strangely enough gave her face an expression not of boredom but of terror.

She was dressed in a worn and wine-stained *peignoir* of mauve velvet trimmed with torn lace and round her neck, which was yellow and piteously thin, was a necklace of diamonds, their brilliance seeming to make a cruel mockery of the fatigue and fear on the face above them.

The woman came quietly into the room, leaving the secret panel open behind her. She did not speak and after a moment Rêve found her voice.

"Do you want to speak to me?" she asked.

The woman hesitated and it seemed to Rêve as if her expression changed.

"You are the Comtesse Rêve de Valmont?" she asked at length. Her accent was that of the bourgeoisie.

"I am," Rêve replied.

"I have come to warn you," the woman said. "You must not marry the Count. If you do, you will regret it."

"Why do you say this to me?" Rêve asked.

The woman's eyes searched her face as if she strove to find the truth there. What she saw seemed to satisfy her, for after a few minutes she said:

"I am right. He did not lie to me. You are young and innocent. But you must do what I tell you! Go away from here; make some excuse, say you are ill or that you have changed your mind; but do not agree to what he asks. You cannot marry him, you must not!"

There was some obscure pain and suffering in the woman's words and Rêve forgot her fear in the realisation that here was someone in trouble, someone who was unhappy.

"Will you give me a reason for what you say?" she asked, "for I believe that you are speaking to me out of the kindness of your heart?"

The woman stared at her.

"Is that why I am doing it? No, it is because I would save him from himself. You must go away! Go now!"

"But how can I?" Rêve asked. "It——"

They were interrupted by a knock on the door. An expression of sheer unbridled terror came into the woman's face and she put a finger over her lips.

"Do not say you have seen me," she whispered.

She moved surprisingly quickly through the aperture in the wall from which she had come.

The panel closed. There was nothing to show where it had opened. For a moment Rêve stood staring at the mirrored wall, feeling that the whole incident must be a dream; then the knock on the door was repeated and she called out: "Come in!"

"Are you ready?" Armand's voice asked.

He was dressed for dinner in a coat of blue satin trimmed with sapphire buttons and she felt her heart

191

turn over at the sight of him. He was so handsome, so lovable.

"Yes, I am ready," she replied, "but Armand—"

"We had best go downstairs," he interrupted, "or we shall be late, and that, you must agree, would be extremely discourteous to our most attentive host."

"Yes—yes—of course," Rêve answered.

He held out his arm and she put her hand on it, feeling somehow secure because she could touch him, because they were close together.

"I want to talk to you, Armand," she whispered. "I have got something to tell you."

"It should not be too difficult to find somewhere where we can be alone in this vast place." Armand replied lightly as they descended the wide staircase.

"It must be somewhere where we cannot be overheard," Rêve said and glanced at the walls apprehensively for she felt that any one of them might open to reveal a secret entrance.

"You sound very secretive," Armand smiled.

To Rêve's consternation his voice rang out, and then from the hall below them a voice said:

"I cannot believe that Mademoiselle has any secrets!"

It was the Count who spoke, and Rêve, looking down at his thin, pale face, tightened her hold on Armand's arm. She knew at last from where the atmosphere of evil in the house emanated.

It was from the Count, she was sure of that now.

11

Despite the fact that Rêve was tense and apprehensive after the warning of the strange woman who had entered her bedroom by the secret panel, the evening passed pleasantly enough.

The Count exerted himself to be charming and succeeded in amusing his guests until Rêve and Armand were surprised to find that the hours had passed so quickly.

The Count had a brilliant, if biting, wit; he was extremely well informed on current affairs and also very well read as regards the past.

About everyone who was mentioned he narrated some anecdotes or drew a character-sketch that was pointed and some cases scurrilous, and after a time Rêve felt some of her fear of him pass away.

She listened to Armand's laugh ringing out again and again and told herself that she must have been mistaken in her premonition of evil. She had been tired after the journey, she thought, and it was natural that, coming to Cruex under false pretences and loving Armand as she did, everything about the Count should antagonise her and make her suspect trouble even where there was none.

Yet if she could dismiss her own feelings as being the result of an overwrought imagination, it was not so easy to find an explanation of the ominous words of the woman in the mauve *peignoir*.

Many explanations presented themselves, but the most obvious was to believe that she was a jealous, displaced mistress of the Count who wished him to remain unmarried.

Yet it had not appeared to be jealousy which moved

her to speak, but some deeper, more fundamental emotion, and Rêve, concentrated on her thoughts, found her attention wandering again and again from the conversation, brilliant though it might be.

There were, however, many other things to think about. The magnificence and luxury in which the Count lived equalled, if it did not surpass, the splendour at Fontainebleau. The Banqueting Hall in which they dined was one of the most splendid in all France and the table was laden with gold plate of incredible antiquity and of priceless value.

The food and wine, too, was superb and it seemed to Rêve that there was a whole army of flunkeys moving quietly around the table with the great gold dishes in their gloved hands, their powdered hair silhouetted against the carved panelling of the hall, the gold lacings on their livery glittering in the light of a hundred candles.

"Tonight we are alone," the Count explained, "because I felt it would be an opportunity for us to get to know each other better. Tomorrow night I am giving a dinner party for you, and the night after that a ball; but now we can talk intimately about ourselves, and what subject is of more interest to any man—or woman, for that matter?"

"Tell us about yourself, Monsieur," Rêve said,

She was anxious that he should not probe too deeply into her feelings or ask questions which might be embarrassing to Armand.

"I am indeed flattered and complimented by your command," the Count said with a smile. "What can I tell you? There are, if I may say so, many sides to my character."

"You are an astrologer, aren't you?" Armand asked.

The Count looked up at him quickly.

"So you have been told that," he said. "Yes, I suppose it is one way to describe my powers."

His voice deepened on the last word and Rêve, anxious to keep the conversation going, said:

"Princess Pauline Borghese said you were a magician. Was she right, or was that just a figure of speech?"

The Count seemed to hesitate before he answered, then after a moment he said slowly:

"She was right, I am a magician!"

Rêve caught a look of sceptical incredulity in Armand's eyes, and quickly, because she was afraid that he might say something which would offend the Count, she said:

"That is indeed exciting! Do show us some of your magic. I would like it above all things."

The Count looked at her and there was something in the darkness of his eyes, which made her suddenly afraid.

"You will see evidence of my magic in due course," he replied. "It is not a thing to be spoken of lightly or to be discussed with an air of frivolity. It is a very serious matter, one indeed of the greatest and most transcending importance."

His voice seemed to ring out almost on a note of triumph, and for a moment Rêve felt that he appeared like a man possessed, a man elated with some secret inner force greater than himself.

Then as her heart began to thump and her lips to go dry, Armand—as if he were quite unaware that anything untoward was occurring—drawled:

"I wish you would tell my fortune. Perhaps you will be able to revive the past for me. It should be damned interesting if it were not too indiscreet."

The fanatical light faded from the Count's eyes. Rêve thought that he drew a deep breath as if of anger; but when he answered Armand, it was in a normal voice although his words were curt.

"I do not tell fortunes, my dear Marquis, as if I were a gipsy at a fair. For the Emperor I make certain prognostications in which he has absolute faith. Sometimes I see things for other people, either intentionally or unintentionally. For those who find it a laughing matter I see only bad luck, ill fortune and disaster."

"What a threat!" Armand said pleasantly. "Well, I suppose that under those circumstances I must let my future come as a surprise to me. It is a pity, though, that you take it so seriously. If you could predict the winner of a race or what card was going to turn up at faro, it would be easy to make a fortune."

"I already have one," the Count said quietly.

Rêve knew that he was angry by the way his long, thin fingers were clasping the wineglass at his side, but Armand appeared to be quite unaware that the Count was in any way incensed.

"So it appears," Armand said happily. "Perhaps you have already found the philosopher's stone which turns everything it touches into gold."

"Perhaps I have," the Count replied.

Rêve could feel that the atmosphere was electric, and to change the subject she said:

"After dinner will you not tell us something about your pictures, Monsieur? I can see that you have a very valuable collection."

"I would like to do that," the Count said, "but you must forgive me if I ask you to retire about eleven o'clock. I have something that I must do for the Emperor tonight, a certain calculation that must be made before midnight."

"More prognostications?" Armand asked with a smile. "He keeps you at it then! I hope you charge him a decent fee. Even the Greeks brought gifts when they consulted the oracle."

"My reward," the Count said stiffly, "is in knowing that I have both the Emperor's friendship and his confidence in all that I predict."

"That will be all right as long as you promise him victories," Armand said; "but wait until the moment comes when you have to mention a defeat. They were telling me at Fontainebleau what he was like when he learnt last week that the British had bombarded Copenhagen. Fouché says he has never seen him in such a fury

"He made frantic threats—foaming at the mouth as he did so—to invade England within a fortnight with a hundred thousand men. He swore to close every port in Europe against the stupid islanders, drive every British minister from the Continent and arrest every individual Englishman.

"A most undignified exhibition it appears to have

been; but then what can one expect from someone who was not born to the purple? Indeed, Count, you had best keep to victories."

Rêve tried to meet Armand's eyes in a warning to say no more, but it was too late. The words were spoken and it was obvious that the Count was deeply offended.

"I am neither a charlatan nor a liar, Monsieur le Marquis," he said in a voice of fury which was almost a snarl, while Armand looked up at him in innocent astonishment.

"Blister it, but I didn't mean to offend you!" he said with smiling good humour. "I know very little about such things, but I find it hard to credit that someone as intelligent as Napoleon should really believe in all this hocus-pocus about stars and the like.

"But you are an authority on such matters and if you say it is all the gospel truth, then far be it from me to argue with you. I will believe you and refrain from talking nonsense. So stop looking as mad as fire, my dear fellow, and let us drink to our future, whether we know what will happen in it or whether we don't."

Armand's voice seemed to mollify to a slight degree the Count's anger, but Rêve had the impression that he was only appeased superficially and that inadvertently Armand had created for himself a bitter enemy.

Agitated and fearful, she forced the Count to talk to her of his pictures, doing her best to keep Armand out of the conversation until gradually with a sense of relief she realised that it was nearly eleven o'clock and they would be able to retire to their rooms.

She was aware that the Count was also watching the clock; and as the time for their departure drew nearer, his features seemed to sharpen and grow eager, there was a light in his eyes and an air of expectancy and excitement about him which was quite unmistakable.

At last their formal adieux were said, and taking leave of the Count in the hall, Rêve and Armand climbed the broad staircase towards their bedrooms. As they reached the landing and were out of earshot of their host, Rêve whispered:

"I must speak with you."

"I will come to your room in five minutes," Armand replied in a low voice.

The fire was lit in the Queen's Bedroom and the candelabra on the dressing-table and by the bedside were ablaze with tapers, yet the room seemed dark and chilly.

Rêve on entering glanced apprehensively towards the secret panel, but there was no sign of anything unusual; and having dismissed the maid who was waiting up for her, she sat in a low chair before the fireplace. Her eyes went again and again towards the panelled wall.

Would Armand believe her, she wondered, not only when she told him about the woman who had appeared in her bedroom before dinner, but also about himself?

There was so much to tell. It all sounded so fantastic, such an incredible story, and she would almost be inclined to sympathise with him were he to say that he did not believe one word of it and the whole thing was a figment of her imagination.

A faint knock on the door made her start to her feet and run across the room to open it. Armand stood there, and at the sight of him she felt somehow reassured.

Nothing could be too frightening, too incredible when Armand was with her, even this strange unfamiliar Armand who treated her as a sister and who had little in common with the ardent lover she had known at Valmont.

"Oh, I am glad you have come," Rêve said quickly, drawing him into the room, shutting the door behind him and locking it.

"What is worrying you?" he asked. "I saw your face at dinner and realised that I was putting my foot into it, but what does it matter? The chap's a pompous fool with no sense of humour. You can't possibly marry him and I shall tell him so tomorrow."

Rêve gave a little sigh that was half a laugh and half a sob.

"Oh, Armand, you take everything so casually. Nothing seems to frighten you, nothing seems to shake your imperturbability. Why, you might not be a Frenchman!"

"What do you expect me to do?" he asked good-humouredly. "Shriek at the sight of my own shadow, or believe all that mumbo-jumbo with which he tried to delude the Emperor? A magician indeed! I credit he cannot even do a decent conjuring trick, if it comes to that."

"That is where you are mistaken," a voice said quietly.

Rêve gave a little shriek. The interruption was so unexpected, but when she turned her head, she saw that the secret panel in the wall was open again and the woman whom she had seen earlier in the evening was advancing slowly into the room.

"Who are you? What do you want?" Armand asked, jumping to his feet.

Even he was startled at the sudden interruption and the strange appearance of the woman advancing towards them.

She had changed the mauve *peignoir* she had worn earlier in the evening for a dress of some dark transparent material which was covered with cabalistic designs—stars, the moon, a twisting snake, all embroidered in silver, and on her breast, hanging from her neck by a chain of diamonds, was a swastika of blood-red rubies.

She came right across the room before she spoke and when she did, her voice was low and had a queer husky quality which was almost hypnotic in its depth and resonance.

"I warned you earlier in the evening," she said to Rêve, "but you did not take my warning. If you are wise, you will leave now, and at once. If you wait until tomorrow, it will be too late—yes, too late for anyone to save you."

Rêve found to her surprise that she was holding tightly on to Armand's hand. She did not even realise that she had drawn closer to him, but there was comfort in the warmth and strength of his fingers.

"Why do you want my sister to leave here?" Armand inquiried.

The woman looked at him.

"She is in danger," she replied simply;

Then, as she looked into Armand's face, a strange expression came into her eyes.

"You too are in danger, Monsieur," she said slowly. "I can see it shadowing you—danger—prison and worse still—death."

Rêve gave a little exclamation.

"Why do you say that?" she cried. "Tell me, why do you say that?"

The woman blinked her eyes as if she would clear her vision.

"I know not," she said dully. "I saw it clearly for the moment, but now it has gone. The danger is for you, Mademoiselle, not for your brother. It is you who must leave here, now and at once."

"But why?" Rêve asked. "You must explain further, you must give us a reason why we must go."

"You need a reason!" the woman said. "My poor child, I will give you one and then you will understand from what I am trying to save you."

"But why should you try to save my sister from this danger whatever it may be?" Armand asked in a tone of logical common sense.

"I am doing it for her sake," the woman replied. "I am doing it for Giles. Because I have worked for him, because in the past I have loved him and he has loved me, and I would save him from the final crime, the final sin against God. There is no salvation for me, I am past it; but because he believes, because he has complete faith in what he does, there is hope for him if he does not commit the greatest crime of all."

"And what is that?" Armand asked.

The woman glanced over her shoulder as if she were afraid of being overheard. She put out her hands and laid one on Rêve's arm, the other on Armand's. Her fingers were cold and Rêve shivered at her touch.

There was something eerie and horrible about the woman and yet it was impossible not to believe that she was acting sincerely. Whatever she said, she was doing it because she must.

"Listen, *mes enfants*," the woman said, "I am Marie-Madeleine, and many years ago Giles de Durieux was my lover. I was young when he first brought me here and asked more of me than love, but I did what he asked me to do because I loved him, because I wished to give him pleasure.

"I was not very religious, you understand, although I had been brought up in the Faith. But my love for Giles was greater than my love for God, and I did what he asked of me.

"Yet what at first had seemed an amusing hobby became gradually with him an obsession, his life's work. He had natural powers, it was true. He had been so since a child and he was clairvoyant. Often he could see things about people which others could not see.

"Then he found old books on necromancy, books which revealed to him the mysteries of sorcery, demonology, vampirism and the hidden secrets of the supernatural. He met other men, as skilled and as knowledgeable as he was himself, and he began to want more and yet more power.

"I became his accomplice, his slave, a creature who must do his bidding because I had no longer any will of my own. I was still infatuated with him, but even I began to be afraid as I saw to what lengths his desire of power would take him—power not as other men want it for riches, for victories, but power over the elements and the spirits that dwell in the universe, power over the dead as well as over the living—that was what Giles wanted, and that is what he is willing to risk everything to obtain."

"Yet what——" Rêve began, but the woman interrupted her with what was almost a fierce gesture.

"There is no time to talk," she said, "we have so little time. I am trying to make you understand, trying to make you see the danger you run in being here.

"Three years ago Giles came into possession of a palaeographic manuscript. It was very old and had been kept hidden from the eyes of the world by a secret society centuries old and of great magic power. It was given to Giles to read and from the moment he had read it he has thought of nothing else. It told him, this manuscript, that to obtain the final initiation, to free himself from the last bondage of mortal man he must make a supreme sacrifice.

"He must sacrifice his first-born child, a child that must be conceived by him of a virgin, born under the right planets and of his equal both in birth and breeding. Giles began to look for a girl who would answer this description, but she was not easy to find."

Rêve gave a little convulsive murmur.

"Yes," Marie-Madeleine said, as if she had spoken, "it was you on whom his choice finally fell. He saw you at the Palace and he told me that when he saw you it was as if you were enveloped in a great white light and he knew that you had been sent there deliberately and for his own purpose.

"He made exhaustive inquiries about your birth and found that you had been born at the right time of the year, under the right stars and the right sign of the Zodiac. From that moment he has never rested until you promised to marry him, until he had got the Emperor to agree to hurry forward the ceremony.

"Tomorrow morning you will receive a communication from the Emperor, instructing you to marry the Count before noon. It will be a command, and one you dare not disobey. That is why I beg you to escape now. Leave at once, fly from the castle while there is yet time."

"But how can we be sure that you are telling us the truth?" Armand asked.

The woman looked up at him and her thin, lined face was somehow infinitely pathetic.

"I cannot blame you for asking that question, Monsieur," she said. "Come with me. Already Giles begins the ceremonies which must take place before he is spiritualised and ready for marriage with your sister.

"If he should know that I had told you this, he would kill me; and yet I am not afraid to die, it is for him I am afraid, for his soul, which he has already

202

dedicated to the Devil, but which I would save from the final act of damnation in the destruction and death of his own child.

"Come, if you must, but do not make a sound, for if he discovers us, we are all lost and for you, like me, there will be no escape."

Marie-Madeleine turned as she spoke and picking up a candle from the dressing-table, she led the way through the panel in the wall. Rêve and Armand found themselves stepping from the Queen's Bedroom into a tiny empty chamber which was obviously a secret room concealed between the panellings of two great adjacent Salons.

Marie-Madeleine touched a spring on the opposite side of the wall and another secret door was revealed. When they had stepped through it, they found themselves in a big, unfurnished room, and passing through it they came into a long, dark passage.

With a finger to her lips to indicate silence Marie-Madeleine led the way. The passage twisted and turned and, although she held the candle high above her head, she moved so quickly that the flame blown by the draught make little light, and only by clinging tightly to Armand's hand did Rêve feel assured that she would not stumble or bruise herself. Finally Marie-Madeleine stopped.

Once again there was no door, only a dark wall. In a voice so low that they could hardly hear her, she said:

"Do not say a word or you will be discovered. Watch for a little while, then creep away and escape from the Castle as speedily as you can. Follow the passage by which we have come. The doors are open into the Queen's Bedchamber. Close them when you return so that your departure will not be connected with me."

"We will do that," Armand answered.

"I will leave the candle here," Marie-Madeleine said. "It will burn for about an hour, not longer."

As she spoke, she put it down on the floor and, searching for a secret spring, pressed the panelling with her fingers. A small narrow piece slid back silently and Rêve saw that in front of them was an organ loft.

It was surrounded by a thick balustrade of carved oak, from which it was possible to see and yet not be seen. From below them came the sound of voices raised in a chant, and under cover of this it was easy to move forward without being heard.

It was very dark and Rêve had to feel her way over the rough surface of the boards which floored the loft; then, kneeling at the balustrade, she peeped through between the carvings to see what lay below.

She felt Armand join her. His shoulder was against hers and his hand gripped her trembling fingers. She glanced up at him but she could not see his face. She turned again to look below.

As she had expected, she was looking down into a Chapel. It was a very beautiful one, structurally Gothic, with carved oak stalls and elaborately painted tombs which had been ornamented and decorated with gilt and mosaic until they shone and glittered with an almost dazzling brilliance. In the chancel were hundreds of lighted candles.

Tall white tapers soared high on the altar and in carved sconces behind the choir stalls. There were sanctuary lamps of shimmering silver whose lights flickered mystically and there was the thick pungent fragrance of incense rising in small purple clouds from a censer of gold set with rubies and swung by a fairhaired, effeminate-looking acolyte clothed in crimson and priceless lace.

The chanting, too, was beautiful, boys' voices transcendent in their quality, rising high and exquisite until the whole building seemed to ring with them.

"What is wrong with this?" Rêve thought. "I do not understand."

Then what she saw made her gasp and tighten her hold on Armand until her nails cut into his flesh. On the altar was a human form.

She had not noticed it at first, for the candles had been so bright, but now she saw that it was the body of a woman, quite naked, lying on the white cloth in an attitude of sensuous abandon.

Above her was a great jewelled crucifix, exquisitely fashioned, glittering with fabulous gems—but it was turned upside down.

It was then that Rêve understood. She was watching the Black Mass! The service of those who had sold themselves to the Devil and who had forfeited even the mercy of God in the degradation to which they had stooped.

Vaguely Rêve remembered hearing that such ceremonies had taken place during the Revolution, but that even the most hardened sinners and atheists spoke of them with horror.

For any son of the Church who took part in the mass was to be damned for all eternity.

With a sense of fear which was almost agonising in its intensity Rêve saw the Count enter from the sacristy.

He was wearing vestments exquisitely embroidered on priceless brocade, but the symbols entwined in golden thread and ornamented with jewels were the symbols of the Devil himself. On his face there was that look of fanatical exaltation and triumph of which she had caught a pale reflection at dinner. The evil was shining forth from him as if from some hidden fire within and his lips were wet with saliva.

As he approached the altar and the body of the naked woman, the voices of the choir rose in exaltation which fell at length into silence and then into the slow repetition of a prayer.

They were repeating the Lord's Prayer backwards, and it seemed to Rêve as if from the body of the Chapel there came up towards her and Armand such an atmosphere of horror, evil and wickedness that she must faint from the very impact of it.

Indeed she felt as if her will-power was leaving her and she was being sucked down into some dread undercurrent of foulness from which she could not free herself.

She felt herself sinking, felt as if she voluntarily surrendered her will, her thoughts and her very soul to an octopus reaching out to encircle her with its tentacles.

But as she gasped for breath, feeling that she was drowning in some ghastly cesspool from which she could never save herself, she felt Armand's arm go around her and knew that he was taking her away.

At that moment she must have completely lost consciousness, for when she opened her eyes again she was back in the Queen's Bedroom, lying on the sofa, and Armand was bending over her with a glass of water in his hand.

"Drink this," he said, and his face was stern in the light of the candles.

"Oh, Armand," she gasped, "save me! Save me!"

"We will get away at once," he answered. "Are you well enough to travel?"

Rêve took another sip of the water and sat up.

"I am well enough to do anything rather than stay here," she said. "Oh, Armand, I am frightened. Supposing he stops us?"

"He will not do that," Armand said quietly.

Looking at his face, Rêve realised that his langour and his air of boredom had gone. Here was a man purposeful, determined, a man whom she could trust utterly and completely.

She felt her heart leap towards him. She knew without his telling her that this was no time to talk. They must go and at once.

With an effort she rose to her feet and, going to the wardrobe, she took down her travelling-cloak of dark velvet trimmed with fur and threw it over her shoulders. There was no time to worry about anything else.

She slipped a handkerchief into the bosom of her dress and remembered thankfully that she was wearing her gown of white *crêpe* which was fashioned on Grecian lines with a full pleated skirt.

If she had to ride a horse, as undoubtedly she would, it would not hamper her movement as many of her other dresses would have done.

"Are you ready?" Armand asked.

As she nodded, he opened the door and glanced out

into the landing. There was no one about, and he drew her after him, closing the door behind them. They crossed the landing to his own room. It took him but a few minutes to find his purse and travelling-cloak.

Now they were ready. The difficulty would be to escape from the Castle. Armand looked over the stairs. Candles illuminated the great hall, but there was no one in attendance.

Quickly he and Rêve descended the stairs side by side, and passing through the Great Hall they came to the other vestibule. It was then, even as Armand put out his hand towards the bolts and chains fastening the front door, that they heard the sound of horses' hoofs outside.

Someone was arriving. They heard horses drawn to a standstill, the clink of harness, a man's voice and the sound of footsteps coming up the marble steps.

Rêve looked at Armand and they both knew there was no time to be lost. Swiftly he drew her back into the Great Hall and with a deft movement drew aside one of the long velvet curtains which were drawn over the nearest window.

She slipped behind it and Armand followed her. They hardly concealed themselves before they heard footsteps approaching from the other end of the Great Hall which led towards the servant's quarters.

Rêve felt as if she must suffocate with sheer terror. She could see nothing, but she could hear the lackey's feet passing their hiding-place, could hear the bolts on the front door being pulled back, the key turned in the lock and the creak as the heavy nail-studded door swung open.

Then a man's voice said:

"I must speak immediately with Comte Giles de Durieux,"

"Monsieur le Comte is engaged at this moment, Monsieur."

There was the sound of heavy footsteps entering the Great Hall, as if someone had pushed past the lackey and entered the Castle.

"Tell the Count with my compliments that Captain

Ettiene, of the Emperor's bodyguard, wishes to speak with him immediately. Make it quite clear that I came here on the Emperor's business and there must be no delay."

"Very good, Monsieur."

There was a sound of footsteps withdrawing and more footsteps entering the Castle. Another man joined the first; Rêve could hear the clink of his spurs.

"Is Prévost staying with the horses?" a man asked.

"Yes, there are apparently no grooms about at this hour of night. They are obviously not expecting visitors."

"Well, why should they be," the man who had called himself Captain Ettiene asked, "especially unwelcome ones?"

"We shall certainly be that," the other man answered. "This is what I call an uncomfortable mission. I wish to God the Emperor had chosen someone else for the job."

"Oh, it's all in the day's work," Captain Ettiene replied. "I must say the fellow looked all right to me, I spoke to him once or twice at Fontainebleau!"

"Miollis says he was suspicious from the first."

"Oh, it's easy to say that afterwards! Besides, what do first suspicions amount to? The whole thing may be a misunderstanding."

"The Duchess de Monestier is certain that he is a spy."

"That's an easy way of getting rid of one's unwanted lovers," Captain Ettiene sneered.

Rêve felt as if a cold hand was squeezing her heart. At first when the men entered the Castle she had been afraid that she and Armand would be discovered in the act of escaping from it, but now she was afraid of something much more sinister.

There was the sound of footsteps coming across the hall, then the Count's voice, angry and rising to a high falsetto. A note of hysteria was in his tone. He brought with him the scent of incense which percolated behind the heavy velvet curtains and made Rêve shudder as if the fragrance in itself was impregnated with evil.

"I am informed that you gentlemen are here on the Emperor's business. It is of the greatest inconvenience that you interrupt me now at this particular moment."

"We apologise for any inconveneince we may have caused you, Monsieur le Comte," Captain Ettiene replied, "but on the Emperor's commands we have come here with all possible speed to arrest a guest in your Castle."

"A guest of mine?" the Count inquired.

"Yes, a man calling himself Monsieur le Marquis d'Augeron."

"But why should he be arrested?"

"He is believed to be an imposter. Information has been given to the Emperor that he is not in fact the Marquis d'Augeron."

"It is the most extraordinary assertion I have ever heard," the Count exclaimed. "The Marquis is the half-brother of the lady who is to be my wife. I must have proof of what you say before I allow you to insult him by such suggestions."

"Proofs have been given to the Emperor, Monsieur, by the Duchess de Monestier and I think I am right in saying by Count Metternich."

"The Austrian Ambassador!" the Count exclaimed. "What has he got to do with it?"

"That I can't tell you, Monsieur," Captain Ettiene replied, "but to convince you that this is not a wild-goose chase I would tell you that the Emperor has seen a portrait of the real Marquis d'Augeron which does not resemble in the slightest the gentleman using that title."

"Portraits are not always a reliable testimony of a man's looks," the Count said testily.

"That may be the usual rule," Captain Ettiene replied, "but in this case the portrait reveals a certain characteristic which we have since confirmed from Monsieur Fouché's office to be indubitably true about the real Marquis d'Augeron."

"And what is that?" the Count inquired.

"That the Marquis has only one eye," Captain Ettiene said. "He lost the other in a duel which took place five years ago in Vienna."

There was a moment's pause.

"My guest undoubtedly has the use of both his eyes," the Count said hesitatingly.

"Then perhaps you will be kind enough to let us proceed at once to his bedchamber. By the Emperor's order he is under arrest and we are to take him immediately to Fontainebleau where further inquiries will be made as to his true identity."

"I cannot of course prevent you from doing your duty," the Count said coldly, "but I must beg that you are as discreet and as quiet as possible in making your arrest. I do not wish my future bride to be disturbed nor is there any reason for her to know that her half-brother has left the Castle."

"You will doubtless think of some tale in the morning to account for his disappearance, Monsieur."

There was a hint of sarcasm in Captain Ettiene's tone.

"That point you may leave with confidence in my hands, Captain."

"Our business, Monsieur le Comte, is entirely with the man calling himself le Marquis d'Augeron," Captain Ettiene replied, "and, as you suggest, we will be as quiet as possible."

"A footman will show you to his room. And now, gentlemen, if you will excuse me, I am engaged on important matters of great delicacy which cannot further be delayed."

"Bon soir, Monsieur le Comte, and thank you," Captain Ettiene said.

"Bon soir, gentlemen."

Rêve heard the Count cross the hall; then she heard the slow footsteps of the officers going upstairs. She hardly dared to breathe for fear of betraying their hiding-place.

But before she had time to think, before she had time to consider what Armand's reactions must be to what he had heard, she felt his hand on her arm as he drew back the curtain and they stepped from their hiding place. Swiftly he led her across the hall and into the vestibule.

There was only one sleepy footman guarding the

front door. He was in the act of yawning as Armand appeared, and with a powerful uppercut, which Armand had learned in Gentleman Jackson's rooms in Bond Street, he was knocked out before he had time to finish stretching.

In a moment the door was open and Armand was hurrying Rêve down the stone steps to where below them three hhorses were standing in the moonlight, an officer holding their bridles.

He turned as they approached, and something in Armand's purposeful advance made his hand reach instinctively towards his sword. But before he could draw it, Armand was upon him.

He was not a very big man and Armand took him up bodily and threw him over the courtyard wall into the lake. Rêve heard a splash as he struck the water, and then Armand's arm was round her waist and he swung her up into the saddle of the nearest horse.

"Pray Heaven you can ride well," he said, and to her own surprise she answered him with a light laugh.

"You will find it hard to keep up with me," she answered confidently, and noted the ease with which he swung himself into the saddle of the other horse.

Now they were away, galloping full speed over the drawbridge and through the open gates which led them through the park and out into the open country-side.

Rêve looked back over her shoulder. The Castle of Creux was bathed in moonlight.

Its grandeur had a magnificent, almost breath-taking beauty yet she knew that she was escaping from something utterly evil and so long as Armand was at her side she was no longer afraid.

12

They had galloped for about two miles across country when they came under the shelter of some thick trees. Here Armand reined in his horse.

"We will ride through this wood," he said. "Follow me."

He turned and rode ahead down a grassy path which led them to a clearing in what appeared to be the very heart of the wood itself.

Armand drew his horse to a standstill and after listening for a moment to hear if he could detect the sound of anyone following them he turned to Rêve and said abruptly:

"Who am I?"

She could see his face in the moonlight, the scar from his wound standing out darkly against his forehead, and she had an urgent impulse to hold out her arms to him and beg him to reassure her of his love and affection before she told him anything.

If they had been alone together in a room, she might have sought the protection of his arms; but now on horseback and in danger of pursuit there was nothing she could do but answer him honestly and with the same abruptness with which he had asked the question.

"You are English," she said, "and your name is the Viscount Sheringham."

She thought he started with surprise at her reply, but it was difficult to read the expression on his face. For a moment he said nothing and then at length in a strange voice the inflection of which she could not understand he said:

"So I am English! I might have known it! I might

have guessed I had nothing in common with these damned Frenchmen."

"Yes, you are English," Rêve said, and there was a hint of anger in her tone.

"Then why——?" Armand began, then checked the words on his lips.

He swung himself down from his horse and, leaving the animal free to crop the short tufts of grass, he walked the few steps to Rêve's side and lifted her down from the saddle.

She felt his arms around her waist and as she swayed towards him she was conscious of his strength and felt a sudden thrill go through her. She loved him, and whatever he said or did, however incensed he might be, however much he might antagonise her, she would still love him now and until her life's end.

But almost before she had realised that he had touched her she was free of him, and standing apart from her he said sternly:

"Now tell me everything, and I want the truth remember; all of it."

Rêve threw back her heavy travelling cloak from her shoulders. The hood had fallen from her head during the ride and now as she raised her face towards Armand's she realised that she was facing the moonlight while his face was in shadow.

She felt that he had arranged this deliberately so that he could watch her eyes and see whether or not she told the truth, and once again she felt her anger rise a little that he should be so arbitrary.

"I will tell you the truth," she said slowly. "I would have told you it long ago had I not been afraid that what you would hear might be detrimental to your health. You know that you have lost your memory, and if what I tell you does not appear to you credible, you have yet got to take my word for it because it is the truth as I know it, that and nothing else."

"Tell me what you know," Armand said, and it was a command.

For a moment Rêve hesitated. Where should she begin? It was hard to tell a man who remembered nothing that he had come upon her bathing in what she had believed was the secret seclusion of her own lake—that he had seen her naked and fallen in love with her.

How could she relate such a story—not to Armand, but to this hard-voiced stranger who appeared to be ready not only to doubt the verity of all that she told him but also to criticise her for having kept the truth from him when he was wounded and very near death.

It was impossible, quite impossible, to tell him what had happened that first evening.

Indeed there were no words in which she could describe the magic of that moment when they had looked into each other's eyes and had known themselves in love, no words in which she could relate that moment of ecstasy when his lips had touched hers and it had seared itself indelibly into her heart for all time.

She could not explain what had happened to her—or to him; she could not translate those moments of divine beauty into the banal, mundane terms of everyday emotions and occurrences.

She had not anticipated that, when the moment came for her to reveal to Armand who he was, this embarrassing situation would arise. She had always believed that his memory would return and that with it would come the realisation of what they had meant to each other.

She had never thought of their love as being dead or even changed, but merely as being laid aside. Yet now that she had to speak, had to make some explanation, she felt as if her voice died in her throat and her lips were too dry to frame the words.

"I am waiting," Armand said sharply.

"It is a long story," Rêve replied quickly. "Are we wise to make this delay? They will be searching for you, and for me too. At any moment we may hear the sound of hoofs. Let us make for the coast while there is still time so that somehow, by some means, you can escape to England."

"I am waiting," Armand repeated.

Rêve gave a little sigh of desperation.

"I was sitting by the lake at Valmont one evening,"

she began, "when a man called Paul de Frémond arrived. He told me that my half-brother, whom I was expecting to arrive from Amsterdam, had been killed in a drunken brawl.

"He—he then insulted me. You—you must have heard my cries, for you—came to my rescue. You made Paul de Frémond release me, and when he turned and saw who you were, he said: 'Faith, if it isn't Sheringham. What the hell are you doing here?'

"He accused you of being a spy on French soil, and said it was an extraordinary thing to find the son of the Prime Minister of England in such a position. You had apparently known each other when you were both at Eton and Oxford. You accused Paul de Frémond of having caused the death of one of your friends, and he did not deny it. Then—then you fought a duel.

"Paul de Frémond fired too soon, only—you seemed to anticipate his action and by some miraculous movement you avoided his bullet, but you shot him through the heart. He crumpled up and lay bleeding on the ground.

"When you went to his aid, he drew a dagger from the inner pocket of his coat and stabbed you in the head. It was a treacherous blow and I thought at first that it was a fatal one.

"It was only after you had been carried to the *Château* that I realised that I had got to make some explanation as to who you were and why I had taken you into my home."

"And why had you?" Armand asked.

Rêve twisted her fingers together nervously.

"You—you were wounded—you had tried to save me—I felt it was the least I could do for you in return."

"And yet you already knew and believed that I was an Englishman spying on your countrymen?"

"Yes—yes," Rêve admitted; "but I knew too that you called yourself Armand de Ségury, and that you were staying at the Inn at St. Benis."

"How did you know that?"

"We—we had met before."

"When?"

"One—one night. I—I found you—er—wandering in the woods. We talked together. You told me that you were a traveller in France. But—when de Frémond came, you were wounded in my defence and I thought that I must save your life, so I pretended that you were my half-brother. It was all done on the impulse of the moment and there was no time to consider whether it was a wise thing to do or not."

"And having done that," Armand said, "knowing that I was a spy, you let me meet the Emperor, let me go with you to Fontainebleau and ever become aide-de-camp to Napoleon Bonaparte. I confess it is extra-ordinary behaviour on the part of a Frenchwoman."

Rêve bowed her head.

"Yes," she said faintly. "I—I suppose it—does seem —extraordinary."

In one step Armand crossed the intervening space between them, and, putting his hand under her chin he turned her face up to his.

"You are not telling me the truth," he said accusing-ly. "There is something behind all this, something you are keeping from me. If you knew me to be an English-man and a spy, you should have handed me over to the authorities immediately. If you had done that, there would have been no need to continue your subter-fuge and lies about a man who might at any moment have assassinated your Emperor."

Rêve felt herself quiver in his hold, but her eyes were forced to meet his. She wondered why he did not read in them her love for him, which seemed to fill her whole being to the exclusion of all else.

"I was not afraid that you would do that," she said in a very small voice.

"Why not?" Armand demanded.

"It would not have been honourable or the action of a gentleman," she replied.

He released her almost roughly.

"How do you know how honourable a spy would be when he is concerned in a foreign country?" Ar-mand said. "I cannot understand how you could have permitted me to come with you to Fontainebleau, be with the Emperor, to learn even the most intimate secrets of his Council."

There was a sudden sound far off in the woods. It might have been but the falling of a branch, but Rêve started violently.

"Now that you have learned those secrets," she said, "and the Emperor already knows you for an imposter, do you imagine that your life will be safe for one single instant?"

"You are right there," Armand said. "We had best go on."

He helped her on to her horse and once again they moved forward. It was only when they were riding down a dark path that Rêve asked:

"Where are we going?"

"I have thought of that," Armand replied. "If we strike north across country, we should come to Valmont. I can leave you there in safety with Antoinette."

"Leave me!" The words were a cry of horror. "But, Armand, you do not understand! However incensed the Emperor may be with me for aiding and abetting you, he will still insist that my marriage to the Count de Durieux should take place."

"I think not," Armand said. "Besides, where else can I take you?"

"Take me with you," Rêve replied passionately. "Take me to wherever you are going."

"But that is impossible," he answered. "I must, of course, return to England. I must find out if I am indeed the man you say I am. At any rate any useful work I might have achieved in France is now at an end. I shall be hunted, pursued, and every loyal Frenchman's hand will be against me. It will be a question of wits—whether the hounds will get the fox before he can run to earth.

"The idea amuses me, for I am not afraid for myself; and if I am captured, I suppose it is as good a way of dying as any other. But you must be saved. There is no one else I can leave you with except Antoinette."

"Neither Antoinette nor anyone else can protect me

217

at the moment," Rêve answered. "Even supposing the Count does not wish to marry me after what has occurred what do you imagine will be my position when it is discovered who you are. I have harboured you, I have sponsored you, I have deliberately deceived—not only you, but the Emperor himself."

"You can say that you did not know who I was, that I told you I was your brother and you believed me," Armand said.

"Do you think they would credit that?" Rêve inquired.

He did not answer and there was a long silence while they jogged along. Rêve realised that Armand was deliberately choosing difficult, obscure paths which led through woods and across country, and with some skill avoiding the roads and villages.

Fortunately the horses were fresh and Rêve thought that Captain Ettiene and his officers must have changed mounts shortly before they arrived at Creux, doubtless thinking of the journey back to Fontainebleau when they would be taking Armand with them.

It was hard to ride in silence, and yet she realised with an instinct which came from her knowledge of Armand's character, that she would gain nothing by pleading with him too desperately until he had thought out the situation as it stood.

She was terrified that he might insist on her remaining at Valmont while he sought to escape alone; and yet some strength and courage within herself told her that, when the moment came, she would somehow continue to prevent him from doing this and that she would go with him whether he desired it or not.

It was sufficient for the moment to know that she had left him doubtful and dismayed about the success of his plan, and that, whether he realised that she loved him or not, he would be too chivalrous to allow her to bear the consequences of the deception which she had practised for him and for his sake alone.

At last after a long time Armand spoke again.

"It is impossible," he said slowly.

"What is?" Rêve asked.

"That I should try to get you away to England," he replied. "It will mean leaving Valmont almost as soon as we get there. It would not be safe to linger in the house, for sooner or later they are bound to look for you in your own home."

"I have thought of that," Rêve replied, "but in some ways it might be the safest place. They would hardly think that, being fugitives, we should seek to conceal ourselves in such an obvious spot."

"There is that point, of course," Armand said, "yet they will remember that we are bound to obtain fresh horses. Fortunately I have a certain amount of money with me, but I should be relieved to have what I left behind at Valmont when we departed for Fontainebleau."

"You left some money behind?" Rêve asked. "You did not tell me so. Did you put it somewhere safe?"

"I think so," Armand replied. "Antoinette showed me the secret panel behind which your father kept his valuables. She was certain that no one else knew of its existence save herself."

"She has never told even me of it," Rêve said.

"We must carry what gold we can," Armand said, "for we must buy horses as we go. Are we likely to obtain two at Valmont?"

"Yes, indeed," Rêve replied. "It will not be difficult there to obtain horses and good ones. Part of the stables and the old paddock are used by a Farmer Barrois who is interested in breeding horse-flesh. He has always proved himself both loyal and devoted in anything I have asked of him."

"Good," Armand said briefly, "that is one problem solved."

"And I may come with you?" Rêve asked in a very small voice.

"I do not know what to reply to that," he answered. "I cannot leave you alone to face the consequences of this or to endure the Emperor's rage. Yet if I take you with me and I am captured, it will be all the worse for you."

"But I am more than ready to take that risk," Rêve

said, and her voice was light and suddenly imbued with happiness. "Let me come with you, Armand."

"To where?" he inquired. "Are you wise to trust me like this? What do you know of me? And what indeed do I know about myself? You tell me I am the Viscount Sheringham. I will be honest with you and admit that, though the words have a vaguely familiar sound, I can remember nothing tangible or concrete about them.

"England, it is true, grows clearer in my mind every day, yet I cannot remember my father, relatives, or even my friends. Napoleon Bonaparte seems very real to me, but I cannot recall what the King of England looks like or if indeed there is one.

"Are you wise to throw in your lot with a man such as I am? Suppose when we get to England—if we are lucky enough to escape from our pursuers, you discover that I am a beggar, a pauper, a thief, what will you do then?"

Rêve knew the answer, but she dared not say it. How could she tell Armand that whoever he was, however humble or however penniless, she would still love him?

Were he a murderer or a felon hanging from the gallows, she would still love him with her whole heart and soul, still ask only that she might be at his side until death finally separated them.

She did not answer, and at last Armand turned his head and said mockingly:

"Well, have I frightened you at last?"

She realised that she had not answered his last question.

"Nothing frightens me," she replied, "except the idea of marriage with the Count de Durieux. Oh, Armand, I did not believe such evil existed in the world."

"Do you suppose Napoleon knows with what sort of man he is dealing?" Armand inquired.

"Princess Pauline said that her brother would never go into battle save when the prophecies of the soothsayers assured him that he would be victorious," Rêve said. "You have seen the Emperor. He is a man whose mind is concentrated entirely on victory.

"If the Count promises him that some battle will go in his favour and the event proves him to be right, I feel sure that the Emperor will think that nothing the Count does in his private life is of the slightest consequence.

"A victory for France is all that matters! A ruler who will sacrifice the lives of a million men to achieve that is not interested in the hearts and souls of individuals."

Armand nodded.

"You are right there. An eagle soaring heavenwards is concerned with nothing but his own flight."

Rêve felt her heart contract at the words. She remembered that day at Valmont when Armand and the old Duchess had talked together and spoken of love as being an eagle.

She had known then that that was how Armand had brought love to her—fierce, strong, ecstatic—and her love had soared like the greatest and strongest of the birds high into the heavens of happiness.

And yet so many things had happened to change and destroy that happiness that now she felt a feeling of utter despair creep over her. Armand no longer loved her, and while she prayed blindly that his love was but forgotten, she must face the fact that it might be dead.

Supposing she went with him back to England and found that he was married or that he had other women who meant more to him than she did?

Supposing that, penniless, friendless and utterly destitute, he left her alone in a strange country and returned to his own life, or his own environment and forgot her very existence?

For a moment everything seemed very dark at the mere idea; then briefly she told herself that she had suffered so deeply and endured so much for the sake of her love that this was no time to surrender herself to dismal forebodings.

For better or worse, whatever the future might bring forth, her life was linked with Armand's. Perhaps they would never reach England, and if he was to die, she must die too. Somewhere in eternity they would still be together.

"We should hurry," she said aloud. "We have a long way to go before we reach England and safety."

Even as she said the words she realised that in the east the first pale flush of dawn was coming up in the sky. At her words Armand suddenly put out his hand and laid it on hers and she held the horse's reins.

"I like your courage," he said, and she flushed as if he had paid her an extravagant compliment.

They rode for another hour until the sun was up and the country-side bathed in sunshine. On the summit of a hill Armand reined in his horse. Down below them they could see several villages, white roads dissecting cultivated fields like so many ribbons.

"We must find a wood and stay there until this evening," Armand said. "It will not be wise to press on."

"Why not?" Rêve asked.

"I have the feeling that it would be stupid to show ourselves," he replied. "Besides, we have got to sleep some time, so why not now?"

He looked at the scene below, then pointed with his right hand.

"Do you see that man riding hard towards that hamlet? He may be a doctor hurrying to a dying patient, a Priest carrying the Last Sacrament, a man going to work or a lover hastening to his mistress.

"He might be any of these things, yet again he might be someone warning the citizens of France that there is a traitor amongst them, a man masquerading as the Marquis d'Augeron, an Englishman impudent enough to have learned the secrets of the Emperor himself."

Armand spoke lightly, but his eyes were grave.

"You are right," Rêve said quietly. "Let us wait here. When night falls, we can go to Valmont and enter the *Château* from the garden. If soldiers are waiting for us, they will not see us if you allow me to lead you into the house by the hidden ways I used as a child."

"We will do that," Armand said briefly.

He turned his horse and led her into the middle of a small wood. The trees were close together and made a perfect shelter from the curious eyes of any passer-by. The ground was covered with pine-needles and moss which offered a comfortable bed, and after they had tied their horses to a tree and Armand had fetched them some armfuls of grass from outside the wood.

Rêve stretched out her travelling-cloak and lay down. She did not know until that moment how tired she was.

While Armand was seeing to the horses, she thought they would talk together, for there was so much she wanted to say; but when he returend, her eyelids were already drooping.

"I wanted—to tell—you some——" she began, her voice seeming in her utter fatigue to come from a very long way away.

"Go to sleep," he said gently. "I will hear all that you have to tell me when you awake."

She hardly heard his last words. Sleep took her completely in its toils. She felt herself relax and knew that delicious moment when she was floating away as if on a cloud into an oblivion which acted like a balm to her tortured nerves.

Her breath came rhythmically and her travelling-cloak fell aside to reveal the soft contours of her young body beneath her evening gown of white *crêpe*.

Armand stood looking down at her. He too was tired, but as his eyes rested on her closed ones, on the curved sweetness of her red lips, on her dark hair curling against the whiteness of her neck, he thought she looked very young and defenceless. After a long moment his mouth tightened as if in pain.

He walked to the edge of the woods to make quite certain that no one could see their place of concealment; then, returning to where Rêve slept, he lay down a little way from her and closed his eyes.

Rêve woke first after wondering wildly for a frightened second where she was, she sat up and saw that the afternoon must be far advanced for the shadows of the trees were pointing eastwards and there was a feeling of heat which seemed almost to rise from the ground after a long day of sunshine.

Armand was still asleep, his head pillowed on his travelling-cloak, his body turned sideways, his knees bent as if he were reclining in the softest and most luxurious bed. Rêve watched him for a moment, then very softly she got to her feet and crept away to where, far in the wood, she had noticed earlier in the day a tiny trickling stream.

It came from a rock and the water was cool and fresh. Having drink of it and washed her face and hands, she felt ready for whatever lay before them.

She wished she had a mirror or a comb with her so that she could tidy her hair, but she thought with joy that in a few hours they would be at Valmont and she would be able to change her dress and make herself look pretty for Armand.

Even as she thought of him she heard his voice. He called her name, and she felt unaccountably glad because there was a note of alarm in his tone.

"Rêve, Rêve, where are you?"

"I am here," she answered.

She came running back through the wood to find him standing distractedly where she had slept, looking in every direction.

"I am here," she replied.

At the sight of her he made a gesture as if he would hold out his arms; but something seemed to check him and he let them fall again to his sides.

"I was worried about you," he said. "I woke and found you had gone."

"I had merely gone to drink and wash," Rêve explained, but her words were a mere formality and unimportant because of an inner singing gladness that Armand had been worried about her.

"You are quite safe?" he asked unnecessarily.

"Quite," she smiled, "and most refreshed. I might have been sleeping in my own bed at Valmont with Antoinette watching over me."

"I should really have stayed awake to protect you," he said, "but no harm has been done. We must both have slept for the best part of the day."

"Surely that is a good thing," Rêve said. "We are

fresh to travel tonight. Besides, if we had been awake, we might have remembered how hungry we are."

"I am ravenous," Armand confessed with a sudden grin, "and I suppose you must be too."

"I can bear it until we get to Valmont," Rêve replied, and glancing up at the setting sun, she said: "How soon can we go?"

"We must wait a little longer," Armand replied. "In the meantime I, too, will wash and drink."

He disappeared towards the stream. Rêve watched him go; then she bent and picked up his travelling-cloak from where he had left it on the ground. She shook it and tried fruitlessly to erase some of the creases from it.

On an impulse she laid it against her cheek. It smelt of pine-needles and a faint fragrance which was characteristic of Armand. She drew a deep breath, then pressed her lips longingly and passionately against the soft material.

As she did so, she thought one day that Armand would remember everything; but if he did not, she determined there and then that she would make him love her all over again.

Once he got used to knowing she was not his sister it would be easy to create between them that magnetic atmosphere which draws an unattached man and woman to each other and makes them acutely conscious of each other's presence.

"Oh, God, make him love me again," Rêve prayed into Armand's coat.

Then she turned with a smile as she heard him coming towards her through the trees.

It was after eleven o'clock before they reached Valmont that night. Armand had insisted that they should not move until the sun had sunk and the twilight made it possible for them to slip along the hedgerows like shadows, even their horses being difficult to distinguish from any distance.

It was not easy to find their way, and more than once Rêve felt frightened lest they were completely lost and moving in the wrong direction.

At last with excitement she recognised two familiar landmarks—a clump of trees on the horizon, a church spire in a valley, and knew at last that they were on their right route and heading straight for Valmont.

There was no sign of soldiers or men lurking in ambush as they drew near to the little village of St. Benis. They did not enter it, but turned towards the fields and came upon the *Château* from the north, from which direction Armand thought it least likely that they would be expected.

The house was in darkness. There were no lights burning in the windows, and Rêve thought that in the moonlight it looked big, empty and very lonely, as if life had moved away from it and it had been forgotten.

They left the horses in a field outside the trees which encircled the gardens, and climbing the fence, Rêve led the way by tiny, overgrown paths to what had once been a lawn.

Here they stood for a little while and listened, to hear only the sound of their quick breathing and the thumping of their apprehensive hearts.

"Antoinette will be in bed," Rêve whispered. "We will go in by the garden door. It used never to be kept locked, and if it is, there is a window outside it which is quite easy to open. Then we can go up a side staircase just in case someone is lurking in the house."

Armand nodded his head in reply. They had already agreed that they would talk only when it was absolutely necessary. Rêve led the way towards the house.

Once she stumbled on an uneven path and Armand's hand came out to save her from falling. She clung to him for a moment but did not speak, and they proceeded on their way until at last they came to a small, inconspicuous garden door which stood as the side of the *Château* near the lake.

Rêve turned the handle and found it was locked. She pointed to the window and it took Armand but a few seconds to manipulate the old and rusted catch. The casement flew open, he swung himself up on the window ledge and disappeared into the house.

There was the sound of a key turning in the lock and the door in front of Rêve stood open. Stealthily she entered her own house.

The passage smelt damp and musty. There was darkness and silence everywhere. Moving quickly and sure-footed because the way was so familiar, Rêve climbed the staircase to the first floor while Armand groped his way behind her.

There was still only silence, not a sound of any sort, until at last Rêve reached Antoinette's room and saw there was a light beneath the door. She listened for a moment before knocking, and then with the tips of her fingers she made a faint sound, too faint to be heard by anyone save the person directly behind the door on which they knocked.

"Entrez!"

There was a note of astonishment in Antoinette's voice as if she wondered who it could be at this hour of night, and then, as Rêve opened the door, she gave a loud cry of surprise.

"Ma petite, it is you! But why? What is the matter?"

Antoinette was sitting in her rocking-chair, embroidering with exquisite stitches a linen chemise which Rêve knew was intended to be a part of her trousseau.

Now her embroidery was thrown aside and she started to her feet. Rêve ran into her arms.

"Oh, Antoinette, thank God you are here," she whispered.

Antoinette's eyes met Armand's as he came into the room and closed the door behind him.

"What has happened?" she inquired.

"Terrible things," Rêve said. "Oh, Antoinette, we are in danger, great danger, and you must save us."

"What danger?" she inquired, but she asked the question of Armand rather than of the girl she held to her breast.

"The Count de Durieux is a madman," Armand said briefly. "It would be impossible for Rêve to marry him, and I have learned that I am not the Marquis d'Augeron, but an Englishman sent over here to obtain information of my country's enemies."

Antoinette's face went if anything a little whiter than it had been before, but she made no movement and gave no exclamation. Then as she did not speak, Rêve murmured:

"We saw the Count performing a Black Mass, Antoinette. It was evil, wicked, terrifying; and when we were about to flee from the Castle, some officers arrived from Fontainebleau to arrest Armand. The Emperor has discovered that he is not my half-brother, because the real Armand d'Augeron had only one eye."

Still Antoinette did not speak. Her eyes were on Armand's face as if she questioned him, as if she asked of him some explanation which would satisfy her own unspoken question.

"We dare not stay here long," Armand said. "We must have fresh horses and food. Rêve has not eaten since dinner last night."

It was as if his more practical demands galvanised Antoinette to action.

"Sit down, my child," she said to Rêve, "and I will fetch you food and a bottle of wine. After that you can tell me more."

She took one of the candles and, opening the door, went from the room. They heard her footsteps going quickly down the passage, then Rêve looked at Armand.

"She is brave," she said. "She has always been like that when there is danger about. She does the practical thing. She says very little, but she suffers terribly because she loves me."

"I understand," Armand said, "and we must ask her what is best for you."

"I know that already," Rêve said in a quiet voice.

"No one has been here as yet," Armand went on as if he had not heard her, "or Antoinette would have been on her guard. They may be waiting on the road between St. Benis and Paris thinking we might come that way."

Rêve rose from the chair on which she had been sitting and crossed to the dressing-table. She took up a comb and tidied her hair, first letting her travelling cloak drop on the bed.

She stood there in her white evening gown, looking as if she were merely a light-hearted girl preparing for a ball. Armand watched her in silence; then as she turned towards him with a smile, he asked:

"Are you quite certain?"

She knew to what he referred.

"If you will not take me with you," she replied, "I will follow you. I cannot stay here, and there is no one else to whom I can go in this country and be free both from the Count and from the Emperor's vengeance. If you will not let me come with you, then there is really only one alternative."

"What is that?"

"I can die."

"You are not to talk like that!"

Armand's voice was abrupt, almost rough in its tone, and she knew that she had shocked and surprised him.

There was a sound outside the door and Armand, as if glad of the interruption, rose to open it. Antoinette stood there with a heavily laden tray. She came into the room before she spoke.

"I wakened Jacques," she said. "He has gone at once to ask Farmer Barrois to saddle two of his best horses and conceal them in the shed at the end of the far lake. They should be there within half an hour."

"We must not delay long," Armand said. "It is dangerous to linger."

"But first you must eat, *mes enfants,*" Antoinette replied.

She placed a whole roast chicken and half a ham on the table, then sliced a long crusted roll of newly baked bread with mathematical precision.

"I was hungry, but I did not realise how hungry until this moment," Rêve said laughingly, seating herself and reaching for a big slice of bread.

Armand smiled at her across the table.

"I am too hungry even to talk," he said.

"If that is an effort to stop me, you have failed," Rêve retorted. "I have always been able to talk and eat, haven't I, Antoinette?"

"Oh, my child, my little one," Antoinette said suddenly.

She sat down on her chair, the tears filling her eyes. Rêve bent forward and took her hand.

"You are not to grieve, darling Antoinette," she said. "I am happy, very happy, and that is what you have always wanted for me, isn't it?"

She met the older woman's eyes steadily as she spoke and Antoinette saw in that moment that the child she had loved and cherished had vanished and there was a woman in her place—a woman who loved and having loved had found the true purpose of life.

"So that's it," Antoinette whispered almost beneath her breath.

Rêve nodded, almost imperceptibly, but her fingers tightened on Antoinette's hand and by her answering pressure she knew that she had understood.

"I must have all the gold you concealed for me in the secret hiding-place," Armand said, pouring himself a glass of wine and apparently quite oblivious of the exchange of understanding between the two women. "It would also be an unmistakable help if we could find a map. Do you think there is one in the house?"

"There is one in the very room where your money is concealed," Antoinete said. "Come and look at it, Monsieur, if you have finished eating."

"We had better take the rest of the ham with us," Armand said. "Will you wrap it up so that it can go in my saddle bag? It would be wiser not to venture into any village until we are at least two days' journey away from here."

"I will do that while you are collecting your gold," Antoinette said. "Come, Monsieur."

She led him from the room along the passage, and Rêve, taking the remaining candle, turned in the opposite direction towards her own bedroom.

It was just as she had left it, her intimate possessions lying about on the tables, the bed covered with a crested white lace cover which Antoinette had worked with her monogram.

She put the candle down on her dressing-table, lit

two others and went to her wardrobe. It took her but a few minutes to change into a travelling gown of blue batiste. It was a pretty dress and she felt glad that Armand was to see her in it. She would wear her travelling-cloak over it.

Quickly she bundled together a few necessaries of underwear, combs, ribbons and washing material. If Armand was to carry the food on his saddle, she at least would have some luggage on hers.

She was so quick that she was ready before she heard Armand and Antoinette coming back from the other end of the house; and when she met them inside Antoinette's bedroom she laughed at the surprise on Armand's face at her changed appearance.

"You have been very quick," he said. "I should have liked to change myself."

"Then hurry," Rêve said. We had best be as inconspicuous as possible. Your white knee-breeches and satin coat are hardly the usual garb for a *bona fide* traveller."

"The clothes that you wore the first night you came here are lying over a chair in your bedroom, Monsieur," Antoinette said. "I laid them out ready for me to pack tomorrow morning."

"I shall be glad to wear my own things again," Armand said. "The clothes of the real Marquis are, I assure you, curst uncomfortable."

He went down the passage, and as soon as he was out of earshot, Antoinette looked at Rêve and her whole expression was one of interrogation. Rêve put her arms round her old nurse and held her very close.

"I love him," Rêve said. "You have guessed that. But he has forgotten that he loved me before he was wounded. I could not tell you who he was. I was too afraid that you might betray him or prevent me from helping him as I wished to do. I love him, and he loves me, only he has forgotten that since he believed me to be his sister."

"I guessed all the time that something unusual had occurred," Antoinette said quietly, "yet I could not trust my own instinct in the matter. I thought it strange

231

that you should care so deeply for your half-brother—
a brother you had never seen before. It disturbed me,
but now everything is very clear."

"You can trust Armand to look after me, Antoinette,
even if he has forgotten that he loves me. He is the
only man in the world for me, now and for ever."

"Yes, I know I can trust him," Antoinette said surprisingly. "I have known that every since he first came
here. He is a gentleman and honourable, whatever his
real name may be. Because of that I shall let him
take you away, *ma petite*— pray God to safety!"

"Oh, Antoinette, I shall miss you so, but somehow,
when we get to England, I shall contrive to send for
you. You will come to me?"

"I would come to you if you wanted me, even if you
asked me to swim the Channel," Antoinette said, and
Rêve had to smile through her tears.

The women were still clinging together when suddenly there came a loud knocking which seemed to rever-
berate throughout the whole house.

For a moment Rêve and Antoinette stared at each
other as if they could hardly believe they had heard
right; then the knocking came again and in the distance a voice cried:

"Open in the name of the Emperor."

"We are too late!"

Rêve could hardly breathe the words. She felt as if
anything she said would choke her. She heard Armand come running down the passage.

"Which way shall we go?" he asked Antoinette.

"By the garden door," Rêve replied quickly.

Antoinette snatched up a candle from the table.

"No," she said, "the house is sure to be surrounded.
There is only one sure way of escape now, and that is
by the secret passage under the lake."

"Then let us hurry," Armand said.

The words were unnecessary, for they all three knew
the urgency. The hammering came once again on the
door and now old Jacques was coming from the pantry,
moving slowly towards the outer door.

Holding the candle high above her head, Antoinette

led the way down another staircase which twisted and turned until finally it became a mere succession of stone steps leading apparently into the cellars of the *Château*.

As they descended, Rêve remembered the hidden door which led into the underground passage. It seemed only a little while ago that she had made this same journey, her hand clasped in Antoinette's, her lips pressed tightly in an effort not to cry out for fear of what was happening to her father.

They reached the bottom of the steps. Antoinette took a key from behind a brick and inserted it in a concealed lock. It was hard to turn, being rusty. They waited, and Rêve slipped her hand into Armand's.

His fingers tightened over hers and the pressure of them was as comforting and as reassuring as Antoinette's had been all those years ago.

13

The door of the underground passage swung open and there was a stench of musty air. Rêve released her hold of Armand's hand and clung to Antoinette.

"Come with us; come with us," she begged, without really thinking how it could be accomplished.

"No, no, *ma petite*," Antoinette replied. "It is best for me to stay here. I shall disclaim all knowledge of you and perhaps put those who are seeking for you off the scent. Go quickly now for there is no time to be lost."

She kissed Rêve's cheeks which were wet with tears, pushed her down the ancient stone steps and slammed the door behind her and Armand.

The draught caused by the closing of the door made the candle in Armand's hand flicker so that for a moment Rêve was afraid they would be in complete darkness. She stood trembling on the steps, afraid lest on taking a step forward she would slip and plunge headlong into the darkness below.

Then as the light flamed up and she saw Armand smiling at her, his hand outstretched to take hers, her courage returned and she smiled back at him, though a little tumultuously.

Frogs jumped ahead of them as they moved. The walls of the passage were damp and slimy while in some places the floor was nearly ankle-deep in water. But there was no time to be fussy about their surroundings.

Armand's hand drew Rêve insistently forward and she knew how anxious he was to get away from the vicinity of the *Château* before a more thorough search was made. If they did not hurry, the horses might be discovered and then they would be trapped with no chance of escape.

On and on they walked until Rêve's feet were soaked and the hem of her dress stained and bedraggled. She began to think that the passage would never come to an end and that they had in fact entered some terrible purgatory in which they must walk in semi-darkness for all eternity. As they advanced, the air became heavier and it was difficult to breathe.

The smell, too, was almost overpowering and Rêve felt she must have fainted had not the thought of the floor on which she must lie disgusted her to the point when it acted as a stimulant and kept her conscious when she thought she must choke or suffocate from the stench around them.

At last, when despite every resolution her feet grew slower and Armmand was literally dragging her along, she saw to her utter relief some steps rising upward and knew they had reached the end of the passage.

It took Armand only a few seconds to bound forward and force open the door which had already rusted off its hinges and was held in place only by the tangle of bushes and brambles outside, which effectively concealed its existence.

It was certainly well hidden for after he had got the door open it took Armand some time to extricate himself and Rêve from the sharp-thorned briars which seemed determined to hold them prisoners.

But at length, drawing deep breaths of the clean night air, they stepped from the bushes to find themselves in the wood at the far end of the lower lake.

Everything seemed very quiet, and Rêve gave a little murmur of relief, then checked herself immediately as Armand turned to her with a warning glance. He put his fingers to his lips and she knew that he was afraid that a sound, however slight, might attract attention.

They could not see the *Château* from where they stood, but a few yards farther on gave them a perfect view of the lake and at the far end of it the little Temple.

They had come, as it happened, almost precisely to the same spot on which Armand had stood that first night nearly a month ago when he had discovered Rêve bathing and had been spell-bound by her beauty.

But Rêve was not thinking of that first meeting, being intent only on their escape and wondering which was the safest and quickest route to the field where by this time the horses should be waiting for them.

Then as Armand did not follow her, she turned in surprise to look back at him and saw that he was staring at the Temple as if transfixed.

The moonlight was full on it and it looked very peaceful, its classic lines silhouetted against the dark trees, its ancient moss-covered steps leading down to the unruffled silver water.

Following the direction of Armand's gaze. Rêve remembered what an important part the Temple had played in both their lives.

It was there that Armand had surprised her and there that, though at first frightened by his presence, she had later known that ecstasy and wonder within her which now seemed but a glorious dream.

There Paul de Frémond had come to destroy their happiness, to denounce Armand as a spy and strike the dastardly blow which had changed him from her ardent, adoring lover to a man who did not even recognise her.

Yes, the Temple had brought them both joy and tragedy, Rêve thought, but now they must leave it for ever and quickly.

"Hurry, Armand," she whispered insistently.

Still he did not move. He was standing immobile as a statue, but there was something about the square set of his jaw and the rigidity of his figure which told Rêve that every muscle was tense, every nerve of his body alert. Impatiently, because of her fear for him, she laid her hand on his arm.

"Come, we must not linger here," she said a little louder.

Still he did not reply, and almost angrily she shook his arm.

"Armand, of what are you thinking? We must get away. We must find the horses."

It was then that he turned his head and looked down at her. For a moment she could not read the expression in his eyes, then slowly in a voice deep and choked with emotion, he said:

"It was you, wasn't it?"

She stared at him and her eyes widened and her breath came quickly.

"You—you have—remembered," she stammered.

"Oh, my beloved—my darling!"

His voice broke on the words. Suddenly he went down on his knee beside her and taking up the hem of her dress, soiled and wet though it was from the secret passage, he pressed it to his lips.

"Armand, your memory has returned?" she gasped.

He rose to his feet and, as she looked at his transfigured face, she felt her heart stop beating at the wonder and excitement of what she saw. He had remembered, and he loved her still.

She could see the love in his eyes, in the expression on his face and in the tender smile on his lips. This was Armand as he had been in those first moments when he had told her of his love, when she had surrendered herself utterly into his keeping.

"Oh, Armand, Armand!"

There were tears in Rêve's eyes, tears of happiness and relief, tears of inexpressible joy. It was difficult to pronounce even his name because of the trembling of her lips.

"My little love!"

He put out his arms and drew her close. She felt for a moment that she must swoon from the very joy and rapture of knowing that he still wanted her.

She looked up at him, knew that in one second she would feel his lips on hers and felt that nothing in the whole world was of consequence now that they had found each other again.

Then, as she trembled in his hold and his mouth drew nearer to hers, there was a sudden sound behind them, and a voice said sharply:

"Seize that man!"

They started apart. Armand turned, ready on the defensive. But it was too late.

Four tall, stalwart men sprang at him and though he fought and struggled, he was overpowered and after a few seconds they had him completely in their power though all four were breathing heavily at the effort of holding him captive.

Rêve, transfixed with horror, could only watch the struggle, her heart pounding in her breast, the blood throbbing in her temples and making it difficult for her to see clearly what was happening.

Then, when finally Armand could fight no more but must stand between his captors, his arms twisted behind him, Rêve saw who stood a little way behind them with a smile on her lips, the moonlight illuminating the contours of her exquisitive figure.

It was the Duchess de Monestier!

She was wearing a travelling-gown of coral velvet. There were diamonds falling like tiny cascades from her ears, and the fingers of her ungloved hands were glittering with rings.

She might have just stepped into the courtyard at Fontainebleau for she seemed curiously out of place in the wood. And with a sinking heart Rêve realised that the men holding Armand wore the Duchess's livery of peacock green trimmed with scarlet facings.

Without having time to think or really consider what she was doing, Rêve took a quick step forward.

"Madame—please—please let us go."

The Duchess ignored her as if she were not there. Her eyes were fixed on Armand's face, and as his eyes met hers, she said:

"We meet again, Monsieur. You have not forgotten me this time, I hope."

Her voice was mocking and there was some under-current of meaning beneath her words which Rêve could not comprehend. Armand managed to bow despite the strangehold of his captors.

"Your servant, Madame," he said as courteously as

238

if they had just encountered each other in a drawing-room.

"It is unfortunate that I must interrupt your travelling plans," the Duchess said, "but the Emperor—who, of course, must be obeyed—is particularly anxious to speak with the gentleman who styles himself the Marquis d'Augeron."

"In that case we must of course alleviate the Emperor's anxiety," Armand said.

"I have arranged that you should do so," Imogène said, "but we will first proceed to the *Château*. It will be more comfortable to continue our conversation in less rustic surroundings."

Still ignoring Rêve, the Duchess turned and led the way through a path which, winding through the wood, brought them to the road along which Armand had walked that very first night he had stayed at St. Benis.

A carriage drawn by four horses was waiting there. Footmen waited at the door, there were postilions on the horses and two coachmen on the coach.

"The prisoners will walk," she said sharply. "See that the girl does not escape."

Her lackeys bowed at her instructions and as the coach moved forward, the four men escorting Armand pulled him roughly on to the road behind it while two others walked on either side of Rêve.

They made no attempt to touch her and only kept pace with her as she hurried her footsteps to draw level with Armand.

"What are we going to do?" she asked, and she spoke in Engllish.

"Do not give up hope," he replied in the same language. "I will think of something."

"Oh, Armand, but what?" Rêve cried. "The Duchess intends to hand you over to the Emperor."

"Silence! Shut your mouths, there is to be no talking," one of the lackeys stormed out in an unnatural, aggressive voice as if by making a noise he could best assert his authority.

Armand and Rêve were silent, though both were busy with their own thoughts. There was indeed little they could say, Rêve thought, as they marched over the rough, dusty road which led them to one of the gates opening into the park.

As they trudged up the drive towards the *Château*, she felt as if she must cry aloud with the horror of what was happening.

If only they could have reached the horses, if only their plan of escape could have succeeded, how happy she might have been at this moment! Armand's memory had returned and he still loved her.

Yet what did the future hold for them now?

Rêve's thoughts turned away from the very thought of it, and yet she knew the answer to her questions. For Armand—imprisonment, then death.

Perhaps quickly, perhaps slowly, according to the will of the Emperor, but the end would be death, however merciful, however honourable an execution.

Her whole being cried out at the misery of it, at the waste and youth and happiness, at the destruction of so much beauty, so much loveliness.

Yet she knew there was no alternative unless by a miracle Armand could be saved, and what could that miracle be?

She did not cry. In fact her eyes were dry and absolutely tearless. She only knew a despair which seemed to freeze her very body, making it difficult for her even to move her limbs.

At last they reached the *Château* and Rêve saw to her surprise that every window was ablaze with light. As the front door was opened for them, there were lights in the passages and the hall, tapers flaring in every sconce.

Then Rêve saw the Duchess standing at the foot of the stairs almost breath-takingly lovely in her beauty, although her mouth was set in a hard line of defiance. Facing her stood a man whom Rêve recognised.

Dressed in his absurd, blue velvet uniform with high Hessian boots, his pale fleshy face contorted with rage, his spiteful, too-closely set eyes ablaze with anger, was Monsieur Fouché.

"I have my instructions from the Emperor himself,

Madame," he was saying, his voice grating and hoarse because he was so angry.

"Your instructions, Monsieur, were to capture the imposter calling himself the Marquis d'Augeron," Imogène replied, "but you are too late. He is already my prisoner, and I have no intention of handing him over to you."

There were perhaps a dozen of Fouché's men standing round the hall, and the Minister glanced towards them now as if in confirmation of his authority.

"You have not the power, Madame la Duchesse, to prevent me from taking this man back to Fontainebleau with me."

"You have no authority to take him from me and you know it," Imogène said sharply. "I, personally, shall on the morrow hand him over to the Emperor."

"But this is absurd, ridiculous; in fact, it is unconstitutional," Fouché spluttered. "As Minister of the Interior I have power over every citizen in this country. The Emperor requires that the man shall be captured, and the fact that you have apprehended him first must not prevent my bringing him to justice."

"And taking all the credit, of course," Imogène sneered. "My dear Monsieur Fouché, surely you are a big enough man to admit the fact that you are beaten. You will undoubtedly remember that it was my information and not yours which revealed that the gentleman in question was not whom he pretended to be.

"He lived in the Palace for nearly three weeks, he has attended the Emperor's councils, he has been treated in a most exceptional and favoured manner by yourself and many other ministers of state.

"Were you suspicious of him? Did you question for one moment his credentials? No, as far as he was comcerned you were blind, deaf and dumb!

"It was left to me, a woman, someone who concerns herself as little as possible with the machinations of your department, to discover that this gentleman was not the Marquis d'Augeron and that in consequence his actions were highly suspect.

"And having told the Emperor of this incredible
241

masquerade, having incited him to take quick, decisive action, what do you do?

"You go blundering up to the front door of this *Château*, shouting and screaming out who you are for half the neighbourhood to hear and giving those within plenty of warning and time to make their escape.

"Such action is hardly one of finesse, my dear Monsieur. I, on the contrary, guessed that there would be a bolt-hole from the *Château*. Most old houses have one. So I sent my lackeys to search the woods while you were marching your policemen up the drive.

"And what did they find? They found horses saddled and waiting in a disused cowshed. After that it was not difficult to make an intelligent deduction and to apprehend the prisoners—my prisoners, Monsieur Fouché."

The Minister of the Interior licked his thin lips.

"Your forethought is to be commended, Madame la Duchesse," he said, "but at the same time I must insist that, now that you have discovered the prisoner and luckily prevented his escape, it is my right and my duty to take him under guard to Fontainebleau."

"I have already told you you have no rights in this matter," Imogène replied. "I have a dozen men with me, and they are well trained in my service. Tomorrow I shall proceed to Fontainebleau and hand over my prisoner to the Emperor in person.

"What His Imperial Majesty does with him after that will doubtless be your business unless as a soldier and an aide-de-camp he is dealt with by the Duke de Tarente, Marshal of France."

This was a telling shot, for it was well known that Fouché loathed the Duke and disputed his powers on every possible occasion. His face grew, if possible, paler and his eyes were mere slits of rage as he replied:

"If Your Grace is determined, there is nothing more I can say in the matter. I can but bid you good night, Madame, and hope that you will not fail to remember that the Emperor and your country should be served before the gratification of your own desires."

His words were pointed and spiteful, but Imogène threw back her head and laughed.

"Your pin-pricks never fail to amuse me, Monsieur," she said. "But their points are too blunt for them to have much effect."

The Minister of the Interior bowed stiffly, and thrusting his hat on to his head, thereby contriving to look more ridiculous than usual, he strode down the passage towards the front door, followed by his men. Imogène laughed again and, turning to her own retainers who were standing behind Armand and Rêve, she said sharply:

"Take the girl and shut her up in her own bedroom. Guard her well. Remember, you are responsible for her with your lives. Bring the gentleman into the Salon. I will talk with him."

She turned and walked up the stairs. But before she had taken one step Rêve sped forward and, falling on her knees, took her hand in hers.

"Madame—Madame la Duchesse," she said, "spare Armand's life. He had lost his memory as you well know. I told him he was my half-brother, the Marquis d'Augeron, and he believed me. He did not know he was deceiving the Emperor or anyone else. He is innocent, Madame. If there is a fault, it is mine and mine alone. Spare him, spare him. Be merciful, as one day you yourself will ask for the mercy of God."

Armand made an impulsive gesture to move forward, but his guards restrained him.

"Do not listen to her, Madame," he cried out to Imogène, agonised that Rêve should try to save him by implicating herself.

But Imogène appeared not to have heard his interruption. She looked down at Rêve and perhaps because the younger woman looked so lovely kneeling there, her eyes were hard.

"Why should I show mercy either to you or to this man?" she asked. "Whoever is responsible, the fact remains that the Emperor himself has been tricked and imposed upon. Give me one good reason why I, as a patriot, should be merciful in such circumstances."

"I—I can think of none," Rêve stammered, "save—save that we love each other."

She could not have said anything more unfortunate, Imogène gave a laugh which had no humour in it, and pulling her hand away from Rêve's clinging fingers, walked on up the stairs. Rêve knelt on the bottom step, looking after her until two lackeys went forward and pulled her to her feet.

"Upstairs, if you please, Mademoiselle," one said.

Quietly she obeyed, not even looking back at Armand following her.

On the first landing Antoinette stood trembling. As Imogène drew level with her, she said in a sharp tone:

"Who are you?"

"If it please Your Grace, I am maid to the Comtesse Rêve de Valmont."

"Tonight you will attend to me," Imogène said. "Prepare the best bedroom and unpack my trunk."

"Very good, Your Grace," Antoinette said almost mechanically, her eyes on Rêve.

As if she sensed what Antoinette was thinking, Imogène said to the lackeys:

"See that these two women have no communication with one another. The Comtesse is to be locked in her room; and make certain she cannot escape through the window."

"Very good, Your Grace."

The two lackeys hurried Rêve down the passage.

"And you, woman, do as I instruct you," Imogène said to Antoinette, "or you will suffer the fate which waits your mistress."

"I am not afraid of that," Antoinette replied, "but if Your Grace will permit it, I would rather wait on my lady."

"You will do as you are told," Imogène said sternly, "or it will be worse not only for you, but for "your lady" as you call her. Every act of disobedience, every insult I endure in this place will be held to her account. Is that clear?"

"Quite clear, Your Grace," Antoinette said steadily, although her face was white.

"Then do as I command you," Imogène said, and she crossed the landing into the Silver Salon.

The candles were lit and, reflected and re-reflected in the silver-paned mirrors, they revealed the pleasing contours of the room, the polished furniture and the draperies of white brocade sprigged with silver flowers.

Imogène crossed to one of the mirrors and drew her hat trimmed with its big, curling ostrich feather from her dark head. She flung it down on a chair, smoothed her hair with skilful fingers and readjusted one of her diamond ear-rings. She was as unhurried and as unselfconscious about her movements as if she were alone in her own bedchamber.

Only when she was satisfied with her appearance did she turn towards the little group of men standing in the doorway.

"Release the prisoner," she said.

The men obeyed her, and Armand's numbed arms fell for a moment to his side before with an effort he raised them and started to massage the circulation back into his wrists and bloodless fingers.

Imogène watched him with a little smile. She seemed to take in every detail of his appearance—his handsome face and dark eyes, his broad shoulders under the well-fitting coat of grey whipcord in which he had come to France, his narrow hips and polished, high riding boots, which had been made by the most famous bootmaker in all St. James's.

There was nothing she missed, from the elegance of his skilfully tied cravat to the chiselled lines of his firm mouth.

At length, when he did not look at her, Imogène seated herself on the satin-covered sofa.

"Well, what have you to say for yourself?" she asked at length, and her tone was low and honeyed.

"Very little," Armand replied coolly. "I must of course be allowed to reserve my defence until I am confronted by my judges."

"That will be tomorrow," Imogène said. "You will

245

find it difficult to convince Napoleon Bonaparte of your innocence."

"I should not, of course, try to do anything so stupid," Armand replied.

"Then you admit that you are guilty?"

"Guilty of what?"

Imogène seemed to hesitate for a moment.

"Of spying," she said.

Armand smiled.

"You are extraordinarily intelligent, Madame, for a lovely woman."

Imogène's expression seemed to soften.

"So now you are prepared to pay me compliments. Last time we met you were not so anxious to do so."

"Last time we met I was suffering from the severe disability of having lost my memory. Tonight it returned to me; it returned just a few moments before you ambushed us so successfully."

"And what have you remembered?" Imogène asked curiously.

"I have remembered who I am, why I came to France, and everything that concerns my past life," Armand replied. "Reprehensible though it may be, it is extraordinary how lost one feels without a past."

Imogène laughed.

"I wonder if I should miss mine," she remarked reflectively.

"You would undoubtedly do so," Armand answered, "if suddenly all memory of yourself, what you had said, done or been was erased as a child might clean a lesson from its slate. You might under those conditions even find it difficult to remember how one should behave in certain circumstances."

Imogène's eyes narrowed a little.

"So that is your excuse for the other night," she said softly.

"Excuse is the wrong word," Armand parried. "Regret is one I find much easier to use."

"It is too late for that," Imogène said. "You must remember that I am angry with you, very angry. That is why I have taken the trouble to denounce you, to

246

bring you to justice. I am not as a rule interested in justice, but for people who hurt me I have no mercy."

Her voice was sharp.

"That I can well understand," Armand said suavely. "I assure you that I ask no mercy for myself. You must forgive the tender-hearted pleas of my little half-sister."

"Do you still think of her like that?" Imogène asked quickly. "I understand that she is no relation of yours."

"She has befriended me and protected me," Armand said evasively. "If it was not the action of a relative, it is that of a woman. Your sex, Madame, invariably shows sympathy and tenderness towards those who are sick or in trouble."

Imogène looked up at him and her eyes were veiled. "I wonder if I can believe you?" she said.

"I am asking you to believe nothing," Armand replied, "save that tonight I am a very different man from the lost, bewildered fool who saw the gates of paradise open before him and ran back to hell."

Imogène's breath came quicker, stirring her high pointed breasts. There was something in Armand's voice which seemed to perturb her. A fire flickered in the depths of her eyes and her red lips parted.

"It is time that Your Grace retired for the night," Armand said surprisingly. "Have I your permission to kiss your hand?"

He glanced at the four men standing at his side as he spoke. Imogène did not reply in words. She raised her arm and the light of the candles glittered on that great diamond she wore on her third finger.

Armand crossed the room, took her hand in his and raised it. She felt his lips hard and insistent no the back of her hand, then he turned it over and kissed the palm. It was the long lingering kiss of passion. She felt herself tremble, as an irresistible languor swept over her in a sensuous wave of desire.

She knew the feeling so well, it was almost as familiar as breathing, yet always it had the power to charm and enchant her. Armand's eyes were looking into hers and as he raised his head from her hand, he said softly:

"Send the men away."

She smiled then, a smile of triumph and elation, the smile of a woman utterly confident of her own beauty, completely sure of herself. She glanced towards the lackeys and there was no hesitation in the order she gave them.

"Leave the room and wait outside in the corridor," she said sharply.

Then, as they turned smartly to obey her, she gave a little low laugh of excitement, and, putting up her hand, she drew Armand's head towards her.

He felt her lips, warm, greedy and lustful; but even as they touched his, as he pressed them for one moment before the closing of the door told him that they were alone, his hands came up towards Imogène's long white neck. His fingers were hard and merciless as, encircling it, he squeezed the rounded column, at first gently, then exerting more and more pressure until finally her arms fell away from his shoulders and her mouth flew open as she gasped again and again for breath.

She could not scream, could not utter a cry of any sort and her eyes, looking up at him, expressed first astonishment, then fear until they began to protrude in an ugly manner.

Still Armand's pressure on Imogène's neck increased until her face grew blotched and purple, and it seemed as if she must suffocate without air.

Only then did he allow her to fall back against the satin pillows, gasping for breath, too weak even to raise her hands.

"Listen to me," Armand said quietly, "and if you make the slightest attempt to cry out, I will kill you before anyone can come to your rescue. You are in my power, completely and absolutely, and remember I am a desperate man. I have nothing to lose by murdering you.

"If you take me to Fontainebleau, my life is forfeit

anyway. Besides that, there is little hope for the woman I love and the woman I intend to marry.

"In your vanity you have played into my hands, you have made yourself my prisoner and I am no longer yours. Obey me or I swear I will throttle you.

"I shall go to the door now and send one of the footmen for Antoinette. When she comes, I will tell you further what I intend to do. If you scream for help, if you make any attempt to recall your men, my hands will be on your throat long before they are in the room, and next time I touch you, you will not survive to remember it."

He saw terror in Imogène's eyes but he knew that she could not speak. He went to the door, opened it a very little and said to the lackey outside:

"Madame la Duchesse requires the maid Antoinette. Fetch her immediately."

"Very good, Sir."

The lackey's voice was quite respectful, and Armand reflected that Imogène's servants would doubtless be used to her vagaries where her lovers were concerned and would not find it unduly surprising that the prisoner —seeing that he was young and handsome—should now be giving them orders.

Armand closed the door and went back to the sofa. Imogène was making a strange sobbing noise in her throat. Her neck was covered with crimson weals from the strength of his hands and her eyes still appeared to be protruding unnaturally.

He said nothing, only stood there and after a moment she gave a little groan and her hands fluttered upwards.

He heard a footstep outside and, giving her a warning glance was at the door before the lackey could open it and usher in Antoinette.

"Come in, Antoinette," Armand said. "Madame wants you."

Antoinette looked surprised at seeing him free, but she said nothing, merely slipped inside the room. Armand shut the door and locked it, then he went back to stand at Imogène's side.

"Antoinette," he said, "I have just given the Duchess a demonstration of what it feels like to be strangled. She is suffering from the effects of my fingers as you will see by the marks on her neck. For the moment she is afraid of me, but very shortly she will be thinking and planning how to have me executed and perhaps Rêve with me.

"It is a question of wits. If I win, I save both Rêve and myself; if the Duchess wins, we know the answer—— Will you help me?"

Antoinette looked up at him.

"You know that I will do anything in my power, Monsieur, for the child I have loved since a baby."

"Then, Antoinette, I have a plan by which we may all three escape," he said.

He turned as he spoke and took up from the table of inlaid ivory standing by the fireplace a little gold-handled paper knife which many generations of de Valmonts had used to cut the leaves of their books.

It was in reality a jewelled dagger fashioned by some Italian craftsman in the Middle Ages. It was an amusing toy in the more civilised world in which it now existed, but it had been intended for sterner tasks—the protection of a lady's virtue—and it was sharp enough to be an adequate defence against robbers or a surprise attack from a fiend. Armand turned it over with his fingers.

"If you love your mistress," he said to Antoinette, "you will not hesitate to do what I ask of you. The woman you see lying here on the sofa is hard, ruthless and utterly without mercy for man or woman. There is only one thing she fears—the destruction of her own beauty. Take this dagger, keep it in your hand, and if she makes the slightest attempt to disobey my commands or betray us, slash her across the face with it. Will you do that?"

"I will do exactly as Monsieur commands," Antoinette said quietly.

Imogène gave a little cry.

"But you could not do that to me," she said, but

250

her voice was tremulous and weak, very unlike her usual authoritative tone.

"Antoinette will do it for the sake of Rêve de Valmont—my future wife," Armand replied. "As I would strangle you willingly to save her one moment of unhappiness, one second of fear or misery. For the first time, Madame la Duchesse, you have met in your life two people who are not slaves to your beauty nor afraid of your venom.

"You have the choice of two things and two only, either to obey us or to lose that beauty which you have used as a weapon to demand what you would of life. Choose, and choose quietly."

Imogène's eyes turned from Armand's face to Antoinette. If she expected the older woman to look shocked or perturbed by what she had been asked to do, she was disappointed.

Antoinette met her gaze steadily and without emotion. Perhaps Imogène sensed the almost fanatical love that Antoinette bore Rêve and knew that behind that calm expression was a strength of purpose which would enable her to go willingly to the guillotine for a girl to whom she had been father and mother, nurse and counsellor for so many years.

Antoinette moved the little jewelled dagger. The light from the candles glittered on the shining steel and its sharp, treacherous point. Imogène looked again at Antoinette's face. It was stern and unyielding and without a hint of mercy or weakness about it.

"Choose," he said briefly, and again in that strange tone which she hardly seemed to recognise as her own, Imogène replied hoarsely:

"I will do what you wish."

14

"You will lean on my arm as if you felt extreme affection towards me," Armand said.

"I hate you," Imogène replied through clenched teeth. "I can only pray that the Emperor's troops will overtake us and that you will die a lingering, painful death—as you well deserve."

"By all the laws of justice your prayers, rusty from long disuse, should not be answered," Armand said.

Imogène stood biting her lip, her eyes roving speculatively round the room as if she sought vainly for some weapon by which she herself could carry out his execution.

But Armand had laid his plans well. He had forced Imogène to send for her major-domo and inform him that they were leaving immediately for the coast.

The man received the news with the imperturbable calm of a well-trained servant and, as Armand guessed, he showed no surprise at receiving such a strange order.

He was used to Imogène's vagaries and merely imagined that she had fallen in love with her handsome prisoner and was therefore driving him out of the reach of Imperial interference or Monsieur Fouché's spies— the latter being as cordially disliked by the Duchess's staff as by their mistress.

After the orders had been given for the carriage to be packed, Armand made Imogène give instructions that Rêve should be brought to the Silver Salon.

She had come into the room, wide-eyed and very pale. She had suspected that the summons meant further trouble, perhaps immediate transportation for all of them to Fontainebleau.

When Armand had explained the position to her, abruptly without mincing his words, the colour had flown back into her cheeks. She had said little, only looked with an expression in her eyes which made him glance quickly away as if he were afraid that to linger might mean a forgetfulness of everything else save their two selves.

It was indeed imperative that nothing should happen to hinder their departure or delay even by a minute their escape towards freedom.

At any moment Monsieur Fouché might think of an excuse to bring him back to the *Château,* a company of soldiers might arrive or even some of the Count de Durieux's bodyguard or retainers.

Armand was well aware that there would be a great number of people searching for him and that to evade capture was not going to be easy.

Everything depended on their acting swiftly and so unexpectedly that their pursuers would be thrown off the scent. Old Jacques was fetched upstairs at Armand's request, their plans were carefully explained to him and he was told what he must say to every inquiry, to every question.

The old man was slow of understanding and his brain was not quick, but he was loyal and devoted and ready to shed his very life-blood in service to the de Valmont family.

He promised complete obedience to every one of Armand's instructions, and then with tears in his eyes he kissed Rêve's hand.

"I am an old man, Mademoiselle," he said. "I am feared that I shall never see you again, but as long as there is breath in my body I shall never forget you and I will pray for you night after night."

"Thank you, Jacques," Rêve replied gently, deeply moved by the old man's words.

Imogène gave a little laugh, disdainful and mocking.

"These sentimental farewells are quite unnecessary," she said. "Tell your old servant that, if he wishes, he will be able to see you meet your death by public execution. A spectacle not without enjoyment! Espe-

253

cially when one watches the traitors to France embrace Madame Guillotine!"

No one had answered Imogène's spiteful words, but it was as if they spurred them all to an ever further realisation of the danger which beset them.

"We must hurry, Monsieur," Antoinette said a little breathlessly to Armand.

He nodded his head.

"I am but waiting for them to announce that the coach is at the door."

Antoinette had fetched Imogène's cloak, an elaborate garment of coral velvet, its hood lined with white ermine so that it framed her dark head as if with a halo. She looked so lovely that for a moment Rêve felt a pang of envy and of jealousy.

But one glance at the expression on Armand's face swept all such thoughts from her mind, for while she was looking at Imogène he had been looking at her. The intensity and passion in his gaze brought the blood to her cheeks.

She felt her heart quicken its beat, she felt that same ecstasy and joy course through her veins that had been hers when they had first met, when they had first known that enchanted magnetism and realised that something untoward was happening to both of them.

That magic had now been recaptured. They were both actually conscious of each other's presence, both kindled with the same fire, tingling with the same infusion of happiness which despite the danger in which they stood seemed to run through their veins like wine.

There was a knock on the door.

"The coach is ready, Your Grace."

Armand glanced at Imogène and held out his arm in courteous formality. She hesitated for a moment, then slipped her arm through it.

"You know what orders to give," he said, "you know, too, what, if you fail to give them or make one cry of help, you may expect?"

"Yes, indeed," Antoinette said quietly. "I shall act at once, Madame."

Her fingers closed over the little jewelled dagger as

she spoke, and Imogène looked away from it with a shudder which she could not almost entirely suppress.

Rêve pulled her own travelling-cloak a little more over her shoulders and picked up the bundles of clothes and small necessities which Antoinette had brought from their rooms while they were waiting. Armand's luggage was very simple.

He merely crossed the room to where, lying under a glass case on a gilt console-table, was a jewelled sword which had belonged to Rêve's father.

The Count had been a noted duellist and he had won a great many prizes and competitions in the art of duelling when he was a young man. When he thought himself too old to continue to give exhibitions of his skill, he had had his favourite *épée de combat* embellished with a beautiful hilt and scabbard and laid out on a bed of crimson velvet in the Silver Salon at Valmont.

"My third hand," he used to call it laughingly, and he had kept the blade polished bright and clean as if it were in frequent use.

The sword was one of the few things Antoinette had been able to hide in a secret place before she left the *Château* with the child Rêve, and although the revolutionaries had sacked the house and had even pulled some of the panelling down in search of treasure, they had not discovered the sword or the other things which Antoinette had concealed so skilfully.

On Rêve's return to Valmont the sword had gone back to its customary place in the Silver Salon, where it reminded Rêve more poignantly of her father than any portrait or statue could have done.

It often seemed to her that the very spirit of him was beside the weapon which he had loved so dearly and which seemed to typify both his courage and his pride.

As Armand walked across the salon to take the sword from its nesting place and clasp it round his waist, she had been glad and in some ways reassured that he had chosen this particular weapon to defend them from whatever lay ahead.

255

Now they were ready. They had only to descend the broad staircase to the hall, walk to the front door, step into the waiting carriage and they would be off. Rêve was conscious that her heart was beating almost suffocatingly as she followed Armand, the Duchess leaning on his arm.

Lackeys bowed them into the coach, Imogène and Rêve seated themselves on the back seat with Armand and Antoinette facing them.

As the door closed they heard the crack of the coachman's whip, the jingle of the harness, a jerk as the horses took the pull of the shafts; then slowly the wheels began to turn. They were on their way.

No one spoke. Rêve knew that both Armand and Antoinette were as tense as she was herself as they drove down the long drive and through the iron gates on to the road which led to St. Benis.

At the beginning of the village they heard the horses' hoofs ringing on the cobbles, and the coach, well-sprung though it was, rattled and rolled a little.

But no one was thinking of discomfort. Instead they were anticipating with horror what would happen if there should come a command to halt.

There were two coachmen on the box, two footmen standing behind, four horses each carrying its own postilion, and the other half-dozen of the Duchess's servants were on horse-back, riding perfectly matched black horses with a touch of Arab in their breeding.

There flashed through Rêve's mind that Armand would be able to escape much quicker if he were to take one of these tireless stallions and ride on alone. But even as the thought came to her she knew that it was hopeless to suggest it. Armand would never leave her.

She was certain of that; and though she might have ridden beside him, neither of them now would abandon Antoinette to the mercy of the Duchess.

No, Armand's plan was the only possible one, and Rêve was surprised how well and how successfully it had succeeded so far. She could hardly believe that Imogène would be so frightened as to agree to everything that was suggested to her.

Yet she had intercepted one glance which the Duchess had given the little dagger that Antoinette carried and she realised that her fear was a very real one.

Only now when they were together in the coach and in no danger of being overheard did Imogène allow her anger to show itself and her fury to blaze forth in the livid fury of her eyes and the twisted bitterness of her mouth.

Rêve could see Imogène's face very clearly by the light of the silver candle lanterns fixed in the corners of the carriage, and, looking at her, she thought to herself that it was strange that such exquisite beauty could be so evil.

There was indeed unbridled evil in Imogène's expression as she rested her head against the soft padded cushions of the coach and spoke directly to Armand.

"You fool!" she said. "What do you think to gain by this? Do you imagine that Fouché, hating me as he does for having been a jump ahead of him, will allow you to escape so easily? The *Château* will have been watched, for he will be waiting to escort us to Paris on the morrow whatever I might have said to prevent him."

"I have thought of that," Armand said simply. "Monsieur Fouché was expecting you to spend what remained of the night at Valmont, and doubtless, knowing your habits, he would not anticipate that you would be on the road much before noon."

Imogène pressed her lips together to prevent an angry exclamation. Fouché would doubtless expect her plans to take that course exactly for, had it not been for Armand's unexpected behaviour, she would undoubtedly have slept at Valmont and allowed nothing to interfere with her own desire to rest.

"I have been reckoning," Armand said, "that we have with any luck got about ten or eleven hours' start. Our only real danger is that we may encounter the Emperor's troops or be questioned by some local authority who, having been informed of my escape, may make inquiries of any unexpected wayfarers."

Rêve spoke for the first time.

"Is there any reason why they should anticipate that you should go north?" she asked. "Do they suspect who you are?"

"That is for Madame la Duchess to answer," Armand said.

Imogène tossed her head.

"I shall tell you nothing which might alleviate your anxiety," she said. "I hope the fear of death stalks beside you until in very terror you betray yourself."

Armand threw back his head and laughed.

"You are trying to frighten us," he said, "and somehow, strange though it may seem to you, Madame, I am not frightened. I have a prophetic presentiment within me that we shall all reach home in safety."

His words made Rêve think for a moment of Valmont. Once again she had left her home, once again penniless she was fleeing from those who would take her life and destroy everything she loved and held dear.

Yet even as the thought came to her with all its melancholy, she knew that, true though it was, it was of no consequence.

When she had left Valmont before, Antoinette had been beside her; now not only was Antoinette still there but she was with Armand; and in that moment clearly and assuredly she knew that, while she might be leaving her home, she was going to another. Wherever Armand might be, wherever they might dwell together, that would be home for her, henceforth and for ever.

In the past she had been utterly and almost overwhelmingly lonely. Now she would no longer be alone.

It was not so much the fact that he was beside her; she was part of him. They belonged together, one in spirit from the very first moment of their meeting when their eyes had met and they had known that strange union of souls.

Yes, Rêve knew that to her Armand meant home, the protection, comfort, love and understanding which she had never known in her childhood and had missed in her adolescence, but which now she had found in her womanhood.

Love had brought her all these things and even in death they would not be divided.

At peace within her own heart she smiled across the coach at Armand, and when he smiled back at her she felt as if the sun was pouring through the window and it was no longer night.

Antoinette bent forward to tuck the rug more closely over her knees.

"Sleep, my little one, and you, Monsieur. I will keep watch over this lady. You can trust me and you can both relax."

"I know that we can trust you, Antoinette," Armand said, "but we will take it in turn, you and I, to act as gaoler. In five hours' time we should be at Amiens. There we will change horses before it is daylight."

"Then sleep until we reach Amiens," Antoinette said.

Under the circumstances Rêve thought it would be impossible to sleep, and yet the strain and emotion of the past hours had taken their toll. After a while, try as she would to keep awake, she felt her eyes closing and her head nodding against the soft cushions.

Before she slept, she realised that Imogène was asleep first, her breath coming evenly and rhythmically, her hands with their heavy diamond rings lying limp in the lap of her dress.

"At least she cannot be overburdened by her guilty conscience," Rêve thought with a little smile as she too fell asleep.

She was wakened by the sound of voices as they drove into the yard of an Inn. Ostlers came running, the coachmen climbed down from the box, and there was the usual interchange of pleasantries, questions and an occasional oath or two.

Armand stepped out from the carriage. Rêve heard his voice, quiet and commadning, say:

"Madame instructs me to tell you that she requires——"

But his words were lost. Imogène, wide awake now, bent forward in an attempt to look out of the window.

There was a great number of people outside, some seeing to the horses, others bringing food and drink for the attendants, the proprietor adding up the accounts and a miscellaneous collection of stable boys, grooms, waiters and spectators who seemed to spring from no-where but to be unaccountably wakeful at such an early hour in the morning.

Suddenly as swift as a panther might spring Imogène put out her hand to grasp the handle of the door. She pulled it open and in one single moment would have been outside the coach had not Antoinette moved as quickly as she did.

The pointed tip of the dagger was slashed against her wrist, inflicting a deep scratch which began im-mediately to bleed.

Imogène gave a little cry and let go of the handle of the door. Antoinette pulled it shut with a slight slam.

"How dare you!" Imogène said. "You have hurt me! Look what you have done!"

In answer Antoinette drew a large clean white linen handkerchief from the pocket of her dress.

"I had my orders, Madame," she said. "I am ready to obey them."

Imogène snatched the handkerchief from her and attempted to stop the flow of blood.

"You have injured me," she said. "We must have a doctor immediately lest I bleed to death."

"It is but a scratch, Madame," Antoinette said suave-ly. "You are fortunate that I did not do as Monsieur had instructed me and strike at your face."

"You wouldn't dare!" Imogène muttered.

Antoinette bent forward, and taking the handker-chief from her, tore it into several strips and skilfully bound up the wound on her wrist.

"Madame is making a great mistake," she said quietly, "if she thinks that I would hesitate in any way to save those I love. And even if it were not a question of saving them and it would be too late to do that, I think I would be justified in despoiling Madame of a beauty which has brought unhappiness and misery to so many."

"What do you mean?" Imogène said angrily.

"The day I left Fontainebleau for Valmont," Antoinette replied, "the maid in the next apartments to us was weeping bitterly. I gave her what comfort I could and inquired what had distressed her to such an extend. She told me that she was personal maid to the old Comtesse de Méry, an old lady who had come to court to petition the Emperor for the return of her son's *Château* near Lyons.

The Emperor had granted her request, but though the *Château* was released, the present owner, Comte Jules de Méry, would not return to it. He would not leave Fontainebleau because he was besotted by a very lovely lady.

Everyone else had ceased to be of consequence to him; but while his mother waited and prayed that he might return to sanity and to an appreciation of the favours which had been granted to him, the lady of his choice tired of him, and so the Comte killed himself.

He was found dead in his room, with his throat cut from ear to ear. It was an ugly sight to a stranger like myself, but much worse for a mother who had loved her only son."

There was a pause as Antoinette stopped speaking, then Imogène remarked with an air of defiance.

"Jules was always an hysterical youth, a more balanced person would not have behaved in such a manner."

"A more balanced person might not have loved you so deeply, Madame," Antoinette replied quietly.

The door of the coach was opened and Armand got in. He carried in his hand a plate piled high with fresh crisp bread, buttured and sandwiched with slices of ham.

"It is the best I could procure," he said, "although it is hardly suitable fare for ladies of quality."

Rêve laughed.

"When one is hungry," she said, "there is a very

obvious equality between ladies of quality and more ordinary folk."

She took a roll and dug her white teeth into the crisp crust. After a moment Imogène put out her hand and helped herself. It was then that Armand saw the bandage round her wrist.

"Have you hurt yourself?" he inquired.

She gave him a glance of unmasked venom, but did not reply. He did not press the question further.

The new horses started off at a brisk rate. Armand had obviously given instructions for the coachmen to drive as quickly as they could, but the journey was by no means smooth and at times the coach rocked dizzily from side to side.

It was Antoinette's turn to sleep, and after a mile or so Rêve felt sleepy too. Her eyelids closed, then she was suddenly aware that Imogène had leant forward towards Armand. She laid her unbandaged hand on his arm and in a whisper which was very soft and beguiling, she said:

"Why do we not stop fighting? Let us be friends—you and I."

"Have you a capacity for friendship?" Armand inquired, and there was a hint of amusement in his tone.

In answer Imogène's fingers tightened over his arm.

"You are going to England," she said. "If you ask me, I will come with you."

"And leave your life here—your position, your wealth, your influence at Court?" Armand inquired.

"What do they matter?" Imogène replied. "The things I have acquired have all been part of a game which I play against the world, against everyone. Have you never thought how amusing it is to realise that one can get anything one wants, anything because one is beautiful?

"I was only a child when I first sensed my power, and then when I began to exploit it I knew that while there were men in the world, whether they be Emperors or crossing-sweepers, I could have everything that I wished from them, and more besides."

"A dangerous philosophy," Armand said.

"Why?" Imogène inquired. "What else does anyone strive for save power? All seek it—some effectively, some ineffectively. Whether they be Napoleon Bonaparte or a man who works in an office, they toil and sweat for one thing and one thing only—power, power, power! To have what they want, to gain what they desire, to achieve in a greater or lesser degree that for which their heart craves."

"And what do you want," Armand asked, "when you have so much?"

"I want you," Imogène replied softly. "You are the only man I have ever met who has turned from me, who has repulsed me. To make you mine I would follow you to the uttermost parts of the earth. Can you refuse me now that I have told you that?"

Armand looked at her and surprisingly his eyes were gentle.

"A few months ago," he said, "I might have been flattered by what you suggest, but I should not have understood what made you offer yourself to me. Now I understand your need and I am desperately sorry for you."

"Sorry?" Imogène queried. "Why should you be sorry for me?"

"Because you are looking for something, because you do not know what that something is, because so far you have failed in your search for it," Armand replied.

Imogène knit her lovely brows together.

"What do you mean?" she queried.

"I mean, Madame, that you are finding life as empty and as boring as I found it but a short while ago when I agreed to come to France in search of adventure. Life has offered you many things, things that seem delectable and infinitely desirable, but they turn to ashes in your mouth.

"You are bored as I was bored with the people around you. You are bored with those who seek you out, you are bored with their desires and your own. You know that something is missing, you know that your life is empty; but you are not quite certain what it is you want, and you won't be happy until you get it."

263

"It is you I want," Imogène said a little defiantly.

"No," Armand shook his head. "You only want me because I have proved difficult. Had I been easy, tractable, you woud have tired of me long since. No, what you are looking for is love, real love, which comes to us but once in a lifetime. Perhaps you will find it, perhaps it will elude you, yet without it you will always be alone, unhappy and unsatisfied."

"It is your love I want," Imogène said desperately.

"My love such as it is," Armand said, and there was a sudden ring in his voice, "is given to someone else. She is asleep beside you, Duchess, and perhaps you will wonder what it is that she has which you have not got. You are both women, both very beautiful. You have had great experience; you have had opportunities for development which Rêve has never had, so that you might easily think that you would find it easier for you to captivate a man than for a girl who is simple, unsophisticated and innocent.

"But actually none of these things are of real consequence. Love is a thing which happens between a man and a woman in its perfection but once in a lifetime and only to those who are fortunate—others may never find it.

"From the moment I first saw Rêve I loved her. I knew then what it was I had missed ever since I was old enough to think, what it was I longed for in every woman but found lacking, what it was I wanted from life and yet had not been able to express in words. It was true love! My love for Rêve and hers for me!"

"And what of me?" Imogène asked and her voice was shrill.

"Our lives have crossed by accident," Armand replied quietly. "Had you not forced the issue between us, we should not be here now."

"I want you! Why should I give you up?"

Imogène's voice was hard. Armand looked across the carriage at her. The dawn was breaking and already the first pale fingers of the sun were creeping up the sky, its light dimming the flickering candles and revealing something haggard and sharp about Imogène's face.

It was not that she looked old, it was just that there was something empty and meaningless in her beauty. There was no light shining behind the mask that was her face, there was no inner spirit to radiate through the translucent depths of her eyes.

Armand sighed, and did not answer her question so that after a moment Imogène said:

"Have you thought of what will happen to me after this? I shall be the laughing stock of all France. The Emperor will accuse me of treachery, of having conspired against him in having allowed you to escape. I shall be fortunate if I can convince him that you outwitted me.

"And if eventually he believes the truth that I let you go unwillingly do you not suppose that my enemies will make capital of it? Fouché, who loathes me, the women who have been jealous of me, the wives and mistresses who have been neglected because their men have left them for me. How they will laugh, how they will sneer!

"There will never be a conversation in which some barbed sentence will not be introduced about how I wished to protect my beauty rather than serve the Emperor. I am not a fool, I have always faced facts and I know exactly what awaits me if I return to Fontainebleau alone.

"Take me with you, take me to England. You talk of love, let me teach you what love means."

Armand sighed.

"What do you know of love but the hunger of the body?" he asked. "A lust which can be easily satisfied and which sooner or later satiates those who hunger for it. No, Madame, I doubt if you could teach me anything of the love such as I have glimpsed for but a brief moment and which I know to be the path which leads to paradise.

"A love of the spirit, a love of the soul! Something which I hardly believed existed until now—a love with an inner beauty more compelling than any superficial loveliness, a love which is the perfect unity of a man and woman who are made for each other."

"You believe that nonsense of souls and spirits?" Imogène exclaimed. "You fool!"

"If I am a fool," Armand replied, "then allow me to be happy in my folly. I ask nothing else. Go back to your Palace, to your Emperor and the intrigues of society. You will soon forget that I existed, and your enemies will have fresh escapades to talk about.

"You said yourself you always got what you wanted. There must be an exception to every rule, in your case perhaps only one exception, but it is easily forgotten."

Imogène put her fingers up to her eyes and after a moment she said in a strangled voice:

"And suppose I cannot forget?"

Before Armand could answer, Antoinette stirred and woke.

"Where am I?" she asked in a voice of fear; then looking round her, she saw Rêve and smiled.

"Pardon, Monsieur," she whispered to Armand, "but I had a bad dream. I dreamt that we were captured."

"Do not perturb yourself. Dreams always go by the contrary," Armand said reassuringly.

But as if Antoinette's words perturbed him, he let down a window and putting his head out, he shouted to the coachman to go faster.

Rêve did not open her eyes. She had no wish for Armand or the Duchess to know that she had overheard their conversation. She did not wish to embarrass them and was only too conscious of her gratitude and the happiness swelling within her heart to have any desire to discomfort the Duchess or add to her unhappiness.

She could find it easy now to be sorry for her. She could understand perhaps better than Armand what fate awaited her on her return to Fontainebleau.

But worse still, Rêve thought, to have lost Armand, to have staked everything, to have sacrificed pride and self-respect in one desperate effort at frankness and to be repulsed. Could anything be worse? Fontainebleau and the jeers of one's enemies could not hurt as much as that.

The day passed slowly. Because they had nothing else to do, they played cards and Imogène was quite childishly delighted when she won not once but continually at whist.

"My luck is changing," she said, looking from under her dark eyelashes at Armand. "Lucky in one thing, lucky in others."

She swept their money off the table into her lap.

"My luck has changed," she repeated. "Are you afraid?"

"If we are honest, we would all admit to being afraid to something," Rêve said.

"Very well, I will be honest and say that I am afraid because things have gone so well," Armand said with a smile. "We got away from the *Château,* we have found posting-horses and good ones, the coach has not broken down and we have not been intercepted as yet."

Rêve gave a little cry.

"I hate those last two words," she said. "Do not speak of things having gone right. It is unlucky. The gods are made jealous."

"*Le Bon Dieu* will understand," Antoinette said quietly.

Imogène gathered up the cards.

"Shall we play again?" she asked.

Armand looked out through the window.

"I think there is hardly time," he said. "We are approaching the environs of Calais."

"When we get there what happens?" Rêve asked apprehensively.

In answer Armand let down the window and spoke to the coachman on his box. After some distance the horses turned down a narrow dusty lane which took them along the cliff side.

"Where are we going?" Rêve asked.

He smiled at her reassuringly.

"There is something else I have remembered," he replied.

The coach came to a halt beside a group of fisher-men's cottages. It was a desolate part of the coast and there were only a few barefooted children playing on the shore who stared at the dusty, mud-splashed carriage with its tired attendants, their gorgeous liveries in strange contrast to the fatigue on their faces.

Armand got out.

"Guard the Duchess," he said to Antoinette, and went slowly down to the huts.

One by one over the horizon fishing boats appeared, their patched sails billowing in the evening breeze. They were heading for home, their catch on board, their men hungry and weary after a long day's fishing.

It grew dark and still Armand did not return.

Rêve bent forward apprehensively and looked out of the window. She could see him standing outside one of the huts, a fisherman by his side. The man held something in his hands; Rêve saw him bending over it and realised that he was kindling a light in a heavy lantern.

Some minutes passed and then the light flickered and grew stronger. The fisherman held the lantern by the handle and swung it backwards and forwards, signalling out to sea. Rêve strained her eyes.

Already it was hard to see anything but the fishing boats which were being pulled in on the beach below them. Again and again the man flashed his lamp. She could see Armand looking at an horizon which was almost indistinct now as the darkness both of sea and sky met and were united.

At length, far away, so small and indistinct that after a moment Rêve felt she must have dreamed it, there came an answering signal. It came and went, came again and then vanished.

Had it been there, she wondered or was it perhaps the reflection in a glass of the coach of the lantern on the shore? Then, as she wondered, the light came again and this time she was certain.

Armand came back to the coach, walking with long impatient strides. He spoke to the coachman.

"Go another mile farther along," he said. "You will

268

find a sandy bay, it is the first we come to. It would be hard to miss it."

He got in and shut the door behind him. There was an air of excitement about him which Rêve sensed instantly. The coach rumbled along, unable to proceed at anything more than a walking pace for the road was rough and untended and little more than a cart track.

Rêve did not ask any questions. She knew without asking that Armand had got in contact with someone who could help them, perhaps a ship of the British fleet lying in the Channel, waiting for just such a message.

She wondered what would have happened if he had not recovered his memory, if he had not known where to go, and yet when she told him her story, he had believed her and they had tried to escape as she had originally intended. She thought now that such an action might well have proved disastrous.

The coach came to a sudden stop. The door was opened and a footman said:

"Is this the place, Monsieur? The coachman says it is impossible to get the horses any farther."

"This will do," Armand replied.

"Is this where we say good-bye?" Imogène inquired. Her voice was languid and betrayed nothing of her feelings whatever they were.

"Not yet," Armand answered. "I regret that for safety's sake you must escort us, Madame, to the very water's edge. We are in a lonely spot, but one never knows what might turn up. If you will be good enough to alight. I will help you down the cliff."

In answer Imogène shrugged her shoulders and allowed Armand to assist her to the ground. It was a rough track, little more than a goat track winding down the cliff side.

It was difficult to see the way and more than once they stumbled, while Imogène's servants, obeying her commands to wait for them at the top, watched them go in amazement.

"They are wondering if I will return," she said to Armand when they were out of earshot of the little

269

band holding their tired horses and staring at their mistress's descent of the perilous cliffs.

"They will not be disappointed," Armand said firmly. "You have them well trained, Madame, in obedience."

"They fear me more than they fear the Emperor himself," Imogène answered. "I have my own methods of dealing with recreant servants."

Her voice was hard and Rêve felt her sympathy for her shrivel and die. This was a woman without mercy, a woman who had driven men to their death without regret, who would not hesitate to inflict misery and unhappiness on anyone who crossed her.

They reached the bay, the sand was soft beneath their feet and the silence was broken only by the ripple of the waves splashing gently on the shore.

The wind seemed to have died, the sea was very calm, and there seemed nothing to break the absolute silence and almost eerie breathlessness which lay over everything.

Armand walked down to the very water's edge and looked out to sea. There were no lights, nothing to be seen, only a vast expanse of dark water.

Still he went on looking into the darkness and Rêve found herself looking too, straining her eyes, thinking that she saw something and then realising that it was but an optical illusion and the movement of a wave.

No one spoke. Even Imogène seemed awed into silence as if the very tenseness of their feelings and the quietness around them left her without words. At length Armand gave a little exclamation.

It was hardly more than the indrawing of his breath, but Rêve heard it and at the same time saw what he had seen.

A dark shape was coming across the water, and a few seconds later they heard the splash of oars. A boat was being rowed towards them, a boat moving swiftly and purposefully to carry them to safety.

Rêve slipped her hand into Armand's. She could feel herself trembling with excitement and knew from the

270

quick, almost painful pressure of his fingers that he was excited too.

It was then they heard a sound behind them, a sound of falling stones, of men scrambling and clambering down the cliffs. Rêve turned her head apprehensievly. For a moment she wondered if the Duchess's servants had become alarmed and were coming in search of her, perhaps, as they thought, to rescue her from abduction.

Then even as the thought crossed her mind, there came a voice, a voice out of the darkness:

"Hurry, you fools, you dolts, hurry! They cannot have gone far."

Rêve stood as if turned to stone. She recognised the voice. There was only one person who spoke in that way, only one person whose voice rose to a high falsetto, curiously feminine and quite unforgettable in its surprising hysteria.

15

As Rêve clung to Armand's hand, her heart pounding, the moon came out from behind the clouds.

It was but rising in the sky and its light had not yet come to its full strength, yet it was strong enough to illuminate everything very clearly so that with one startled and apprehensive glance Rêve could see all that was happening.

She had her back to the sea, facing towards the direction from which the noise came. The first thing she saw was half a dozen soldiers in red and blue uniform, scrambling down the cliff side, slipping and slithering in their heavy boots, the loose stones cascading in front of them like miniature avalanches.

Coming down the path, picking his way fastidiously, was Comte Giles de Durieux.

He was dressed in his habitual black and with his cloak swinging behind him he looked in the light of the moon like some revengeful bird of prey.

It seemed to Rêve that his hands were like talons and his face, white and evil, resembling some monstrous apparition from the supernatural.

As Rêve was able to see the Count, so he was able to see them, and pointing to the little crowd on the shore he cried in a voice rising high almost to a shriek:

"There they are, there they are! Seize them, men, seize them!"

The soldiers were, however, unable to obey him as they had not yet descended on to the shore, for having missed the path, they had found it imperative in some places to retrace their steps lest they should fall from the overhanging rocks.

Then as Rêve stood, too frightened even to cry out,

she heard a sound beside her and turned to see that the boat had come right into shore, the oars were being shipped, and two sailors were springing over the side to drag it stern first into shallow water.

It was a large boat manned by eight men and to Rêve's utter relief she saw that four of them held muskets in their hands. A petty officer reached shore first, the water splashing high against his boots as he came quickly through the softly breaking waves.

He came up to Armand and saluted him.

"From H.M.S. *Triumphant,* m'lord," he said in English. "We are ready to take you aboard."

Nothing could have been more reassuring and in a way more contemptuous than his utter disregard for the French soldiers scrambling about on the cliff or the Count advancing across the sands, crying out as he did so for his escort to make speed.

"Get the ladies into the boat," Armand said.

"Very good, Sir."

He picked up Antoinette without more ado. She gave a little startled exclamation, then submitted to being carried through the water to the boat. Rêve turned to Armand with a touch of panic in her eyes.

"Hurry," she said, "the soldiers have muskets."

In answer Armand gathered her up in his arms and with a few strides deposited her beside Antoinette in the bows of the boat. Yet even in that brief second she clung to him and as he set her down she felt his lips against her hair and knew a thrill which even terror and fear could not supplant.

Then, as she expected him to jump into the boat beside her, he turned and walked back through the water. She gave a little cry:

"Armand, where are you going?"

But he did not reply, and she saw that he was going to meet the Count who was nearing the water's edge, Imogène, too, had obviously the same intention for she moved along the sand until she reached the Count one split second before Armand.

"Giles," she said urgently, "seize the man. He is about to escape us."

273

"That is just what I intend doing," the Count replied, and facing Armand he said: "Sir, you can consider yourself under arrest."

"I shall consider myself nothing of the sort," Armand replied coolly, and turning to the petty officer who was close beside him, he said: "Instruct your men to hold these soldiers at bay. Do not shoot unless you have to. I have a debt to settle with this gentleman before we embark."

"Very good, m'lord."

The order was barked out, and the four sailors sprang from the boat to stand ready with their muskets trained on the French soldiers who by this time were running across the sand from the bottom of the cliff.

At the sight of the English sailors, they hesitated for a moment, reduced their speed to a walk, then stopped and looked at each other as if for guidance.

"Resistance is useless," the Count said angrily. "There is a full company of the Imperial Guard but a few miles behind us. If you attempt to escape, I shall have you shot immediately."

"Pistols," Armand said pleasantly, "were never to my liking. I see, Count, that you have a sword. I have one also. I therefore challenge you to a duel and one which shall be fought to the death."

The Count's eyes narrowed, then he looked round quickly. He saw the soldiers who had come with him standing sheepishly some way away. Their muskets were in their hands, but they were making no attempt to use them.

Kneeling on one knee on the sand and covering them were the four sailors with the petty officer in charge. The Count glanced up at the cliff. There was no one in sight.

"We have time to fight our duel before your reinforcements arrive," Armand said gently.

"Why are you hesitating, Giles?" Imogène said impatiently. "Everyone knows you are one of the best swordsmen in France. Kill this imposter, kill him, he deserves to die."

Armand's lips twisted into a smile.

"You were offering me a very different fate but a short while ago, Madame," he said.

Imogène's eyes flashed.

"And you refused it," she said, and her tone was bitter.

"Are you ready, Count?" Armand asked.

Still the Count seemed to hesitate. He glanced again towards his men, opened his mouth as if he would call them, then realised the futility of such an action.

"Why should I fight with a traitor?" he inquired, and his voice was petulant.

"I can tell you one very good reason why a traitor, as you call me, should wish to fight with you," Armand said. "Because you are rotten and evil, because it is the job of all decent men to abhor and destroy all that you are and believe in."

His words seemed to touch the Count on the raw. He drew himself up as if in affront and his eyes began to gleam fanatically as he said:

"You fool! What do you know of such things? It was my powers, which you dare to call evil, which showed me where to come in search of you. I was guided here, yes, guided, by the greatest force on earth."

"If that is true," Armand retorted, "then the sooner I rid the earth of your devil-infested body the better. On guard, Sir."

He drew his sword as he spoke and almost reluctantly the Count followed his lead. Then he paused to unfasten his long velvet cloak and flung it on the sands. Imogène drew aside to give the men more space in which to move.

Her fingers were clasped together, her face alight with excitement. So that she could see better she pushed back her ermine-lined hood and her head was bare in the moonlight.

In the boat Rêve turned and put out her hands towards Antoinette.

"The Count will kill him," she whispered. "Oh, Antoinette what can I do?"

"Nothing, *ma petite,*" Antoinette answered softly, "save pray for Monsieur and know deep in your heart that right will triumph. See, the soldiers are quiet for fear of these brave Englishmen. Monsieur will win his battle, you can be certain of that."

"But I cannot be," Rêve answered. "Did you not hear the Duchess say that the Count was the best swordsman in France?"

"Monsieur is doubtless the best swordsman in England," Antoinette said steadily. "Pray, child, pray for him and hide your eyes if you are afraid to watch such a fight."

It was impossible of course to do any such thing. Rêve turned her head to look at the two men already fighting. The moonlight was growing stronger, its rays glinted on the shining steel of the crossed swords and revealed the tense expressions on the duellists' faces.

Armand's jaw was set square, his eyes were alert, and his breath came quickly, otherwise he appeared to Rêve to wear his usual expression when something serious was occurring and needed his full concentration. But the Count was very different.

His face was contorted almost diabolically. His eyes were pools of madness, his lips quivered and now and then some foul oath was spat from them as he was forced to retreat before Armand's blade or when they were locked together hilt to hilt.

Armand never spoke. The Duchess cried out, continually spurring the Count on with cries of encouragement, sneering and jeering at Armand when he lost a point or his opponent seemed to have got the upper hand.

There was no doubt from the first moment of the fight that the two men were very evenly matched.

The Count was older and therefore not quite as quick as Armand, but he was more experienced and had a kind of tricky finesse which Armand found at first a trifle disconcerting.

Yet he managed to stand his ground, to avoid the traps which the Count set for him, to fight steadily without apparently over-exerting himself.

As the minutes went by the pace and fury of the attack seemed to take its toll of the Count. They must have been fighting for perhaps ten minutes when Rêve, glancing towards the soldiers, saw a strange sight.

The Frenchmen had laid down their arms and had drawn nearer to watch the duel with interest and excitement. The English sailors still held their muskets, but they were no longer at their shoulders, and they too had turned to watch.

Shoulder to shoulder the men stood, bitter enemies as far as their countries were concerned, but united together as man to man in a common interest. On all their faces there was but one expression, that of a keen love of sport.

Thrust and counter-thrust, an attack repulsed and the incessant clash of steel. Both men were warming up by this time. Their faces were flushed and even the Count's habitual pallor had been replaced by a faint glow on his thin cheeks.

Armand had the advantage—no, he had lost it— now he was retreating before a vicious, deadly attack on the part of the Count.

The quickness of his movements saved his life. He was no longer on the defensive—in his turn he was attacking. The Count was parrying his thrusts, giving a superb exhibition of swordsmanship.

If it had not been a matter of life and death, Rêve felt that like the soldiers and sailors watching she might have been thrilled by the very expert quality of the swordsmanship.

But it was difficult to remember anything save what was at stake. Armand's life and hers as well. If he should fail, if he should fall to the ground wounded and incapable of getting away, then as far as she was concerned life was finished and she would ask nothing more than to be allowed to die with him.

Then as Rêve watched, as her apprehensions grew for Armand's safety, it seemed to her that she was indeed watching an age-old battle between good and evil. There was something young and virile, strong and clean about Armand.

He fought in a controlled, decent manner without ever attempting to take unfair advantage of his opponent or to infringe upon the rules pertaining to duelling, rules which had been in existence for hundreds of years.

There was, too, something fine and even noble about his appearance, and the same adjectives could be applied to his swordsmanship. He fought as a gentleman might fight, but the Count was very different.

Twisting his lips, uttering insults, oaths, expletives, trying by every trick and every possible cheat to take advantage of his opponent, he was becoming more and more fantastic and in a way more fanatical as the duel proceeded.

Rêve felt she had not realised until now how utterly evil he was in appearance and how in moments of stress it was possible to see in everyone's face their true character, a revelation of their innermost soul.

If that was true of the Count, evil and bestial as he was, it was also true of Imogène.

Hovering on the outskirts of the fight, she was like a cobra waiting to strike, standing at times quite immobile, at other times gesticulating and shrieking, a fiend rather than a human being and reflecting, so it seemed to Rêve, the same evil which seemed to emanate from the Count.

Good and evil, evil and good matched against each other, and fighting perhaps for far greater issues than an individual life and a personal desire for survival.

Rêve's lips were moving in prayer, but she was hardly conscious of what she said. She only knew that her whole being went out towards Armand as if in her very love and intensity it would give him her strength on which he could draw as well as on his own.

Then when it seemed as if the duel might go on for ever and there was no chance of it ever ending, there came a sudden shout from the cliffs.

Everyone turned and Rêve clung convulsively to Antoinette's arm as she saw there, silhouetted against the sky, a company of horsemen and some foot soldiers.

The reinforcements had arrived.

The British sailors turned to face the new intruders, while Imogène gave a shriek of delight. It was perhaps this which attracted the Count's attention. Just for a moment his blade seemed to falter, he made as if to turn his head, then checked himself.

Only Armand remained quite unperturbed, quite impervious to everything that was happening around him.

But that moment's lapse on the part of the Count was enough to give Armand an advantage. He lunged forward slipped through the Count's guard and the point of his sword entered the Count's body just above the heart.

He hung for a second on Armand's blade and the expression of surprise on his face was almost ludicrous, then without a sound, his tongue silenced for the first time since the duel had commenced, he toppled forward to fall face downwards on the sand.

As he drew his blade clear of the body, Armand looked up and saw what was happening. He saw the British sailors retreating slowly towards the sea, their muskets in their hands. He saw the petty officer look at him for instructions.

With a cry that was one of triumph, elation and happiness, all rolled into one he roared out the order: "Embark!"

A line of soldiers was filing down the path from the top of the cliffs. They were moving at the double and they reached the shore at almost the same moment as Armand leaped into the boat beside Rêve. The sailors splashed through the water, pushing the boat before them, then sprang in. It took them but a moment to get out the oars and pull into deeper water; but as they did so, the French soldiers came hurrying down to the sea.

Their onrush was checked for a moment at the sight of the Count. Imogène was bending over him and with an effort and by exerting all her strength she had turned him on to his back.

As she did so, a stream of dark blood poured from his open mouth and his sightless eyes gaped upwards at the sky.

She gave a little shudder of horror and rose to her feet. She saw the boat drawing away and the soldiers staring.

"What are you waiting for, you idiots?" she screamed. "Shoot them, shoot them before they escape."

The soldiers, however, hesitated to obey her orders. An officer was approaching and they waited for him to join them. He was very young, pink-faced and breathless from his descent down the cliff.

He stared at Imogène, his eyes full of admiration for her beauty as she stood there, her head uncovered, the ringlets of her dark hair moving in the breeze against her white forehead.

"The man we seek—the man who styles himself the Marquis d'Augeron—he has gone?"

"They are in that boat," Imogène said angrily. "Will you give the order for these imbeciles to fire?"

"Yes, yes, Madame, of course," the officer replied.

In the boat they were already out of earshot, but they could see what was happening on the shore. Armand drew Rêve from the bows down on to the floor of the boat.

"Keep low, my love," he said. "They will fire at us, though they are an unaccountably long time in doing so."

"Come on, men," roared the petty officer's voice from the stern, "put your backs into it. A few more pulls and we are safe."

There was a roar from the muskets on shore. Bullets whistled across the water. One struck the boat and they heard the splintering of wood. Rêve turned to Armand with a little convulsive gesture and he gathered her into his arms.

"We are quite safe, my darling," he said. "We have not come through all this to be killed by a stray bullet."

"Pull together, pull!" the petty officer cried.

The oars seemed to lift the boat almost out of the water as if it had wings. There was another report, and yet another, but this time the bullets did not reach them. They were out of range.

Rêve's face was hidden against Armand's neck. She was trembling uncontrollably, aware, now that the strain and anxiety were over, how much she had suffered, how much her anxiety and agony of mind has cost her.

"Ship ahoy!"

Rêve raised her head at the shout. Looming up above them, great guns pointing from her wooden sides, her masts silhouetted high against the sky, was a British Man-Of-War.

The boat drew alongside, a rope ladder was let down, and Rêve found herself climbing it, frightened yet aware that Armand was close behind her, his arms ready for any assistance she might need.

Eager hands were bending down to assist her. She was lifted almost bodily on deck and with a sigh of relief she found herself standing firmly on her own feet. An officer resplendent in gold braid kissed her hand, and then he was greeting Armand.

"Welcome, my lord," he said. "I am delighted to see you safe and in such good health. We have been worried as to why you were so long delayed."

"You must forgive me," Armand said, "but many things, including a lapse of memory, presented me from being here a fortnight earlier, as originally planned."

"But now that you are on board we will take you at all possible speed to England," the Captain said. "The Prime Minister will not unnaturally be deeply concerned at not hearing from us."

"I have news for my father which will make him find it easy to overlook my unpunctuality," Armand said with a smile.

Even as they moved towards the Captain's cabin the anchor was being hauled aboard, sails were being run up, and long before they had sat down to the meal which was prepared for them Rêve felt the ship begin to move.

She was too tired to eat although she was glad of the glass of wine Armand put into her hand.

Purposely it seemed to her he did not look at her while the meal was in progress; he engaged the Captain in conversation, allowing her time to collect her thoughts, to let the thumping of her heart subside.

At length when the table was cleared, the Captain made his excuses, saying that he was required on deck, and left them alone.

The room in which they had dined was low-ceilinged with oak beams, carved oak tables and chairs, and was illuminated by two big hanging lanterns. In their light Rêve could see Armand's eyes searching her face as if he had never seen her before.

With a sudden sense of panic she rose from the table. She could feel the ship moving steadily but without much motion on the calm sea. It was easy to keep her balance, yet she held on to one of the chairs as if for support.

Antoinette had tidied her hair and arranged a fresh fichu around her shoulders before dinner, but now she wished she was wearing something really beautiful, something which would give her confidence and courage.

She had fallen in love with Armand when she had had no idea of his rank and position in life. He was just a man, a man who had walked into her life and into her heart with no other attributes save that he had attracted her and she had known that he was the only person who would ever matter to her.

She had accepted his love unquestioningly, but then she had been the possessor of an estate, the bearer of a proud title, a woman of consequence and in the hierarchy of an *ancien régime*.

Now she was nobody, a refugee from her own country, a fugitive from justice, penniless and without any assets save a heart full of love and adoration for the man with whom she had escaped.

It seemed to her as she stood there, her fingers on the dark carved oak of the chair, that Armand was waiting for her to speak, waiting for her to say something, but she had no idea what he asked of her.

For a moment she dared not turn round and face him, and when at length as she forced herself to do so she saw that he had moved from the table and was standing a little way behind her.

His eyes were grave, but there was a faint smile at the corners of his lips. She looked up into his face and drew a deep breath.

"I have something I would say to you," she whispered at last.

"I am waiting," he said, and she was thankful that he made no attempt to come nearer to her.

"It is this," Rêve said, twisting her fingers together in her agitation. "We are on our way to England. It is only tonight, since I came aboard, since I noticed the courtesy and respect paid to you by the Captain of this ship, that I have realised a little of what lies ahead.

"You are the son of the Prime Minister of a great country. You have your home to go to, your place in society, your position and an inheritance both of wealth and of importance. I am nobody. I have no country, no home, no money.

"We met under unusual circumstances, we . . . we fell in love with each other; but then a treacherous blow made you forget that love and you believed for a long time that our relationship was a very different one.

"Now that your memory has returned, we have had little time to talk of it; in fact we have not been alone together for one moment since you recalled what happened that first night we met at the little Temple."

Rêve's voice faltered for a moment. Armand took a step forward but before he could speak her raised hands checked the very words on his lips.

"No, no," she said, "let me finish. You have now had time to think, to remember, to know what we said to each other and also to recall who you are and where you come from.

"You have brought me away from France and in doing so have doubtless saved my life, but I would not be a burden to you. I would also not have you grateful for what I had done. Anything that I was able to do I did willingly and gladly, for my own sake as well as yours.

"You owe me no gratitude, there is no debt left

unpaid, and therefore please consider now whether it would not be much better, when we reach England, for our paths to diverge.

"I would not have you feel that you are under any obligation to me, I would not have you be kind to me out of consideration for . . . my feelings. That I . . . could not . . . bear"

Rêve's voice broke completely now. For a moment her eyes were full of tears. Almost angrily she brushed them away.

"Please, Armand, please," she faltered at length, "be quite certain before you make any decisions, before you decide . . . our . . . future . . ."

She stopped because it was impossible for her to say more. She felt as if the very words were choked in her throat; then mistily, half blinded by her tears, she looked up to see that Armand's face was very near to hers.

"My darling—my dear ridiculous little love," he said very softly.

His arms went round her, and she started at his touch. Then, as he did not release her, she quivered in his hold, her hands pressing against him as if to ward him off from too close a contact.

"Think . . . before you say anything," she said a little wildly.

"What about?" Armand asked.

Now purposefully, masterfully he overcame her resistance and drew her closer until she could no longer fight against his strength. With a little quivering sigh her head fell back against his shoulder.

"You know the answer to all your questions," he said, "but I will spoil you by telling you the truth once and for all. I love you, Rêve, I have loved you from the first moment I saw you. It was not an ordinary love that came upon me as a blinding flash of lightning from the sky. I saw you, I loved you and knew that you were mine.

"Whatever our position in life, whatever the future holds, we will face it together, you and I, as man and wife, as man and woman if you like, one and undivided. Darling, I love you."

He bent his head, but he did not kiss her. Instead he waited as if he asked rather than commanded the surrender of herself.

Then because she understood what he asked, because her heart was throbbing in unison with his, because the last barrier which stood between them was down for all time, she put her arms round his neck and with a sob turned her mouth to his.

She felt a quickening of her whole being, she felt herself drawn up into an ecstasy of joy and happiness until it seemed as if her very soul passed from between her lips into his keeping.

Then Armand raised his head and looked down at her.

"I love you," he said. "I love you now and for all time, even in eternity you can never escape from me."

She looked up at him now, her lips parted, her eyes wide and radiant. She felt as if he drew her up into the very heaven of happiness, so that it was almost as if they were both flying in a clear translucent sky to a glory beyond all human imagination.

"You are like . . . an eagle," she said, and was hardly aware that she had said the words.

"An eagle, then, of love," Armand replied. "But an eagle who takes what he most desires. You are mine, my darling—mine, now and for ever."

Their lips met again and they were oblivious of everything in the whole world.

Outside the wind freshened and the great sails, full-bellied, sped the Man-Of-War towards the English coast.

ON SALE WHEREVER PAPERBACKS ARE SOLD
— or use this coupon to order directly from the publisher.

BARBARA CARTLAND

	V2705	Again This Rapture $1.25 £ (#36)
	V3389	Against The Stream $1.25 £ (#68)
	V2823	Audacious Adventuress $1.25 £ (#41)
	V3491	Coin Of Love $1.25 £ (#3)
	V2921	Debt Of Honor $1.25 £ (#16)
	V3473	Desire Of The Heart $1.25 £ (#1)
	V3271	The Dream Within $1.25 £ (#62)
	V3537	A Duel of Hearts $1.25 £ (#8)
	V2560	Elizabethan Lover $1.25 £ (#28)
	V2769	Enchanted Evil $1.25 £ (#5)
	V2795	Enchanted Moment $1.25 £ (#40)
	V3048	The Enchanted Waltz $1.25 £ (#26)
	V3019	A Ghost In Monte Carlo $1.25 £ (#48)
	V3627	Golden Gondola $1.25 £
	V3239	A Halo For The Devil $1.25 £ (#55)
	V2706	A Hazard of Hearts $1.25 £ (#2)
	V3358	A Heart Is Broken $1.25 £ (#66)
	V2539	Hidden Evil $1.25 £ (#27)
	V3538	The Hidden Heart $1.25 £ (#10)
	V2636	The Innocent Heiress $1.25 £ (#15)
	V3564	An Innocent In Paris $1.25 £ (#24)
	V3326	Josephine, Empress Of France $1.25 £ (Biographical Romance)

Send to: PYRAMID PUBLICATIONS,
Dept. M.O., 9 Garden Street, Moonachie, N.J. 07074

NAME

ADDRESS

CITY

STATE   ZIP

I enclose $_____, which includes the total price of all books ordered plus 50¢ per book postage and handling for the first book and 25¢ for each additional. If my total order is $10.00 or more, I understand that Pyramid will pay all postage and handling.
No COD's or stamps. Please allow three to four weeks for delivery.
Prices subject to change.   P-15

ON SALE WHEREVER PAPERBACKS ARE SOLD
— or use this coupon to order directly from the publisher.

BARBARA CARTLAND

V2734	**Open Wings** $1.25 £ (#37)	
V3242	**Out Of Reach** $1.25 £ (#60)	
V3243	**The Price Is Love** $1.25 £ (#61)	
V3373	**The Private Life Of Elizabeth Empress Of Austria** $1.25 £ (Biographical Romance)	
V2650	**Reluctant Bride** $1.25 £ (#34)	
V3518	**Royal Pledge** $1.25 £ (#18)	
V3428	**The Runaway Heart** (#69) $1.25 £	
V3331	**The Scandalous Life Of King Carol** $1.25 £	
V3565	**The Secret Heart** $1.25 £ (#7)	
V2429	**Stars In My Heart** $1.25 £ (#21)	
V2887	**Stolen Halo** $1.25 £ (#44)	
V2689	**Sweet Adventure** $1.25 £ (#17)	
V3189	**Sweet Enchantress** $1.25 £ (#58)	
V2920	**Sweet Punishment** $1.25 £ (#45)	
V3388	**Theft Of The Heart** $1.25 £ (#67)	
V3272	**The Thief Of Love** $1.25 £ (#63)	
V2577	**The Unknown Heart** $1.25 £ (#29)	
V2146	**The Unpredictable Bride** $1.25 £ (#6)	
V2996	**Wings on My Heart** $1.25 £ (#47)	
V2504	**Wings of Love** $1.25 £ (#25)	
V3293	**Woman, The Enigma** $1.25 £ (Nonfiction)	

Send to: PYRAMID PUBLICATIONS,
Dept. M.O., 9 Garden Street, Moonachie, N.J. 07074

NAME

ADDRESS

CITY

STATE   ZIP

. I enclose $_____, which includes the total price of all books
ordered plus 50¢ per book postage and handling for the first book and
25¢ for each additional. If my total order is $10.00 or more, I understand
that Pyramid will pay all postage and handling.
No COD's or stamps. Please allow three to four weeks for delivery.
Prices subject to change.   P-17

are you missing out on some great Pyramid books?

You can have any title in print at Pyramid delivered right to your door! To receive your Pyramid Paperback Catalog, fill in the label below (use a ball point pen please) and mail to Pyramid . . .

PYRAMID PUBLICATIONS
Mail Order Department
9 Garden Street
Moonachie, New Jersey 07074

NAME_____

ADDRESS_____

CITY_____ STATE_____

P-5   ZIP_____